The Prairie, Volume 1

James Fenimore Cooper

J. M. HODGES LEARNING CENTER
WHARTON COUNTY JUNIOR COLLEGE
WHARTON, TEXAS 77488

Table of Contents

J. M. HODGES LEARNING CENTER
WHARTON COUNTY JUNIOR COLLEGE
WHARTON, TEXAS 77488

PS
1416
.A1
2004

The Prairie, Volume 1

James Fenimore Cooper

Kessinger Publishing reprints thousands of hard–to–find books!

Visit us at http://www.kessinger.net

PREFACE.

The manner in which the writer of this book came into possession of most of its materials, is mentioned in the work itself. Any well bred reader will readily conceive that there may exist a thousand reasons, why he should not reveal any more of his private sources of information. He will only say, on his own responsibility, that the portions of the tale for which no authorities are given, are quite as true as those which are not destitute of this peculiar advantage, and that all may be believed alike.

There is, however, to be found in the following pages an occasional departure from strict historical veracity, which it may be well to mention. In the endless confusion of names, customs, opinions, and languages, which exists among the tribes of the west, the Author has paid much more attention to sound and convenience than to literal truth. He has uniformly called the Great Spirit, for instance, the Wahcondah, though he was not ignorant that there were different names for that Being among the nations he has introduced. So, in other matters he has rather adhered to simplicity, than sought to make his narrative strictly correct at the expense of all order and clearness. It was enough for his purpose that the picture should possess the general features of the original: in the shading, attitude, and disposition of thefigures, a little liberty has been taken. Even this brief explanation would have been spared, did not the Author know that there is a certain class of learned Thebans who are just as fit to read a work of the imagination, as they are qualified to write one.

It may be necessary to meet much graver and less easily explained objections, in the minds of a far higher class of readers. The introduction of one and the same character, as a principal actor in no less than three books, and the selection of a comparative desert, which is aided by no historical recollections, and embellished by few or no poetical associations, for the scene of a legend, in these times of perilous adventure in works of this description, may need more vindication. If the first objection can be removed, the latter must fallof course, as it would become the duty of a faithful chronicler to follow his hero wherever he might choose to go.

It is quite probable that the narrator of these simple events has deceived himself as to the importance they may have in the eyes of other people. But he has seen, or thought he has seen, something sufficiently instructive and touching in the life of a veteran of the forest, who, having commenced his career near the Atlantic, had been driven by the increasing and unparalleled advance of population, to seek a final refuge against society in the broad and tenantless plains of the west, to induce him to hazard the experiment of publication. That the changes which might have driven a man so constituted to such an expedient have actually occurred within a single life, is a matter of undeniable history; that theydid produce such an effect on the Scout of the Mohicans, the Leatherstocking of the Pioneers, and the Trapper of the Prairie, rests on an authority no less imposing than those veritable pages, from which the reader shall no longer be detained, if he still be disposed to peruse them, after this frank avowal of the poverty of their contents.

CHAPTER I.

"I pray thee, shepherd, if that love, or gold

Can in this desert place buy entertainment,

Bring us where we may rest ourselves and feed."

—— As you like it

Much was said and written, at the time, concerning the policy of adding the vast regions of Louisiana, to the, already, immense and but half—tenanted territories of the United States. As the warmth of controversy, however, subsided, and personal considerations gave place to more liberal views, the wisdom of the measure began to be, generally, conceded. It soon became apparent to the meanest capacity, that, while nature had placed a barrier of desert to the extension of our population in the west, the measure had made us the masters of a belt of fertile country, which, in the revolutions of the day, might have become the property of a rival nation. It gave us the sole command of the great thoroughfare of the interior, and placed the countless tribes of savages, who lay along our borders, entirely, within our control; it reconciled conflicting rights, and quieted national distrusts; it opened a thousand avenues to the inland trade, and to the waters of the Pacific; and, if ever time or necessity should require a peaceful division of this vast empire, it assures us of a neighbour that would possess our language, our religion, our institutions, and it is also to be hoped, our sense of political justice.

Although the purchase was made in 1803, the spring of the succeeding year was permitted to open, before the official prudence of the Spaniard, who held the province for his European master, admitted the authority, or even of the entrance, of its new proprietors. But the forms of the transfer were no sooner completed, and the new government acknowledged, than swarms of that restless people, which is ever found hovering on the skirts of American society, plunged into the thickets that fringed the right bank of the Mississippi, with the same careless hardihood, as had, already, sustained so many of them in their toilsome progress from the atlantic states, to the eastern shores of the "father of rivers."

Time was necessary to blend the numerous and affluent colonists of the lower province with their new compatriots; but the sparser and more humble population, above, was almost immediately swallowed in the vortex which attended the tide of instant emigration. The inroad from the east was a new and sudden out–breaking of a people, who had endured a momentary restraint, after having been rendered, nearly, resistless by success. The toils and hazards of former undertakings were forgotten, as these endless and unexplored regions, with all their fancied as well as real advantages, were laid open to their enterprise. The consequences were such as might easily have been anticipated, from so tempting an offering, placed, as it was before the eyes of a race long trained in adventure and nurtured in difficulties.

Thousands of the elders, of what were then called the New States, broke up from the enjoyment of their hard earned indulgencies, and were to be seen leading long files of descendants, born and reared in the forests of Ohio and Kentucky, deeper into the land, in quest of that which might be termed, without the aid of poetry, their natural and more congenial atmosphere. The distinguished and resolute forester who first penetrated the wilds of the latter state, was of the number. This adventurous and venerable patriarch was now seen making his last remove; placing the "endless river" between him and the multitude, his own success had drawn around him, and seekingfor the renewal of enjoyments which were rendered worthless in his eyes, when trammelled by the forms of human institutions.

In the pursuit of adventures, such as these, men are ordinarily governed by their previous habits or deluded by their secret wishes. A few, led by the phantoms of hope, and, ambitious of sudden affluence, sought the mines of the virgin territory; but, by far the greater portion of the emigrants were satisfied to establish themselves along the margins of the larger water–courses, content with the rich returns that the generous, alluvial, bottoms of the rivers never fail to bestow on the most desultory industry. In this manner were communities formed with magical rapidity; and most of those who witnessed the purchase of the empty empire, have lived to see already a populous and sovereign state, parcelled from its inhabitants, and received into the bosom of the national confederacy, on terms of political equality.

The Prairie, Volume 1

The incidents and scenes which are connected with our present legend, occurred in the earliest periods of the enterprises which have led to so great and so speedy a result.

The harvest of the first year of our possession had long been passed, and the fading foliage of a few scattering trees was, already, beginning to exhibit the hues and tints of autumn, when a train of wagons issued from the bed of a dry rivulet, to pursue its course across the undulating surface, of what, in the language of the country of which we write, is called a "rolling prairie." The vehicles, loaded with household goods and implements of husbandry, the few straggling sheep and black cattle that were herded in the rear, and the rugged appearance and careless mien of the sturdy men who loitered at the sides of the lingering teams, united to announce a band of emigrants seeking for the Elderado of their desires. Contrary to the usual practice of the men of their caste, this party had leftthe fertile bottoms of the low country, and had found its way, by means only known to such adventurers, across glen and torrent, over deep morasses and arid wastes, to a point far beyond the usual limits of civilized habitations. In their front were stretched those broad plains, which extend, with so little diversity of character, to the bases of the Rocky Mountains; and many long and dreary miles in their rear, foamed the swift and turbid waters of La Platte.

The appearance of such a train, in that bleak and solitary place, was rendered the more remarkable by the fact, that the surrounding country offered so little, that was tempting to the cupidity of speculation, and, if possible, still less that was flattering to the hopes of an ordinary settler of new lands.

The meagre herbage of the prairie, promised nothing, in favour of a hard and unyielding soil, over which the wheels of the vehicles rattled as lightly as though they travelled on a beaten road; neither wagons nor beasts making any deeper impression, than to mark that bruised and withered grass, which the cattle plucked, from time to time, and as often rejected, as food too sour, for even their hunger to render palatable.

Whatever might be the final destination of these adventurers, or the secret causes of their apparent security in so remote and unprotected a situation, there was no visible sign of uneasiness or alarm betrayed in the countenance or the deportment of any among them. Including both sexes, and every age the number of the party exceeded twenty.

At some little distance in front of the whole, march ed the individual, who, both by his position and air appeared to be the leader of the band. He was a tall, sun−burnt, man, past the middle age, whose dull countenance and listless manner denoted any other emotion than that of compunction for the past or anxiety for the future. His frame appeared loose and flexible; but it was vast, and in reality of prodigious power. It was, only at moments, however, as some slight impediment opposed itself to his loitering progress, that his person, which, in its ordinary gait seemed so lounging and nerveless, displayed any of those energies, which lay latent in his system, like the slumbering and unwieldy, but terrible, strength of the elephant. The inferior lineaments of his countenance were coarse, extended and vacant; while the superior, or those nobler parts which are thought to affect the intellectual being, were low, receding and mean.

The dress of this individual was a mixture of the coarsest vestments of a husbandman with the leathern garments, that fashion as well as use, had in some degree rendered necessary to one engaged in his present pursuits. There was, however, a singular and wild display of prodigal and ill judged ornaments, blended with his motley attire. In place of the usual deer−skin belt, he wore around his body a tarnished silken sash of the most gaudy colours; the buck−horn haft of his knife was profusely decorated with plates of silver; the martin's fur of his cap was of a fineness and shadowing that a queen might covet; the buttons of his rude and soiled blanket−coat were of the glittering coinage of Mexico; the stock of his rifle was of beautiful mahogany, riveted and banded with the same precious metal, and the trinkets of no less than three worthless watches dangled from different parts of his person. In addition to the pack and the rifle which were slung at his back, together with the well filled, and carefully guarded pouch and horn, he had carelessly cast a keen and bright wood−axe across his shoulder, sustaining the weight of the whole with as much apparent ease, as though he moved, unfettered in his limbs, and free from the smallest incumbrance.

A short distance in the rear of this man, came a groupe of youths very similarly attired, and bearing sufficient resemblance to each other, and to their leader, to distinguish them as the children of one family. Though the youngest of their number could not much have passed the period, that, in the nicer judgment of the law is called the age of discretion, he had proved himself so far worthy of his progenitors as to have reared already his aspiring person to the standard height of his race. There were one or two others, of different mould, whose descriptions must however be referred to the regular course of the narrative.

Of the females, there were but two who had arrived at womanhood; though several white–headed, olive–skin'd faces were peering out of the foremost wagon of the train, with eyes of lively curiosity and characteristic animation. The elder of the two adults, was the sallow and wrinkled mother of most of the party, and the younger was a sprightly, active, girl, of eighteen, who in figure, dress and mien seemed to belong to a station in society several gradations above that of any one of her visible associates. The second vehicle was covered with a top of cloth so tightly drawn, as to conceal its contents, with the nicest care. The remaining wagons, were loaded, with nothing more valuable than such rude furniture and other personal effects, as might be supposed to belong to one, ready at any moment, to change his abode, without reference to season or distance.

Perhaps there was little in this train, or in the appearance of its proprietors, that is not daily to be encountered on the highways of our changeable and moving country. But the solitary and peculiar scenery in which it was so unexpectedly exhibited, gave to the party a marked character of wildness and adventure.

In the little vallies, which, in the regular formation of the land, occurred at every mile of their progress, the view was bounded, on two of the sides, by the gradual and low elevations, which give name to that description of prairie, we have mentioned; while onhe others, the meagre prospect ran off in long, narrow, barren perspectives, but slightly relieved by a pitiful show of coarse, though, somewhat, luxuriant vegetation. From the summits of the swells, the eye became fatigued with the sameness and chilling dreariness of the landscape. The earth was not unlike the Ocean, when its restless waters are heaving heavily after the agitation and fury of the tempest have begun to lessen. There was the same waving and regular surface, the same absence of foreign objects, and the same boundless extent to the view. Indeed so very striking was the resemblance between the water and the land, that, however much the geologist might sneer at so simple a theory, it would have been difficult for a poet not to have felt, that the formation of the one had been produced by the subsiding dominion of the other. Here and there a tall tree rose out of the bottoms, stretching its naked branches abroad, like some solitary vessel; and, to strengthen the delusion, far in the utmost distance, appeared two or three rounded thickets, looming in the misty horizon like islands resting on the bosom of the waters. It is unnecessary to warn the practised reader, that the sameness of the surface, and the low stands of the spectators exaggerated the distances; but still, as swell appeared after swell, and island succeeded island, there was a disheartening assurance that long, and seemingly interminable, tracts of territory must be passed, before the wishes of the humblest agriculturist could be realized.

Still, the leader of the emigrants steadily pursued his way, with no other guide than the sun, turning his back resolutely on the abodes of civilization, and plunging, at each step, more deeply if not irretrievably, into the haunts of the barbarous and savage occupants of the country. As the day drew nigher to a close, however, his mind, which was, perhaps, incapable of maturing any connected system of forethoughtbeyond that which related to the interests of the present moment, became, in some slight degree, troubled with the care of providing for the wants of the coming hours of darkness.

On reaching the crest of a swell that was a little higher than the usual elevations, he lingered a minute, and cast a half curious eye, on either hand, in quest of those well known signs, which might indicate a place, where the three grand requisites of, water, fuel and fodder were to be obtained in conjunction.

It would seem that his search was fruitless; for after a few moments of indolent and listless examination, he suffered his huge frame, to descend the gentle declivity, in the same sluggish manner that an over fatted beast would have yielded to the downward pressure.

His example was silently followed by those who succeeded him, though not until the young men had manifested much more of interest, if not of concern in the brief inquiry, which each, in his turn, made on gaining the same look−out. It was now evident by the tardy movements both of beasts and men, that the time of necessary rest, was not far distant. The matted grass of the lower land, presented obstacles which fatigue began to render formidable, and the whip was becoming necessary to urge the lingering teams to their labour. At this moment, when, with the exception of the principal individual, a general lassitude was getting the mastery of the travellers, and every eye was cast, by a sort of common impulse, wistfully forward, the whole party was brought to a halt, by a spectacle, as sudden as it was unexpected.

The sun had fallen below the crest of the nearest wave of the prairie leaving the usual, rich and glowing, train on its track. In the centre of this flood of fiery light, a human form appeared, drawn against the gilded background, as distinctly, and, seemingly as palpable, as though it would come within the graspof any extended hand. The figure was colossal; the attitude musing and melancholy, and the situation directly in the route of the travellers. But imbedded, as it was, in its setting of garish light, it was impossible to distinguish more concerning its proportions or character.

The effect of such a spectacle was instantaneous and powerful. The man in front of the emigrants came to a stand, and remained gazing at the mysterious object, with a dull interest, that soon quickened into a species of superstitious awe. His sons, so soon as the first emotions of surprise had a little abated, drew, slowly, around him, and, as they who governed the teams, gradually, followed their example, the whole party was soon condensed in one, silent, and wondering groupe. Notwithstanding the impression of a supernatural agency was very general among the travellers, the ticking of gun–locks was heard, and one or two of the bolder of the youths cast their rifles forward, in guarded readiness for any service.

"Send the boys off to the right," exclaimed the resolute wife and mother, in a sharp, dissonant voice, "I warrant me, Asa, or Abner will give some account of the creatur!"

"It may be well enough, to try the rifle," muttered a dull looking man, whose features both in outline and expression, bore no small resemblance, to the first speaker, and who loosened the stock of his piece and brought it dexterously to the front, while delivering this decided opinion; "the Pawnee Loups are said to be hunting by hundreds in the plains; if so, they'll never miss a single man from their tribe."

"Stay!" exclaimed a soft toned, but fearfully alarmed female voice, which was easily to be traced to the trembling lips of the younger of the two women; "we are not all, together; it may be a friend!"

"Who is scouting, now?" demanded the father, scanning, at the same time, the cluster of his stoutsons, with a displeased and sullen eye. "Put by the piece, put by the piece;" he continued, diverting the other's aim, with the finger of a giant, and with the air of one it might be dangerous to deny. "My job is not yet ended; let us finish the little that remains, in peace."

The man, who had manifested so hostile an intention, appeared to understand the other's allusion, and suffered himself to be diverted from his object. The sons turned their inquiring looks, on the girl, who had so eagerly spoken, to require an explanation; but, as if content with the respite she had obtained for the stranger, she had already sunk back, in her seat, and now chose to affect a maidenly silence.

In the mean time, the hues of the heavens had often changed. In place of the brightness, which had dazzled the eye, a gray and more sober light had succeeded, and as the setting lost its brilliancy, the proportions of the fanciful form became less exaggerated, and finally quite distinct. Ashamed to hesitate, now, that the truth was no longer doubtful, the leader of the party resumed his journey, using the precaution, as he ascended the slight acclivity, to release his own rifle from the strap, and to cast it into a situation more convenient for sudden use.

There was little apparent necessity, however, for such watchfulness. From the moment when it had thus unaccountably appeared, as it were, between the heavens and the earth, the stranger's figure had neither moved nor given the smallest evidence of hostility. Had he harboured any such evil intention, the individual who now came plainly into view, seemed but little qualified to execute them.

A frame that had endured the hardships of more than eighty seasons was not qualified to awaken apprehension, in the breast of one as powerful as the emigrant. Notwithstanding his years, and his look of emaciation if not of suffering, there was that aboutthis solitary being, however, which said that time, and not disease, had laid his hand too heavily on him. His form, had withered, but it was not wasted. The sinews and muscles, which had once denoted great strength, though shrunken, were still visible; and his whole figure had attained an appearance of induration, which, if it were not for the well known frailty of humanity, would have seemed to bid defiance to the further approaches of decay. His dress was chiefly of skins, worn with the hair to the weather; a pouch and horn were suspended from his shoulders; and he leaned on a rifle of uncommon length, but which like its owner, exhibited the wear of long and hard service.

As the party drew nigher to this solitary being, and came within a distance to be heard, a low growl issued from the grass at his feet, and then, a tall, gaunt, toothless, hound, arose lazily from his lair, and shaking himself made some show of resisting the nearer approach of the travellers.

"Down, Hector, down;" said his master, in a voice, that was a little tremulous and hollow with age. "What have ye to do, pup, with men who journey on their lawful callings."

"Stranger, if you ar' much acquainted in this country," said the leader of the emigrants, "can you tell a traveller where he may find necessaries for the night."

"Is the land filled on the other side of the Big River?" demanded the old man, solemnly, and without appearing to hearken to the other's question; "or why do I see a sight, I had never thought to behold again!"

"Why, there is country left, it is true, for such as have money, and ar' not particular in the choice," returned the emigrant; "but to my taste, it is getting crowdy. What may a man call the distance, from this place to the nighest point on the main river."

"A hunted deer could not cool his sides, in the Mississippi, without travelling a long five hundred miles."

"And in what way may you name the district, hereaway?"

"By what name," returned the old man, pointing significantly upward, "would you call the spot, where you see yonder cloud?"

The emigrant looked at the other, like one who did not comprehend his meaning and who half suspected he was trifled with, but he contented himself by saying——

"You ar' but a new inhabitant, like myself, I reckon, stranger, otherwise you would'n't be backward in helping a traveller to some advice; which costs but little, seeing it is only a gift in words."

"It is not a gift, but a debt that the old owe to the young. What would you wish to know?"

"Where I may 'camp for the night. I'm no great difficulty maker, as to bed and board, but, all old journeyers, like myself, know the virtue of sweet water, and a good browse for the cattle."

"Come then with me, and you shall be master of both; and little more is it that I can offer on this hungry prairie."

As the old man was speaking, he raised his heavy rifle to his shoulder, with a facility a little remarkable for his years and apearance, and without further words led the way over the acclivity into the adjacent bottom.

CHAPTER II.

"Up with my tent: here will I lie to night,

But where, to–morrow?——Well, all's one for that."

—— Richard the Third

The travellers soon discovered the usual and unerring evidences, that the several articles necessary to their situation were not far distant. A clear and gurgling spring burst out of the side of the declivity, and joining its waters to those of other similar little fountains, in its vicinity, their united contributions formed a run, which was easily to be traced for miles, along the prairie, by the scattering foliage and verdure which occasionally grew within the influence of its moisture. Hither, then, the stranger held his way, eagerly followed by the willing teams, whose instinct gave them a prescience of refreshment and of rest from labour.

On reaching what he deemed a suitable spot, the old man halted, and with an inquiring look, he seemed to demand if it possessed the needful conveniences. The leader of the emigrants cast his eyes, understandingly, about him, and examined the place with the keenness of one competent to judge of so nice a question, though in that dilatory and heavy manner, which rarely permitted him to betray any unmanly precipitation.

"Ay, this may do," he said, when satisfied with his scrutiny; "boys, you have seen the last of the sun; be stirring."

The young men manifested a characteristic obedience to the injunction. The order, for such, in tone and manner it was, in truth, was received with respect; but the utmost movement was the falling of an axe or two from the shoulder to the ground, whiletheir owners continued to regard the place with listless and incurious eyes. In the mean time, the elder traveller, as if familiar with the nature of the impulses by which his children were governed, disencumbered himself of his pack and rifle, and, assisted by the man already mentioned as disposed to appeal so promptly to the rifle, he quietly proceeded to release the cattle from the gears.

At length the eldest of the sons stepped heavily forward, and, without any apparent effort, he buried his axe to the eye, in the soft body of a cotton-wood tree. He stood, a moment, regarding the effect of his blow, with that sort of contempt with which a giant might be supposed to contemplate the puny resistance of a dwarf, and then flourishing the implement above his head, with the grace and dexterity with which a master of the art of offence would wield his nobler though less useful weapon, he quickly severed the trunk of the tree bringing its tall top crashing to the earth, in submission to his prowess. His companions had regarded the operation with indolent curiosity, until they saw the prostrate trunk stretched along the ground, when, as if a signal for a general attack had been given, they advanced in a body to the work, and in a space of time, and with a neatness of execution that would have astonished an ignorant spectator, they stripped a small but suitable spot of its burden of forest, as effectually, and almost as promptly, as if a whirlwind had passed along the place.

The stranger, had been a silent but attentive observer of their progress. As tree after tree came whistling down, he cast his eyes upward, at the vacancies they left in the heavens, with a melancholy gaze, and finally turned away, muttering to himself with a bitter smile, like one who disdained giving a more audible utterance to his discontent. Pressing through the groupe of active and busy children, whohad already lighted a cheerful fire, the attention of the old man became next fixed, on the movements of the leader of the emigrants and of his savage looking assistant.

These two had, already, liberated the cattle, which were eagerly browsing the grateful and nutritious extremities of the fallen trees, and were now employed about the wagon, which has been described, as having its contents concealed with so much apparent care. Notwithstanding it appeared to be as silent, and as tenantless as the rest of the vehicles, the men applied their strength to its wheels, and rolled it apart from the others, to a dry and elevated spot, near the edge of the thicket. Here they brought certain poles, which had, seemingly, been long employed in such a service, and fastening their larger ends firmly in the ground, the smaller were attached to the hoops that supported the covering of the wagon. Large folds of cloth were next drawn out of the vehicle, and after being spread around the whole, were pegged to the earth in such a manner as to form a tolerably capacious and exceedingly convenient tent. After surveying their work with inquisitive, and perhaps jealous eyes, arranging a fold here and driving a peg more firmly there, the men once more applied their strength to the wagon, pulling it, by its projecting tongue, from the centre of the canopy, until it appeared in the open air, deprived of its covering, and destitute of any other freight, than a few light articles of furniture. The latter were immediately removed, by the traveller, into the tent with his own hands, as though to enter it, were a privilege, to which even his bosom companion was not entitled.

As curiosity is a passion that is rather quickened than destroyed by seclusion, the old inhabitant of the prairies did not view these precautionary and mysterious movements, without experiencing some of itsimpulses. He approached the tent, and, was about to sever two of its folds, with the very obvious intention of examining, more closely, into the nature of its contents, when the man who had once already placed his life in jeopardy, seized him by the arm, and with a somewhat rude exercise of his strength threw him from the spot he had selected as the one most convenient for his object.

"It's an honest regulation, friend," the fellow, drily observed, though with an eye that threatened volumes, "and sometimes it is a safe one, which says, mind your own business."

"Men seldom bring any thing to be concealed into these deserts," returned the old man, as if willing, and yet a little ignorant how to apologize for the liberty he had been about to take, "and I had hoped no offence, in looking into the place."

"They seldom bring themselves, I reckon," the other roughly answered; "this has the look of an old country, though to my eye it seems not to be overly peopled."

"The land is as aged as the rest of the works of the Lord, I believe; but you say true, concerning its inhabitants. Many months have passed since I have laid eyes on a face of my own colour, before your own. I say again, friend, I had hoped, no harm; I didn't know, whether there was not, something behind the cloth, that might bring former days to my thoughts."

As the stranger ended his simple explanation, he walked meekly away, like one who felt the deepest sense of the right which every man has to the quiet enjoyment of his own, without any troublesome interference on the part of his neighbour; a wholesome and just principle that he had, also, most probably imbibed from the habits of his secluded life. As he passed back, towards the little encampment of the emigrants, for such the place had now become, he heard the voice of the leader calling aloud, in its hoarse and authoritative tones, the name of——

"Ellen Wade."

The girl who has been already introduced to the reader, and who was occupied with others of her sex, around the fires, sprang willingly forward, at this summons, and passing the stranger with the activity of a young antelope, she was instantly lost, behind the forbidden folds of the fent. Neither her sudden disappearance, nor any of the arrangements we have mentioned, seemed, however, to excite the smallest surprise, among the remainder of the party. The young men who had already completed their tasks, with the axe, were all engaged after their lounging and listless manner; some in bestowing equitable portions of the fodder, among the different animals; others in plying the heavy pestle of a moveable hommony–mortar, and one or two, in wheeling the remainder of the wagons aside and arranging them, in such a manner as to form a sort of outwork for their, otherwise, defenceless bivouac.

These, several, duties were soon performed, and, as darkness, now, began to conceal the objects on the surrounding prairie, the shrill toned termagant, whose voice since the halt had been diligently exercised among her idle and drowsy offspring, announced in tones that might have been heard at a dangerous distance, that the evening meal waited only for the approach of those who were to consume it. Whatever may be the other qualities of a border man, he is seldom deficient in the virtue of hospitality. The emigrant no sooner heard the sharp call of his wife, than he cast his eyes about him in quest of the stranger, in order to proffer to him the place of distinction, in the rude entertainment to which they were so unceremoniously summoned.

"I thank you, friend," the old man replied to therough invitation to take a seat nigh the smoking kettle; "you have my hearty thanks; but I have eaten for the day, and I am not one of them, who dig their graves with their teeth. Well; as you wish it, I will take a place, for it is long sin' I have seen people of my colour, eating their daily bread."

"You ar' an old settler, in these districts, then," the emigrant rather remarked than inquired, with a mouth filled nearly to overflowing with the delicious hommony, prepared by his skilful, though repulsive spouse. "They told us below, we should find settlers something thinnish, hereaway, and I must say, the report was mainly true; for, unless, we count the Canada traders on the big river, you ar' the first white face I have met, in a good five hundred miles; that is calculating according to your own reckoning."

"Though I have spent some years, in this quarter, I can hardly be called a settler, seeing that I have no regular abode, and seldom pass more than a month, at a time, on the same range."

"A hunter, I reckon?" the other continued, glancing his eyes aside, as if to examine the equipments of his new acquaintance; "your fixen seem none of the best, for such a calling."

"They are old, and nearly ready to be laid aside, like their master," said the old man, regarding his rifle, with a look in which affection and regret were singularly blended; "and I may say they are but little needed, too. You are mistaken, friend, in calling me a hunter; I am nothing better than a trapper."

"If you ar' much of the one, I'm bold to say you ar' something of the other; for the two callings, go mainly together, in these districts."

"To the shame of the man who is able to follow the first be it so said!" returned the trapper, whom in future we shall choose to designate by his pursuit; "for more than fifty years did I carry my rifle in thewilderness, without so much as setting a snare for even a bird that flies the heavens;——much less, a beast that has nothing but legs, for its gifts."

"I see but little difference whether a man gets his peltry by the rifle or by the trap," said the ill-looking companion of the emigrant, in his rough and sullen manner. "The 'arth was made for his comfort; and, for that matter, so ar' its creatur's."

"You seem to have but little plunder, stranger, for one who is far abroad," bluntly interrupted the emigrant, as if he had a reason for wishing to change the conversation. "I hope you ar' better off for skins."

"I make but little use of either," the trapper, quietly replied. "At my time of life, food and clothing be all that is needed, and I have little occasion for what you call plunder, unless it may be, now and then, to barter for a horn of powder or a bar of lead."

"You ar' not, then, of these parts, by natur', friend!" the emigrant continued, having in his mind the exception which the other had taken to the very equivocal word, which he himself, according to the customs of the country, had used for "baggage" or "effects."

"I was born on the sea–shore, though most of my life has been passed in the woods."

The whole party, now looked up at him, as men are apt to turn their eyes on some unexpected object of general interest. One or two of the young men, repeated the words "sea–shore," and the woman tendered him one of those civilities, with which, uncouth as they were, she was little accustomed to grace her hospitality, as if in deference to the travelled dignity of her guest. After a long, and, seemingly a meditating silence, the emigrant, who had, however, seen no apparent necessity to suspend the functions of his powers of mastication, resumed the discourse.

"It is a long road, as I have heard, from the waters of the west to the shores of the main sea?"

"It is a weary path, indeed, friend; and much have I seen, and something have I suffered in journeying over it."

"A man would see a good deal of hard travel in going its length!"

"Seventy and five years have I been upon the road, and there are not half that number of leagues in the whole distance, after you leave the Hudson, on which I have not tasted venison of my own killing. But this is vain boasting! of what use are former deeds, when time draws to an end!"

"I once met a man, that had boated on the river he names," observed one of the sons, speaking in a low tone of voice, like one who distrusted his knowledge, and deemed it prudent to assume a becoming diffidence in the presence of a man who had seen so much; "from his tell, it must be a considerable stream, and deep enough for a keel, from top to bottom."

"It is a wide and deep water–course, and many sightly towns, are there growing on its banks," returned the trapper; "and yet it is but a brook, to the waters of the endless river!"

"I call nothing a stream, that a man can travel round," exclaimed the ill–looking associate of the emigrant; "a real river must be crossed; not headed, like a bear in a country hunt."

"Have you been far towards the sun–down, friend?" again interrupted the emigrant, as if he desired to keep his rough companion, as much as possible out of the discourse. "I find it is a wide tract of clearing, this, into which I have fallen."

"You may travel weeks, and you will see it the same. I often think the Lord has placed this barren belt of prairie, behind the states, to warn men to what their folly may yet bring the land! Ay! weeks if not months, may you journey in these open fields, in which there is neither dwelling, nor habitation for man or beast. Even the savage animals travel mileson miles to seek their dens. And yet the wind seldom blows from the east, but I conceit the sounds of axes, and the crash of falling trees are in my ears."

As the old man spoke with the seriousness and dignity that age seldom fails to communicate, even, to less striking sentiments, his auditors were deeply attentive, and as silent as the grave. Indeed, the trapper was left to renew the dialogue, himself, which he soon did by asking a question, in the indirect manner so much in use by the border inhabitants.

"You found it no easy matter to ford the water–courses, and make your way so deep into the prairies, friend, with teams of horses, and herds of horned beasts?"

"I kept the left bank of the main river," the emigrant replied, "until I found the stream leading too much to the north, when we rafted ourselves across, without any great suffering. The woman lost a fleece or two from the next year's shearing, and the girls have one cow less to their dairy. Since then, we have done bravely, by bridging a creek, every day or two."

"It is likely you will continue west, until you come to land more suitable for a settlement?"

"Until I see reason to stop, or to turn ag'in," the emigrant bluntly answered, rising at the same time, and cutting short the dialogue, by an air of dissatisfaction, no less than by the suddenness of the movement. His example, was followed by the trapper, as well as the rest of the party, and then, without much deference to the presence of their guest, the travellers proceeded to make their dispositions to pass the night. Several little bowers, or rather huts, had already been formed of the tops of trees, blankets of coarse country manufacture, and the skins of buffaloes, united without much reference to any other object than temporary comfort. Into these covers the children with their mother soon drew themselves,and where, it is more than possible, they were all speedily lost in the oblivion of sleep. Before the men, however, could seek their rest, they had sundry little duties to perform; such as completing their works of defence; carefully concealing the fires; replenishing the fodder of their cattle, and setting the watch that was to protect the party in the approaching hours of deeper night.

The former was effected by dragging the trunks of a few trees, into the intervals left by the wagons, and along the open space, between the vehicles and the thicket, on which, in military language, the encampment would be said to have rested; thus forming a sort of chevaux−de−frise on three sides of the position. Within these narrow limits (with the exception of what the tent contained,) both man and beast were now collected; the latter being far too happy in resting their weary limbs, to give any undue annoyance to their scarcely more intelligent associates. Two of the young men took their rifles, and first renewing the priming and examining the flints, with the utmost care, they proceeded, the one to the extreme right and the other to the left of the encampment, where they posted themselves, within the shadows of the thicket, but in such positions, as enabled each to overlook his proper portion of the prairie.

The trapper had loitered about the place, declining to share the straw of the emigrant, until the whole arrangement was completed; and then without the ceremony of an adieu, he slowly retired from the spot.

It was now in the first watch of the night, and the pale, quivering, and deceptive light, from a new moon, was playing over the endless waves of the prairie, tipping the swells with gleams of brightness, and leaving the interval land in deep shadow. Accustomed to scenes of solitude like the present, the old man, as he left the encampment proceeded aloneinto the wide waste, like a bold vessel leaving its haven to trust itself on the trackless field of the ocean. He appeared to move for some time, without object, or indeed, without any apparent consciousness, whither his limbs were carrying him. At length, on reaching the rise of one of the undulations, he came to a stand, and for the first time, since leaving the band, who had caused such a flood of reflections and recollections to crowd upon his mind, the old man became aware of his present situation. Throwing one end of his rifle to the earth, he stood leaning on the other, again lost in deep contemplation for several minutes, during which time his hound came and crouched close at his feet. It was a deep, menacing, growl from the faithful animal, that first aroused him from his musing.

"What now, dog?" he said, looking down at his companion, as though he addressed a being of an intelligence equal to his own, and speaking in a voice of great affection. "What is it, pup? ha! Hector; what is it nosing, now? It won't do, dog; it won't do; the very fa'ns play in open view of us, without minding two such worn out curs, as you and I. Instinct is their gift, Hector; and, they have found out how little we are to be feared, now; they have!"

The dog stretched his head upward, and responded to the words of his master by a long and plaintive whine, which he even continued after he had again buried his head in the grass as if he held an intelligent communication with one who so well knew how to interpret dumb discourse.

"This is a manifest warning, Hector!" the trapper continued, dropping his voice, to the tones of caution and looking warily about him. "What is it, pup; what is it?"

The hound had, however, already laid his nose to the earth, and was silent; appearing to slumber. But the keen quick glances of his master, soon caught aglimpse of a distant figure, which seemed, through the deceptive light, floating along the very elevation on which he had placed himself. Presently its proportions became more distinct, and then an airy, female form appeared to hesitate, as if considering whether it would be prudent to advance. Though the eyes of the dog, were now to be seen glancing in the rays of the moon, opening and shutting lazily, he gave no further signs of displeasure.

"Come nigher; we are friends," said the trapper, associating himself with his companion by long use and, probably, through the strength of the secret tie that connected them together; "we are your friends; none will harm you."

Encouraged by the mild tones of his voice, and perhaps led on by the earnestness of her purpose, the female approached, until, she stood at his side; when the old man perceived his visiter to be the young woman, with whom the reader, has already become acquainted by the name of "Ellen Wade."

"I had thought you were gone," she said, looking timidly and anxiously around. "They said you were gone; and that we should never see you again. I did not think, it was you!"

"Men are no common objects in these empty fields," returned the trapper, "and I humbly hope, though I have so long consorted with the beasts of the wilderness, that I have not yet lost the look of my kind."

"Oh! I knew you to be a man, and I thought I knew the whine of the hound, too," she answered, hastily, as if willing to explain she knew not what, and then checking herself, as though fearful of having, already, said too much.

"I saw no dogs, among the teams of your father," the trapper dryly remarked.

"Father!" exclaimed the girl, feelingly, "I have no father! I had nearly said no friend." The old man, turned towards her, with a look of kindness and interest, that was even more conciliating than the ordinary, upright, and benevolent expression of his weather–beaten countenance.

"Why then do you venture in a place where none but the strong should come?" he demanded. "Did you not know that, when you crossed the big river, you left a friend behind you that is always bound to look to the young and feeble, like yourself."

"Of whom do you speak?"

"The law——'tis bad to have it, but, I sometimes think, it is worse, where it is never to be found. Yes ——yes, the law is needed, when such as have not the gifts of strength and wisdom are to be taken care of. I hope, young woman, if you have no father, you have at least a brother."

The maiden felt the tacit reproach conveyed in this covert question, and for a moment remained in an embarrassed silence. But catching a glimpse of the mild and serious features of her companion, as he continued to gaze on her with a look of interest, she replied, firmly, and in a manner that left no doubt she comprehended his meaning:

"Heaven forbid that any such as you have seen, should be a brother of mine or any thing else near or dear to me! But, tell me, do you then actually live alone, in this desert district, old man; is there really none here besides yourself?"

"There are hundreds, nay, thousands of the rightful owners of the country, roving about the plains; but few of our own colour."

"And have you then met none who are white, but us?" interrupted the girl, like one too impatient to await the tardy explanation his age and deliberation were about to make.

"Not in many days——Hush, Hector, hush," he added in reply to a low, and nearly inaudible, growl from his hound. "The dog scents mischief in thewind! The black bears from the mountains sometimes make their way, even lower than this. The pup is not apt to complain of the harmless game. I am not so ready and true with the piece as I used–to–could–be, yet I have struck even the fiercest animals of the prairie, in my time; so, you have little reason for fear, young woman."

The girl, raised her eyes, in that peculiar manner which is so often practised by her sex, when they commence their glances, by examining the earth at their feet, and terminate them by noting every thing within the power of human vision; but she rather manifested the quality of impatience, than any feeling of alarm.

A short bark from the dog, however, soon gave a new direction to the looks of both, and then the real object of his second warning became dimly visible.

CHAPTER III.

"Come, come, thou art as hot a Jack in thy mood, as any in Italy; and as soon mov'd to be moody, and as soon moody to be moved."

—— Romeo and Juliet

Though the trapper manifested some surprise when he perceived that another human figure was approaching him, and that, too, from a direction opposite to the place where the emigrant had made his encampment, it was with the steadiness of one long accustomed to scenes of danger.

"This is a man," he said; "and one who has white blood in his veins, or his step would be lighter. It will be well to be ready for the worst, as the half–and–halfs, that one meets, in these distant districts, are altogether more barbarous than the real savage."

He raised his rifle while he spoke, and assuredhimself of the state of its flint, as well as of the priming by manual examination. But his arm was arrested, while in the act of throwing forward the muzzle of the piece, by the eager and trembling hands of his companion.

"For God's sake, be not too hasty," she said; "it may be a friend——an acquaintance——a neighbour."

"A friend!" the old man repeated, deliberately releasing himself, at the same time, from her grasp. "Friends are rare in any land, and less in this, perhaps, than in another; and the neighbourhood is too thinly settled, to make it likely, that he who comes towards us is even an acquaintance."

"But though a stranger, you would not seek his blood!"

The trapper earnestly regarded her anxious and frightened features, a moment, and then he dropped the butt of his rifle on the ground, again, like one whose purpose had undergone a sudden change.

"No," he said, speaking rather to himself, than to his timid companion, "she is right; blood is not to be spilt, to save the life of one so useless, and so near his allotted time. Let him come on; my skins, my traps, and even my rifle shall be his, if he sees fit to demand them."

"He will ask for neither——He wants neither," returned the girl; "if he be an honest man, he will surely be content with his own, and ask for nothing that is the property of another."

The trapper had not time to express the surprise he felt at the incoherent and contradictory language he heard, for the man who was advancing, was, already, within fifty feet of the place where they stood.—— In the mean time, Hector had not been an indifferent witness of what was passing. At the sound of the distant footsteps, he had arisen, from his warm bed at the feet of his master; and now, as the stranger appeared in open view he stalked slowly towards him,crouching to the earth like a panther about to take his leap.

"Call in your dog," said a firm, deep, manly voice, in tones of friendship, rather than of menace; "I love a hound, and should be sorry to do an injury to the animal."

"You hear what is said about you, pup?" the trapper answered; "come hither, fool. His growl and his bark are all that is left him now; you may come on, friend; the hound is toothless."

The stranger instantly profited by the intelligence. He sprang eagerly forward, and at the next instant stood at the side of Ellen Wade. After assuring himself of the identity of the latter, by a hasty but keen glance, he turned his attention, with a quickness and impatience, that proved the interest he took in the result, to a similar examination of her companion.

"From what cloud have you fallen, my good old man?" he said in a careless, off-hand, heedless manner that seemed too natural to be assumed. "Or do you actually live, hereaway, in the prairies."

"I have been long on earth, and never I hope nigher to heaven, than I am at this moment," returned the trapper; "my dwelling, if dwelling I may be said to have, is not far distant. Now may I take the liberty with you, that you are so willing to take with others? Whence do you come, and where is your home?"

"Softly, softly; when I have done with my catechism, it will be time to begin with your's. What sport is this, you follow by moonlight? You are not dodging the buffaloes at such an hour!"

"I am, as you see, going from an encampment of travellers, which lies over yonder swell in the land, to my own wigwam; in doing so, I wrong no man."

"All fair and true. And you got this young woman to show you the way, because she knows it so well and you know so little about it."

"I met her, as I have met you, by accident. For ten tiresome years have I dwelt on these open fields, and never, before to-night, have I found human beings with white skins on them, at this hour. If my presence here gives offence, I am sorry; and will go my way. It is more than likely that when your young friend, has told her story, you will be better given to believe mine."

"Friend!" said the youth, lifting a cap of skins from his head, and running his fingers leisurely through a dense mass of black and shaggy locks, "if I ever laid eyes on the girl before to-night, may I..."

"You've said enough, Paul," interrupted the female, laying her hand on his mouth, with a familiarity, that gave something very like the lie direct, to his intended asseveration. "Our secret will be safe, with this honest old man. I know it by his looks, and kind words."

"Our secret! Ellen, have you forgot..."

"Nothing. I have not forgotten any thing I should remember. But still I say we are safe with this honest trapper.

"Trapper! is he then a trapper? Give me your hand, father; our trades should bring us acquainted."

"There is little call for handicrafts in this region," returned the other, examining the athletic and active form of the youth, as he leaned carelessly and not ungracefully, on his rifle; "the art of taking the creatur's of God, in traps and nets, is one that needs more cunning than manhood; and yet am I brought to practise it, in my age! But it would be quite as seemly, in one like you, to follow a pursuit better becoming your years and courage."

"Me! I never took even a slinking mink or a paddling musk-rat in a cage; though I admit having peppered a few of the dark-skin'd devils, when I had much better have kept my powder in the horn andthe lead in its pouch. Not I, old man; nothing that crawls the earth is for my sport."

"What then may you do for a living, friend; for little profit is to be made in these districts, if a man denies himself his lawful right in the beasts of the fields."

"I deny myself nothing. If a bear crosses my path, he is soon no bear. The deer begin to nose me; and as for the buffaloe, I have kill'd more beef, old stranger, than the largest butcher in all Kentuck."

"You can shoot, then!" demanded the trapper, with a glow of latent fire, glimmering about his small, deep-set, eyes; "is your hand true, and your look quick?"

"The first is like a steel trap, and the last nimbler than a buck-shot. I wish it was hot noon, now, grand'ther; and that there was an acre or two of your white swans or of black feathered ducks going south, over our heads; you or Ellen, here, might set your heart on the finest in the flock, and my character against a horn of powder, that the bird would be hanging head downwards, in five minutes, and that too, with a single ball. I scorn a shot-gun! No man can say, he ever knew me carry one, a rod."

"The lad has good in him! I see it plainly by his manner;" said the trapper, turning to Ellen with an openly, encouraging air; "I will take it on myself to say, that you are not unwise in meeting him, as you do. Tell me, lad; did you ever strike a leaping buck atwixt the antlers? Hector; quiet, pup; quiet. The very name of venison, quickens the blood of the cur;——did you ever take an animal in that fashion, on the long leap?"

"You might just as well ask me, did you ever eat? There is no fashion, old stranger, that a deer has not been touched by my hand, unless it was when asleep."

"Ay, ay; you have a long, and a happy——ay, and an honest life afore you! I am old, and I suppose Imight also say, worn out and useless; but, if it was given me to choose my time, and place, again,——as such things are not and ought not ever to be given to the will of man——though if such a gift was to be given me, I would say, twenty and the wilderness! But, tell me; how do you part with the peltry?"

"With my pelts! I never took a skin from a buck, nor a quill from a goose, in my life! I knock them over, now and then, for a meal, and sometimes to keep my finger true to the touch; but when hunger is satisfied, the prairie wolves get the remainder. No ——no——I keep to my calling; which pays me better, than all the fur I could sell on the other side of the big river."

The old man appeared to ponder a little; but shaking his head, he soon musingly continued——

"I know of but one business that can be followed here with profit——"

He was interrupted by the youth, who raised a small cup of tin, which dangled at his neck before the other's eyes, and springing its lid, the delicious odour of the finest flavoured honey, diffused itself over the organs of the trapper.

"A bee hunter!" observed the latter, with a readiness that proved he understood the nature of the occupation, though not without some little surprise at discovering one of the other's spirited mien engaged in so humble a pursuit. "It pays well in the skirts of the settlements, but I should call it a doubtful trade, in the open districts."

"You think a tree is wanting for a swarm to settle in! But I know differently; and so I have stretched out a few hundred miles farther west, than common, to taste your honey. And, now, I have bated your curiosity, stranger, you will just move aside, while I tell the remainder of my story to this young woman."

"It is not necessary, I'm sure it is not necessarythat he should leave us," said Ellen, with a haste that implied some little consciousness of the singularity if not of the impropriety of the request. "You can have nothing to say that the whole world might not hear."

"No! well, may I be stung to death by drones, if I understand the buzzings of a woman's mind! For my part, Ellen, I care for nothing nor any body; and am just as ready to go down to the place where your uncle, if uncle you can call one, who I'll swear is no relation, has hoppled his teams, and tell the old man my mind now, as I shall be a year hence. You have only to say a single word, and the thing is done; let him like it or not."

"You are ever so hasty and so rash, Paul Hover, that I seldom know when I am safe with you. How can you, who know the danger of our being seen together, speak of going before my uncle and his sons!"

"Has he done that of which he has reason to be ashamed?" demanded the trapper, who had not moved an inch from the place he first occupied.

"Heaven forbid! But there are reasons, why he should not be seen, just now, that could do him no harm if known, but which may not yet be told. And, so, if you will wait, father, near yonder willow bush, until I have heard what Paul can possibly have to say, I shall be sure to come and wish you a good night, before I return to the camp."

The trapper drew slowly aside, as if satisfied with the somewhat incoherent reason Ellen had given why he should retire. When completely out of ear shot of the earnest and hurried dialogue, that instantly commenced between the two he had left, the old man, again paused, and patiently awaited the moment when he might renew his conversation with beings in whom he felt a growing interest, no less from the mysterious character of their intercourse, than from a natural sympathy in the welfare of a pair soyoung, and who, as in the simplicity of his heart he was also fain to believe, were also so deserving. He was accompanied by his indolent, but attached dog, who once more made his bed at the feet of his master, and soon lay slumbering as usual, with his head nearly buried in the dense fog of the prairie grass.

It was a spectacle so unusual to see the human form amid the solitude in which he dwelt, that the trapper bent his eyes on the dim figures of his new acquaintants, with sensations to which he had long been a stranger. Their presence awakened recollections and emotions, to which his sturdy but honest nature had latterly paid but little homage, and his thoughts began to wander over the varied scenes of a life of hardships, that had been strangely blended with scenes of wild and peculiar enjoyment. The train taken by his thoughts had, already, conducted him, in imagination, far into an ideal world, when he was, once more suddenly, recalled to the reality of his situation, by the movements of his faithful hound.

The dog, who, in submission to his years and infirmities, had manifested such a decided propensity to sleep, now, arose, and stalked from out the shadow cast by the tall person of his master, and looked abroad into the prairie, as though his instinct apprised him of the presence of still another visiter. Then, seemingly, content with his examination, he returned to his comfortable post and disposed of his weary limbs, with the deliberation and care of one who was no novice in the art of self-preservation.

"What; again, Hector!" said the trapper in a soothing voice, which he had the caution, however, to utter in an under tone; "what is it, dog? tell his master, pup; what is it?"

Hector answered with another growl, but was content to continue in his lair. These were evidences of intelligence and distrust, to which one as practised as the trapper could not turn an inattentive ear.He again spoke to the dog, encouraging him to watchfulness, by a low, guarded, whistle. The animal however, as if conscious of having, already, discharged his duty, obstinately refused to raise his head from the grass.

"A hint from such a friend is far better than man's advice!" muttered the trapper, as he slowly moved towards the couple who were yet, too earnestly and abstractedly, engaged in their own discourse, to notice his approach; "and none but a conceited settler would hear it and not respect it, as he ought. Children," he added, when nigh enough to address his companions, "we are not alone in these dreary fields; there are others stirring, and, therefore, to the shame of our kind, be it said, danger is nigh."

"If one of them lazy sons of Skirting Ishmael is prowling out of his camp to-night," said the young bee–hunter, with great vivacity, and in tones that might easily have been excited to a menace, "he may have an end put to his journey, sooner than either he or his father is dreaming!"

"My life on it, they are all with the teams," hurriedly answered the girl. "I saw the whole of them asleep, myself, except the two on watch; and their natures have greatly changed, if they, too, are not both dreaming of a turkey hunt or a court–house fight, at this very moment."

"Some beast, with a strong scent, has passed between the wind and the hound, father, and it makes him uneasy; or, perhaps, he too is dreaming. I had, a pup, of my own in Kentuck, that, would start upon a long chase from a deep sleep; and all upon the fancy of some dream. Go to him, and pinch his ear, that the beast may feel the life within him."

"Not so——not so," returned the trapper, shaking his head as one who better understood the qualities of his dog.——"Youth sleeps, ay, and dreams too; but age is awake and watchful. The pup is never falsewith his nose, and long experience tells me to heed his warnings."

"Did you ever run him upon the trail of carrion?"

"Why, I must say, that the ravenous beasts have sometimes tempted me to let him loose, for they are as greedy as men, after the venison, in its season; but then I knew the reason of the dog, would tell him the object——No——no, Hector is an animal known in the ways of man, and will never strike a false trail when a true one is to be followed!"

"Ay, ay, the secret is out! you have run the hound on the track of a wolf, and his nose has a better memory than his master!" said the bee-hunter, laughing.

I have seen the creatur' sleep for hours, with pack after pack, in open view. A wolf might eat out of his tray without a snarl, unless there was a scarcity; then, indeed, Hector would be apt to claim his own."

"There are panthers down from the mountains; I saw one make a leap at a sick deer, as the sun was setting. Go; go you back to the dog, and tell him the truth, father; in a minute, I..."

He was interrupted by a long, loud and piteous howl from the hound, which rose on the air of the evening, like the wailing of some spirit of the place, and passed off into the prairie, in cadences that rose and fell, like its own undulating surface. The trapper was impressively silent, listening intently. Even the reckless bee-hunter, was struck with the wailing wildness of the sounds. After a short pause the former whistled the dog to his side, and then turning to his companions he said with the seriousness, which, in his opinion, the occasion demanded——

"They who think man enjoys all the knowledge of the creaturs of God, will live to be disappointed, if they reach, as I have done, the age of fourscore years. I will not take upon myself to say what mischiefis brewing, nor will I vouch that, even, the hound himself knows so much; but that evil is nigh, and that wisdom invites us to avoid it, I have heard from the mouth of one who never lies. I did think, the pup had become unused to the footsteps of man, and that your presence made him uneasy; but his nose has been on a long scent the whole evening, and what I mistook as a notice of your coming, has been intended for something much more serious. If the advice of an old man, is, then, worth hearkening to, children, you will quickly, go different ways to your places of shelter and safety."

"If I quit Ellen, at such a moment," exclaimed the youth, "may I never..."

"You've said enough!" the girl interrupted, by again interposing a hand that might, both by its delicacy and colour, have graced a far more elevated station in life; "my time is out; and we must part, at all events——So good night, Paul——Father——good night."

"Hist!" said the youth, seizing her arm, as she was in the very act of tripping from his side—— "Hist! do you hear nothing? There are buffaloes playing their pranks, at no great distance——That sound beats the earth like a mad herd of the scampering devils!"

His two companions listened, as people in their situation would be apt to lend their faculties to discover the meaning of any doubtful noises, especially, when heard after so many and such startling warnings. The unusual sounds were now unequivocally though still faintly audible. The youth and his female companion, had made several hurried, and vacillating conjectures concerning their nature, when a current of the night air brought the rush of trampling footsteps, too sensibly, to their ears, to render mistake any longer possible.

"I am right!" said the bee–hunter; "a panther is driving a herd before him; or may be there is a battle among the beasts."

"Your ears are cheats;" returned the old man, who, from the moment his own organs had been able to catch the distant sounds, had stood like a statue made to represent deep attention——"The leaps are too long for the buffaloe, and too regular for terror. Hist! now they are in a bottom where the grass is high, and the sound is deadened! Ay, there they go on the hard earth! And now they come up the swell, dead upon us; they will be here afore you can find a cover!"

"Come, Ellen," cried the youth, seizing his companion by the hand, "let us make a trial for the encampment."

"Too late! too late!" exclaimed the trapper, "for the creaturs are in open view; and a bloody band of accursed Siouxs they are, by their thieving look, and the random fashion in which they ride!"

"Siouxs or devils, they shall find us men!" said the bee-hunter, with a mien as fierce as though he led a party of superior strength, and of a courage equal to his own——"You have a piece, old man, and will pull a trigger in behalf of a helpless, christian, girl!"

"Down, down into the grass——down with ye both," whispered the trapper, intimating to them to turn aside to the tall weeds, which grew, in a denser body than common, near the place where they stood. "You've not the time to fly, nor the numbers to fight, foolish boy. Down into the grass, if you prize the young woman, or value the gift of your own life!"

His remonstrance, seconded, as it was, by a prompt and energetic action, did not fail to produce the submission to his order, which the occasion now seemed, indeed, so imperiously to require. The moon had fallen behind a sheet of thin, fleecy, clouds, whichskirted the horizon, leaving just enough of its faint and fluctuating light, to render objects visible, dimly revealing their forms and proportions. The trapper, by exercising that species of influence, over his companions, which experience and decision usually assert, in cases of emergency, had effectually succeeded in concealing them in the grass, and by the aid of the feeble rays of the luminary, he was enabled to scan the disorderly party which was riding, like so many madmen, directly upon them.

A band of beings, who resembled demons rather than men, sporting in their nightly revels across the bleak plain, was in truth approaching, at a fearful rate, and in a direction to leave little hope that some one among them, at least, would not pass over the spot were the trapper and his companions lay. At intervals, the clattering of hoofs was borne along by the night wind, quite audibly in their front, and then, again, their progress through the fog of the autumnal grass, was swift and silent; adding to the unearthly appearance of the spectacle. The trapper, who had called in his hound, and bidden him crouch at his side, now kneeled in the cover, also, and, kept a keen and watchful eye on the route of the band, soothing the fears of the girl, and restraining the impatience of the youth, in the same breath.

"If there's one, there's thirty of the miscreants!" he said in a sort of episode to his whispered comments. "Ay, ay; they are edging towards the river ——Peace, pup——peace——no, here they come this way again——the thieves don't seem to know their own er rand! If there were just six of us, lad, what a beautiful ambushment we might make upon them, from this very spot——it wont do, it wont do, boy; keep yourself closer, or your head will be seen——besides, I'm not altogether strong in the opinion it would be lawful, as they have done us no harm——There they bend ag'in to the river——no; here they come up theswell——now is the moment to be as still, as if the breath had done its duty and departed the body."

The figure of the old man sunk into the grass while he was speaking, as though the final separation to which he alluded, had, in his own case, actually occurred, and, at the next instant, a band of wild horsemen, whirled by them, with the noiseless rapidity in which it might be imagined a troop of spectres would pass. The dark and fleeting forms were already vanished, when the trapper ventured, again, to raise his head to a level with the tops of the bending herbage, motioning, at the same time to his companions, to maintain their positions and their silence.

"They are going down the swell, towards the encampment," he continued, in his former guarded tones; "no, they halt in the bottom, and are clustering together like deer, in council. By the Lord, they are turning, ag'in, and we are not yet done with the reptiles!"

Once more he sought his friendly cover, and at the next instant, the dark troop were to be seen riding, in a disorderly manner, on the very summit of the little elevation. It was now soon apparent that they had returned to avail themselves of the height of the ground, in order to examine the dim horizon.

Some dismounted, while others rode to and fro, like men engaged in a local inquiry of much interest. Happily, for the hidden party, the grass in which they were concealed, not only served to skreen them from the eyes of the savages, but opposed an obstacle to prevent their horses, which were no less rude and untrained than their riders, from trampling on them, in their irregular and wild paces.

At length an athletic and dark looking Indian, who, by his air of authority, would seem to be the leader, summoned his chiefs about him, to a consultation, which was held, mounted. This body was collected on the very margin of that mass of herbagein which the trapper and his companions were hid. As the young man looked up and saw the threatening and fierce aspect of the groupe, which was increasing at each instant by the accession of some countenance and figure, apparently more forbidding than any which had preceded it, he drew his rifle, by a very natural impulse, from beneath him, and commenced putting it in a state for instant service. The female, at his side, buried her face in the grass, by a feeling that was, possibly, quite as natural to her sex and habits, leaving him to follow the impulses of his hot blood, but his aged and more prudent adviser, whispered, sternly, in his ear,

"The tick of the lock is as well known to the knaves, as the blast of a trumpet to a soldier! lay down the piece——lay down the piece——should the moon touch the barrel, it could not fail to be seen by the devils, whose eyes are keener than the blackest snake's! The smallest motion, now, would be sure to bring an arrow among us."

The bee—hunter so far obeyed as to continue immoveable and silent. But there was still sufficient light to convince his companion, by the contracted brow and threatening eye of the young man, that a discovery would not bestow a bloodless victory on the savages. Finding his advice disregarded, the trapper took his measures accordingly, and awaited the result with a resignation and calmness that were characteristic of the individual.

In the mean time, the Siouxs (for the sagacity of the old man was not deceived in the character of his dangerous visiters) had terminated their council, and were again dispersed along the ridge of land as if they sought some hidden object.

"The imps have heard the hound!" whispered the trapper, "and their ears are too true to be cheated in the distance. Keep close, lad, keep close; down with your head to the very earth, like a dog that sleeps."

"Let us rather take to our feet, and trust to manhood," returned his impatient companion——

He would have proceeded, but feeling a hand laid rudely on his shoulder, he turned his eyes upward, and beheld the dark and savage countenance of an Indian gleaming full upon him. Notwithstanding the surprise and the disadvantage of his attitude, the youth was not disposed to become a captive, so easily. Quicker than the flash of his own gun, he sprang upon his feet, and was throttling his opponent with a power that would soon have terminated the contest, when he felt the arms of the trapper thrown around his body, confining his exertions by a strength very little inferior to his own. Before he had time to reproach his comrade for this apparent treachery, a dozen Siouxs, were around them, and the whole party were compelled to yield themselves as prisoners.

CHAPTER IV

"With much more dismay,

I view the fight, than those that make the fray."

—— Merchant of Venice

The unfortunate bee–hunter and his companions had now become the captives of a people, who might, without exaggeration, be called the Ishmaelites of the American deserts. From time immemorial, the hands of the Siouxs had been turned against their neighbours of the prairies, and even at this day, when the influence and authority of a civilized government are beginning to be felt around them, they are considered as a treacherous and dangerous race. At the period of our tale, the case was far worse; few white men trusting themselves in the remote and unprotected regions where so false a tribe was known to dwell.

Notwithstanding the peaceable submission of the trapper, he was quite aware of the character of the band, into whose hands he had fallen. It would have been difficult, however, for the nicest judge to have determined whether fear, policy or resignation formed the secret motive of the old man, in permitting himself to be plundered as he did, without a murmur. So far from opposing any remonstrance to the rude and violent manner in which his conquerors performed the customary office, he even anticipated their cupidity, by tendering to the chiefs such articles as he thought might prove the most acceptable. On the other hand Paul Hover, who had been literally a conquered man, manifested the strongest repugnance to submit to the violent liberties that were taken with his person and property. He even, gave several, exceedingly, unequivocal demonstrations of his displeasure during the summary process, and would, more than once, have broken out, in open and desperate resistance, but for the admonitions and intreaties of the trembling girl, who clung to his side, in a manner so dependant, as to show the youth, that her hopes were now placed, no less on his discretion, than on his disposition to serve her.

The Indians had, however, no sooner deprived the captives of their arms and ammunition, and stript them of a few articles of dress of little use and perhaps of less value, than they appeared disposed to grant them a respite. Business of greater moment pressed on their hands, and required their instant attention. Another consultation of the chiefs was con vened, and it was apparent, by the earnest and vehement manner of the few who spoke, that the warriors conceived their success as yet to be far from complete.

"It will be well," whispered the trapper, who knew enough of the language he heard to comprehend perfectly the subject of the discussion, "if thetravellers who lie near the willow brake are not awoke out of their sleep by a visit from these miscreants. They are too cunning to believe that a woman of the "pale–faces" is to be found so far from the settlements, without having a white man's inventions and comforts at hand."

"If they will carry the tribe of wandering Ishmael to the Rocky Mountains," said the young bee–hunter, laughing in his vexation with a sort of bitter merriment, "I may forgive the rascals."

"Paul! Paul!" exclaimed his companion in a tone of reproach, "you forget all! Think of the dreadful consequences!"

"Ay, it was thinking of what you call consequences, Ellen, that prevented me from putting the matter, at once, to yonder red–devil, and making it a real knock–down and drag–out! Old trapper, the sin of this cowardly business lies on your shoulders! But it is no more than your daily calling, I reckon, to take men, as well as beasts, in the snares."

"I implore you, Paul, to be calm——to be patient."

"Well, since it is your wish, Ellen," returned the youth, endeavouring to swallow his spleen, "I will make the trial; though, as you ought to know, it is part of the religion of a Kentuckian, to fret himself, a little, at a mischance."

"I fear your friends in the other bottom will not escape the eyes of the imps!" continued the trapper, as coolly as though he had not heard a syllable of the intervening discourse——"They scent plunder; and it would be as hard to drive a hound from his game as to throw the varmints from its trail."

"Is there nothing to be done!" asked Ellen, in an imploring manner which proved the sincerity of her concern.

"It would be an easy matter to call out, in so loud a voice as to make old Ishmael dream that the wolves were among his flock," Paul replied; "I can makemyself heard a mile in these open fields, and his camp is but a short quarter from us."

"And get knocked on the head for your pains," returned the trapper——"No, no; cunning must match cunning, or the hounds will murder the whole family."

"Murder! no——no murder. Ishmael loves travel so well, there would be no harm in his having a look at the other sea, but the old fellow is in a bad condition to take the long journey! I would try a lock myself before he should be quite murdered."

"His party is strong in number, and well armed; do you think it will fight?"

"Look here, old trapper——Few men love Ishmael Bush and his seven sledge–hammer sons less than one Paul Hover; but I scorn to slander even a Tennessee shot–gun. There is as much of the true stand–up courage among them, as there is in any family that was ever raised in Kentuck. They are a long–sided and a double–jointed breed; and let me tell you, that he who takes the measure of one of them on the ground, must be a workman at a hug."

"Hist! The savages have done their talk, and are about to set their accursed devices in motion Let us be patient; something may yet offer in favour of your friends."

"Friends! call none of the race a friend of mine, trapper, if you have the smallest regard for my affection! What I say in their favour is less from love than honesty."

"I did not know but the young woman was of the kin," returned the other, a little drily——"But no offence should be taken, where none was intended."

The mouth of Paul was again stopped by the hand of Ellen, who took on herself to reply, in her gentle and conciliating tones, "We should be all of a family, when it is in our power to serve each other. We depend entirely on your experience, honest old man,to discover the means to apprise our friends of their danger."

"There will be a real time of it," muttered the bee–hunter, laughing, "if the boys get at work in good earnest with these red skins!"

He was interrupted by a general movement which took place among the band. The Indians dismounted to a man, giving their horses in charge to three or four of the party, who were also intrusted with the safe keeping of the prisoners. They then formed themselves in a circle around a warrior, who appeared to possess the chief authority; and at a given signal the whole array moved slowly and cautiously from the centre in straight and consequently in diverging lines. Most of their dark forms were soon blended with the brown covering of the prairie; though the captives, who watched the slightest movement of their enemies with vigilant eyes, were now and then enabled to discern a human figure, drawn against the horizon, as some one, more eager than the rest, rose to his greatest height in order to extend the limits of his view. But it was not long before even these fugitive glimpses of the moving, and constantly increasing circle, were lost, and uncertainty and conjecture were added to apprehension. In this manner passed many anxious and weary minutes, during the close of which the listeners expected at each moment to hear the whoop of the assailants and the shrieks of the assailed, rising together on the stillness of the night. But it would seem, that the search which was so evidently making, was without a sufficient object; for at the expiration of half an hour the different individuals of the band began to return singly, gloomy and sullen, like men who were disappointed.

"Our time is at hand," observed the trapper, who noted the smallest incident, or the slightest indication of hostility among the savages; "we are now to bequestioned; and if I know any thing of the policy of our case, I should say it would be wise to choose one among us to hold the discourse, in order that our testimony may agree. And furthermore, if an opinion from one as old and as worthless as a hunter of fourscore, is to be regarded, I would just venture to say, that man should be the one most skilled in the natur' of an Indian, and that he should also know something of their language——Are you acquainted with the tongue of the Siouxes, friend?"

"Swarm your own hive," returned the discontented bee–hunter. "You are good at buzzing, old trapper, if you are good at nothing else."

"'Tis the gift of youth to be rash and heady," the trapper calmly retorted. "The day has been, boy, when my blood was like your own, too swift and too hot to run quietly in my veins. But what will it profit to talk of silly risks and foolish acts at this time of life! A grey head should cover a brain of reason, and not the tongue of a boaster."

"True, true," whispered Ellen; "and we have other things to attend to now! Here comes the Indian to put his questions."

The girl, whose apprehensions had quickened her senses, was not deceived. She was yet speaking when a tall, half naked savage, approached the spot where they stood, and after examining the whole party as closely as the dim light permitted, for more than a minute in perfect stillness, he gave the usual salutation in the harsh and guttural tones of his own language. The trapper replied as well as he could, which it seems was sufficiently well to be understood. In order to escape the imputation of pedantry we shall render the substance, and, so far as it is possible the form of the dialogue that succeeded, into the English tongue.

"Have the pale–faces eaten their own buffaloes, and taken the skins from all their own beavers," continuedthe savage, allowing the usual moment of decorum to elapse, after his words of greeting, before he again spoke, "that they come to count how many are left among the Pawnees?"

"Some of us are here to buy, and some to sell," returned the trapper; "but none will follow, if they hear it is not safe to come nigh the lodge of a Sioux."

"The Siouxes are thieves, and they live among the snow; why do we talk of a people who are so far, when we are in the country of the Pawnees?"

"If the Pawnees are the owners of this land, then white and red are here by equal right."

"Have not the pale–faces stolen enough from the red men, that you come so far to carry a lie? I have said that this is a hunting–ground of my tribe."

"My right to be here is equal to your own," the trapper rejoined with undisturbed coolness; "I do not speak as I might——It is better to be silent. The Pawnees and the white men are brothers, but a Sioux dare not show his face in the village of the Loups."

"The Dahcotahs are men!" exclaimed the savage, fiercely; forgetting in his anger to maintain the character he had assumed, and using the appellation of which his nation was most proud; "the Dahcotahs have no fear! Speak; what brings you so far from the villages of the pale–faces?"

"I have seen the sun rise and set on many councils, and have heard the words only of wise men. Let your chiefs come, and my mouth shall not be shut."

"I am a great chief!" said the savage, affecting an air of offended dignity. "Do you take me for an Assiniboine! Weucha is a warrior often named, and much believed!"

"Am I a fool not to know a burnt-wood Teton!" demanded the trapper, with a steadiness that did great credit to his nerves. "Go; it is dark, and you do not see that my head is grey!"

The Indian now appeared convinced that he had adopted too shallow an artifice to deceive one so practised as the man he addressed, and he was deliberating what fiction he should next invent, in order to obtain his real object, when a slight commotion among the band put an end at once to all his schemes. Casting his eyes behind him, as if fearful of a speedy interruption, he said in tones much less pretending than those he had first resorted to——

"Give Weucha the milk of the Long-Knives, and he will sing your name in the ears of the great men of his tribe."

"Go;" said the trapper, motioning him away, with strong disgust. "Your young men are speaking of Mahtoree——My words are for the ears of a chief."

The savage cast a look on the other, which, notwithstanding the dim light, was sufficiently indicative of implacable hostility. He then stole away among his fellows, anxious to conceal the counterfeit he had attempted to practise, no less than the treachery he had contemplated against a fair division of the spoils, from the man named by the trapper, whom he now also knew to be approaching, by the manner in which his name passed from one to another, in the band. He had hardly disappeared before a warrior of powerful frame advanced out of the dark circle, and placed himself before the captives, with that high and proud bearing for which a distinguished Indian chief is ever so remarkable. He was followed by all the party, who arranged themselves around his person, in a deep and respectful silence.

"The earth is very large," the chief commenced, after a pause of that true dignity which his counterfeit had so miserably affected——"Why can the children of my great white

40

father never find room on it?"

"Some among them have heard that their friends in the prairies are in want of many things," returned the trapper; "and they come to see if it be true. Some want, in their turns, what the red men are willing to sell, and they come to make their friends rich, with powder and blankets."

"Do traders cross the big river with empty hands?"

"Our hands are empty because your young men thought we were tired, and they lightened us of our load. They were mistaken, I am old, but I am strong."

"It cannot be. Your load has fallen in the prairies. Show my young men the place, that they may pick it up, before the Pawnees find it."

"The path to the spot is crooked, and it is now, night. The hour is come for sleep," said the trapper, with perfect composure——"Bid your warriors go over yonder hill; there is water and there is wood; let them light their fires and sleep with warm feet. When the sun comes again I will speak to you."

A low murmur, but one that was clearly indicative of great dissatisfaction, passed among the attentive listeners, and served to inform the old man that he had not been sufficiently wary in proposing a measure that he intended should notify the travellers in the brake of the presence of such dangerous neighbours. Mahtoree, however, without betraying in the slightest degree, the excitement which was so strongly exhibited by his companions, continued the discourse in the same lofty manner as before. "I know that my friend is rich," he said; "that he has many warriors not far off, and that horses are plentier with him, than dogs among the red-skins."

"You see my warriors, and my horses."

"What! has the woman the feet of a Dahcotah, that she can walk for thirty nights in the prairies, and not fall! I know the red men of the woods make long marches on foot, but we, who live where the eye cannot see from one lodge to another, love our horses."

The trapper now hesitated, in his turn. He was perfectly aware that deception, if detected, might prove dangerous, and for one of his pursuits and character, he was strongly troubled with an unaccommodating regard to the truth. But, recollecting that he controlled the fate of others as well as of himself, he quickly decided to let things take their course, and to permit the Dahcotah chief to deceive himself if he would.

"The women of the Siouxes and of the white men are not of the same wigwam," he answered evasively. "Would a Teton warrior make his wife greater than himself! I know he would not; and yet my ears have heard that there are lands where the councils are held by squaws."

Another slight movement in the dark circle apprised the trapper that his declaration was not received without surprise, if entirely without distrust. The chief alone seemed unmoved or disposed, in any degree, to relax from the loftiness and high dignity of his air.

"My white fathers who live on the great lakes have declared," he said, "that their brothers towards the rising sun are not men; and now I know they did not lie! Go——what is a nation whose chief is a squaw! Are you the dog and not the husband of this woman?"

"I am neither. Never did I see her face before this day. She came into the prairies, because they had told her a great and generous nation called the Dahcotahs lived there, and she wished to look on men. The women of the pale–faces, like the women of the Siouxes, open their eyes to see things that are new; but she is poor, like myself, and she will want corn and buffaloes, if you take away the little that she and her friend still have."

"Now do my ears listen to many wicked lies!" exclaimed the Teton warrior, in a voice so stern thatit startled even his red auditors. "Am I a woman! Has not a Dahcotah eyes! Tell me, white hunter; who are the men of your colour, that sleep near the fallen trees?"

As he spoke, the indignant chief pointed in the direction of Ishmael's encampment, leaving the trapper no reason to doubt, that the superior industry and sagacity of this man had effected a discovery, which had eluded the search of the rest of his party. Notwithstanding his regret at an event that might prove fatal to the sleepers, and some little vexation at having been so completely outwitted, in the dialogue just related, the old man continued to maintain his former air of inflexible composure.

"It may be true," he answered, "that white men are sleeping in the prairie. If my brother says it, it is true; but what men are thus trusting to the generosity of the Tetons, I cannot tell. If there be strangers asleep, send your young men to wake them up, and let them say why they are here; every pale–face has a tongue."

The chief shook his head with a wild and fierce smile, answering abruptly, as he turned away to put an end to the conference——

"The Dahcotahs are a wise race, and Mahtoree is their chief! He will not call to the strangers, that they may rise and speak to him with their carabines. He will whisper softly in their ears. Then let the men of their own colour come and awake them!"

As he uttered these words, and turned on his heel, a low and approving laugh passed around the dark circle, which instantly broke its order and followed him to a little distance from the stand of the captives, where those who might presume to mingle opinions with so great a warrior, again gathered about him in consultation. Weucha profited by the occasion to renew his importunities; but the trapper, who had now discovered how great a counterfeit hewas, shook him off in high displeasure. An end was, however, more effectually put to the annoyance of this malignant savage, by a mandate for the whole party, including men and beasts, to change their position. The movement was made in dead silence, and with an order that would have done credit to far more enlightened beings. A halt, however, was soon made, and when the captives had time to look about them, they found they were in view of the low, dark outline of the copse, near which lay the slumbering party of Ishmael.

Here another short but exceedingly grave and deliberative consultation was held.

The beasts, which seemed trained to such covert and silent attacks, were once more placed under the care of keepers, who as before were again charged with the duty of watching the prisoners. The mind of the trapper was in no degree relieved from the uneasiness which was, at each instant, getting a stronger possession of him, when he found Weucha was placed nearest to his own person, and, as it appeared by the air of triumph and authority he assumed, at the head of the guard also. The savage, however, who doubtless had his secret instructions, was content, for the present, with making a significant gesture with his tomahawk, which threatened instant destruction to Ellen. After admonishing in this expressive manner his male captives of the fate that would instantly attend their female companion, on the slightest alarm proceeding from any of the party, he was content to maintain during the whole of the succeeding scene a rigid and deep silence. This unexpected forbearance, on the part of Weucha, enabled the trapper and his two associates to give their undivided attention to the little that might be seen of those interesting movements which were passing in their front.

Mahtoree took the entire disposition of the arrangementson himself. He pointed out the precise situation he wished each individual to occupy, like one intimately acquainted with the qualifications of his respective followers, and he was obeyed with the deference and promptitude with which an Indian warrior is wont to submit to the instructions of his chief, in moments of trial. Some he despatched to the right, and others to the left. Each man departed with the noiseless and quick step peculiar to the race, until all had assumed their alloted stations, with the exception of two chosen warriors, who remained nigh the person of their leader. When the rest had disappeared, Mahtoree turned to these select companions, and intimated by a sign that the critical moment had now arrived, when the enterprise he contemplated was to be put in execution.

Each man laid aside the light fowling–piece which, under the name of a carabine, he carried in virtue of his rank, and then divesting himself of every article of exterior or heavy clothing, he stood resembling a dark and fierce looking statue, in the attitude and nearly in the garb of nature. Mahtoree assured himself of the right position of his tomahawk, felt that his knife was secure in its sheath of skin, tightened his girdle of wampum, and saw that the lacing of his fringed and highly ornamented leggings was secure and likely to offer no impediment to his exertions. Thus prepared at all points, and ready for his desperate undertaking, the Teton chieftain gave the signal to proceed.

The three advanced in a line with the encampment of the travellers, until, in the dim light by which they were seen, their dusky forms were nearly lost to the eyes of the prisoners. Here they paused, looking around them like men who deliberate and ponder long on the consequences before they take a desperate leap. Then sinking together, they became lost in the grass of the prairie.

It is not difficult to imagine the distress and anxiety of those different spectators of these threatening movements, who felt so deep an interest in their results. Whatever might be the reasons of Ellen for entertaining no strong attachment to the family in which she has first been seen by the reader, the feelings of her sex, and, perhaps, some lingering seeds of kindness, asserted their existence in her bosom. More than once she felt tempted to brave the awful and instant danger that awaited such an offence, and to raise her feeble and in truth impotent voice in the notes of warning. So strong, indeed, and so very natural was the inclination, that she would most probably have put it in execution, but for the often−repeated though whispered remonstrances of Paul Hover. In the breast of the young bee−hunter himself, there was a singular union of emotions. His first and chiefest solicitude was certainly in behalf of his gentle and dependant companion; but the sense of her danger was mingled in the breast of the reckless woods−man with a consciousness of a high and wild, and by no means unpleasant excitement. Though united to the emigrants by ties still less binding than those of Ellen, he longed to hear the crack of their rifles, and, had occasion offered, he would gladly have been among the first to rush to their rescue. There were in truth moments when he felt in his turn an impulse, that was nearly resistless, to spring forward and awake the unconscious sleepers; but a glance at Ellen would serve to recall his tottering prudence, and to admonish him of the consequences. The trapper, alone, remained calm and observant, as though nothing that involved his personal comfort or safety had occurred. His evermoving, vigilant eyes, watched the smallest change with the composure of one too long inured to scenes of danger to be easily moved, and with an expression of cool determination which denoted the intentionhe actually harboured, of profiting by the smallest oversight on the part of the captors.

In the mean time the Teton warriors had not been idle. Profiting by the high fog which grew in the bottoms, they had wormed their way through the matted grass, like so many treacherous serpents stealing on their prey, until the point was gained, where an extraordinary caution became necessary to their further advance. Mahtoree, alone, had occasionally elevated his dark, grim countenance above the herbage, straining his eye−balls to penetrate the gloom which skirted the border of the brake. In these momentary glances he gained sufficient knowledge, added to that he had obtained in his former search, to be the perfect master of the position of his intended victims, though he was still profoundly ignorant of their numbers, and of their means of defence.

His efforts to possess himself of the requisite knowledge concerning these two latter and essential points were, however, completely baffled by the stillness of the camp, which lay in a quiet as deep as though it were literally a place of the dead. Too wary and distrustful to rely, in circumstances of so much doubt, on the discretion of any less firm and crafty than himself, the Dahcotah bade his companions remain where they lay, and pursued the adventure alone.

The progress of Mahtoree was now slow, and to one less accustomed to such a species of exercise, it would have proved painfully laborious. But the advance of the wily snake itself is not more certain or noiseless than was his approach. He drew his form, foot by foot, through the bending grass, pausing at each movement to catch the smallest sound that might betray any knowledge on the part of the travellers of his proximity. He succeeded, at length, in dragging himself out of the sickly light of the moon, into the shadows of the brake, where not only hisown dark person was much less liable to be seen, but where the sorrounding objects became more distinctly visible to his keen and active glances.

Here the Teton paused long and warily to make his observations, before he ventured further. His position enabled him to bring the whole encampment, with its tent, wagons and lodges, into a dark but clearly marked profile; furnishing a clue by which the practised warrior was led to a tolerably accurate estimate of the force he was about to encounter. Still an unnatural silence pervaded the spot, as though men suppressed even the quiet breathings of sleep, in order to render the appearance of their confidence more evident. The chief bent his head to the earth, and listened intently. He was about to raise it again in disappointment, when the long drawn and trembling respiration of one who slumbered imperfectly met his ear. The Indian was too well skilled in all the means of deception to become himself the victim of any common artifice. He knew the sound to be natural, by its peculiar quivering, and he hesitated no longer.

A man of nerves less tried than those of the fierce and conquering Mahtoree would have been keenly sensible of all the hazard he now so fearlessly incurred. The reputation of those hardy and powerful white adventurers, who so often penetrated the wilds inhabited by his people, was well known to him; but while he drew nigher, with the respect and caution that a brave enemy never fails to inspire, it was with the vindictive animosity of a red man, jealous and resentful of the lawless inroads of the stranger.

Turning from the line of his former route, the Teton dragged himself directly towards the margin of the thicket. When this material object was effected in safety, he arose to his seat, and took a still better survey of his situation. A single moment served to apprise him of the place where the unsuspectingtraveller lay. The reader will readily anticipate that the savage had succeeded in gaining a dangerous proximity to one of those slothful sons of Ishmael, who were deputed to watch over the isolated encampment of the travellers.

When certain that he was undiscovered, the Dahcotah raised his person again, and bending forward, he moved his dark visage above the face of the sleeper, in that sort of wanton and subtle manner with which a reptile is often seen to play about its victim before it strikes the deadly blow. Satisfied at length, by his scrutiny, not only of the condition but of the character of the stranger, Mahtoree was in the act of withdrawing his head when a slight movement on the part of the sleeper announced the symptoms of reviving consciousness. The savage seized the knife which hung at his girdle, and in an instant it was poised above the breast of the young emigrant. Then changing his purpose, with an action as rapid as his own flashing thoughts, he sunk back behind the trunk of the fallen tree against which the other reclined, and lay in its shadow, as dark, as motionless, and apparently as insensible as the wood itself.

The slothful sentinel opened his heavy eyes, and after gazing upward for a moment at the hazy heavens, he made an extraordinary exertion and raised his powerful frame from the support of the log. Then he looked about him, with an air of something like watchfulness, suffering his dull glances to run over the misty objects of the encampment until they finally settled on the distant and dim field of the open prairie. Meeting with nothing more attractive than the same faint outlines of swell and interval, which everywhere rose before his drowsy eyes, he changed his position so as completely to turn his back on his dangerous neighbour, and suffered his person to sink sluggishly down into its former recumbent attitude. A long, and, on the part of the Teton, an anxious andpainful silence succeeded, before the deep breathing of the traveller again announced that he was indulging in his slumbers. The savage was, however, far too jealous of a counterfeit to trust to the first appearance of sleep. But the fatigues of a day of unusual toil lay too heavy on the sentinel to leave the other long in doubt. Still the motion with which Mahtoree again raised himself to his knees was so noiseless and guarded, that even a vigilant observer might have hesitated to believe he stirred. The change was, however, at length effected, and the Dahcotah chief, then bent again over his enemy, without having produced a noise louder than that of the cotton−wood leaf which fluttered at his side in the currents of the passing air.

Mahtoree now felt himself master of the sleeper's fate. At the same time that he scanned the vast proportions and athletic limbs of the youth, in that sort of admiration which physical excellence seldom fails to excite in the breast of a savage, he very coolly prepared to extinguish the principle of vitality which could alone render them formidable. After making himself sure of the seat of life, by gently removing the folds of the intervening cloth, he raised his keen weapon, and was about to unite his strength and skill in the impending blow, when the young man threw his brawny arm carelessly backward, exhibiting in the action the vast volume of its muscles.

The sagacious and wary Teton paused. It struck his acute faculties that sleep was less dangerous to him, at that moment, than even death itself might prove. The smallest noise, the agony of struggling, with which such a frame would probably relinquish its hold of life, suggested themselves to his rapid thoughts, and were all present to his experienced senses. He looked back into the encampment, turned his head into the thicket, and glanced his glowing eyes abroad into the wild and silent prairies. Bendingonce more over the respited victim, he assured himself that he was sleeping heavily, and then abandoned his immediate purpose in obedience alone to the suggestions of a more crafty policy.

The retreat of Mahtoree was as still and guarded as had been his approach. He now took the direction of the encampment, stealing along the margin of the brake, as a cover into which he might easily plunge at the smallest alarm. The drapery of the solitary hut attracted his notice in passing. After examining the whole of its exterior, and listening with painful intensity, in order to gather counsel from his ears, the savage ventured to raise the cloth at the bottom, and to thrust his dark visage beneath. It might have been a minute before the Teton chief drew back and seated himself again with the whole of his form without the linen tenement. Here he sat, seemingly brooding over his own reflections, for many moments, in rigid inaction. Then he resumed his crouching attitude, and once more projected his visage beyond the covering of the linen dwelling. His second visit to the interior was longer, and, if possible, more ominous than the first. But it had, like every thing else, its termination, and the savage again withdrew his glaring eyes from the secrets of the place.

Mahtoree had drawn his person many yards from the spot, in his slow progress towards the cluster of objects which pointed out the centre of the position, before he again stopped. Then he made another pause, and looked back at the solitary little dwelling he had left, as if doubtful whether he should not return. But the chevaux−de−frise of branches now lay within reach of his arm, and the very appearance of precaution it presented, as it announced the value of the effects it encircled, tempted his cupidity the more strongly, and induced him to proceed.

The passage of the savage through the tender andbrittle limbs of the cotton–wood could be likened only to the sinuous and noiseless winding of the reptiles which he imitated no less in sagacity than in the manner of his approach. When, however, he had effected his object, and had taken an instant to become acquainted with the nature of the localities within the enclosure, the Teton used the precaution to open a way through which a retreat might be made with fewer impediments to obstruct its rapidiity. Then raising himself on his feet, he stalked through the encampment, like the master of evil, seeking whom and what he should first devote to his fell purposes. He had already ascertained the contents of the lodge in which were collected the woman and her young children, and had passed several gigantic frames, stretched on different piles of brush, which happily for him lay in unconscious helplessness, when he at last reached the spot occupied by Ishmael in person. It could not escape the sagacity of one like Mahtoree, that he had now within his power the principal man among the travellers. He stood long hovering above the recumbent and Herculean form of the emigrant, keenly debating in his own mind the chances of his enterprise, and the most effectual means of reaping its richest harvest.

He had sheathed the knife, which, under the hasty and burning impulse of his thoughts, he had been tempted to draw, and was passing on, when Ishmael turned in his lair, and demanded roughly who it was that he dimly saw moving before his half–opened eyes. Nothing short of the readiness and cunning of a savage could now have evaded bringing the crisis to an immediate issue. Imitating the gruff tones and nearly unintelligible sounds he heard, Mahtoree threw his body heavily on the earth, and appeared to dispose himself to sleep. Though the whole movement was seen by Ishmael in a sort of stupid observation. the artifice was too bold and too admirablyexecuted to fail of success. The drowsy father once more closed his eyes, and soon slept heavily, with this treacherous inmate in the very bosom of his family.

It was necessary for the Teton to maintain the position he had taken for many long and weary minutes, in order to make sure that he was no longer watched. Though his body lay so motionless, his active mind was not idle. He profited by the delay to mature a plan which he intended should put the whole encampment, including both its effects and their proprietors, entirely at his mercy. The instant he could do so with safety, the indefatigable savage was again in motion. He now took his way towards the slight pen which contained the domestic animals, worming himself along the ground in his former subtle and guarded manner.

The first animal he encountered among the beasts occasioned a long and hazardous delay. The weary creature, perhaps conscious through its secret instinct that in the endless wastes of the prairies its surest protector was to be found in man, was so exceedingly docile as quietly to submit to the close examination it was doomed to undergo. The hand of the wandering Teton passed over the downy coat, the meek countenance and the slender limbs of the gentle animal, with untiring curiosity; but he finally abandoned the prize, as useless in his predatory expeditions, and offering too little temptation to the appetite. As soon, however, as he found himself among the beasts of burden, his gratification was extreme, and it was with difficulty that he restrained the customary ejaculations of pleasure that were more than once on the point of bursting from his lips. Here he lost sight of the hazards by which he had gained access to his dangerous position, and the watchfulness of the wary and long practised warrior was momentarily forgotten in the exultation of a savage.

CHAPTER V.

"Why, worthy father, what have we to lose?"

—— ——The law

Protects us not. Then why should we be tender

To let an arrogant piece of flesh threat us!

Play judge and executioner."

—— Cymbeline

While the Teton warrior thus enacted his subtle and characteristic part, not a sound broke the stillness of the surrounding prairie. The whole band lay at their several posts, waiting, with the wellknown patience of the natives, for the signal which was to summon them to action. To the eyes of the anxious and deeply interested spectators who occupied the little eminence already described as the position of the captives, the scene merely presented the broad, solemn view of a waste, dimly lighted by the glimmering rays of a clouded moon. The place of the encampment was marked by a gloom deeper than that which faintly shadowed out the courses of the bottoms, and here and there a brighter streak tinged the rolling summits of the ridges. As for the rest, it was the deep, imposing, breathing quiet of a desert.

But to those who so well knew how much was brooding beneath this mantle of stillness and night, it was a scene of high and wild excitement. Their anxiety gradually increased, as minute after minute passed away, and not the smallest sound of life arose out of the calm and darkness which enveloped the brake. The breathing of Paul grew louder and deeper, and more than once Ellen trembled at she knew not what, as she felt the quivering of his active frame, while she leaned dependantly on his arm for support.

The shallow honesty, as well as the besetting infirmity of Weucha, have already been exhibited.The reader, therefore, will not be surprised to learn that he was the first to forget the regulations he had himself imposed. It was at the precise moment when we left Mahtoree yielding to his nearly ungovernable delight, as he surveyed the number and quality of Ishmael's beasts of burden, that the man he had selected to watch his captives chose to indulge in the malignant pleasure of tormenting those it was his duty to protect. Bending his head nigh to the ears of the trapper, the savage rather muttered than whispered——

"If the Tetons lose their great chief by the hands of the Long—knives, old shall die as well as young!"

"Life is the gift of the Wahcondah," was the unmoved reply——"The burnt—wood warrior must submit to his laws, as well as his other children. Men only die when he chooses; and no Dahcotah can change the hour."

"Look!" returned the savage, thrusting the blade of his knife before the face of his captive. "Weucha is the Wahcondah of a dog."

The old man raised his eyes to the fierce visage of his keeper, and, for a moment, a gleam of honest and powerful disgust shot from their deep cells; but it instantly passed away, leaving in its place an expression of commiseration, if not of sorrow.

"Why should one made in the real image of God suffer his natur' to be provoked by a mere effigy of reason!" he said in English, and in tones much louder than those in which

Weucha had chosen to pitch the conversation. The latter profited by the unintentional offence of his captive, and seizing him by the thin, grey locks, that fell from beneath his cap, was on the point of passing the blade of his knife in malignant triumph around their roots, when a long, shrill, yell rent the air, and was instantly echoed from the surrounding waste, as though a thousand demons had opened their throats in common at thesummons. Weucha relinquished his grasp and uttered a cry of savage exultation.

"Now!" shouted Paul, unable to control his impatience any longer, "now, old Ishmael, is the time to show the native blood of Kentucky! Fire low, boys——Level into the swales, for the red skins are settling to the very earth!"

His voice was, however, lost, or rather unheeded, in the midst of the shrieks, shouts, and yells, that were by this time, bursting from fifty mouths on every side of him. The guards still maintained their posts at the side of the captives, but it was with that sort of difficulty with which steeds are restrained at the starting–post, when expecting the signal to commence the trial of their speed. They tossed their arms wildly in the air, leaping up and down more like exulting children than sober men, and continued to utter the most frantic and savage cries.

In the midst of this tumultuous disorder a rushing sound was heard, similar to that which might be expected to precede the passage of a flight of buffaloes, and then came the flocks and cattle of Ishmael into view, in one confused and frightened drove.

"They have robbed the squatter of his beasts!" said the attentive trapper. "The reptiles have left him as hoofless as a beaver!" He was yet speaking when the whole body of the terrified animals rose the little acclivity and swept by the place where he stood, followed by a band of dusky and demon–like looking figures, who pressed madly on their rear.

The impulse was communicated to the Teton horses, who were long accustomed to sympathize in the untutored passions of their owners, and it was with difficulty that their keepers were enabled to restrain them. At this moment, when all eyes were directed to the passing whirlwind of men and beasts, the trapper caught the knife from the hands of his inattentive keeper, with a power that his age would have seemed to contradict, and at a single blow severed the thong of hide which connected the whole of the drove. The wild animals snorted with joy and terror, and tearing the earth with their heels, they dashed away into the broad prairies, in a dozen different directions.

Weucha turned upon his assailant with the ferocity and agility of a tiger. He felt for the weapon of which he had been so suddenly deprived, fumbled with impotent haste for the handle of his tomahawk, and at the same moment glanced his eyes after his flying cattle, with all the longings of a Western Indian. The struggle between thirst for vengeance and cupidity was short but severe. The latter quickly predominated in the bosom of one whose passions were proverbially grovelling, and scarcely a moment intervened between the flight of the animals and the swift pursuit of all the guards. The trapper had continued calmly facing his foe, during the instants of suspense that succeeded his own hardy act, and now that Weucha was seen following his companions, he pointed after the dark train, saying, with his deep and nearly inaudible laugh——

"Red–natur' is red–natur', let it show itself on a prairie, or in a forest! A knock on the head would be the smallest reward to him who should take such a liberty with a Christian sentinel; but there goes the Teton after his horses as if he thought two legs as good as four in such a race! And yet the imps will have every hoof of them afore the day sets in, because its reason ag'in instinct. Poor reason, I allow; but still there is a great deal of the man in an Indian. Ah's me! your Delawares were the red–skins of which America might boast; but few and scattered is that mighty people, now! Well! the traveller may just make his pitch where he is; he has plenty of water, though natur' has cheated him of the pleasure of stripping the 'arth of its lawful trees. Hehas seen the last of his four–footed creatures, or I am but little skilled in Sioux cunning."

"Had we not better join the party of Ishmael," said the bee–hunter. "There will be a regular fight about this matter, or the old fellow has suddenly grown chicken–hearted."

"No——no——no," hastily exclaimed Ellen.

She was stopped by the trapper, who laid his hand gently on her mouth as he answered——

"Hist!——hist!——the sound of voices might bring us into danger. Is your friend," he added turning to Paul, "a man of spirit enough——"

"Don't call the squatter a friend of mine!" interrupted the youth. "I never yet harboured with one who could not show hand and seal for the land which fed him."

"Well——well. Let it then be acquaintance. Is he a man to maintain his own stoutly by dint of powder and lead?"

"His own! ay, and that which is not his own, too! Can you tell me, old trapper, who held the rifle that did the deed for the sheriff's deputy, that thought to rout the unlawful settlers who had gathered nigh the Buffaloe lick in old Kentucky! I had lined a beautiful swarm that very day into the hollow of a dead beech, and there lay the people's officer at its roots, with a hole directly through the "grace of God;" which he carried in his jacket pocket covering his heart, as though he thought a bit of sheepskin was a breastplate against a squatter's bullet! Now, Ellen, you need'n't, be troubled; for it never strictly was brought home to him; and there were fifty others who had pitched in that neighbourhood with just the same assistance from the law."

The poor girl shuddered, struggling powerfully to suppress the sigh which arose in spite of her efforts, as if from the very bottom of her heart.

Thoroughly satisfied that he understood the characterof the emigrants, by the short but comprehensive description conveyed in Paul's reply, the old man raised no further question concerning the readiness of Ishmael to revenge his wrongs, but rather followed that train of thoughts which was suggested to his experience by the occasion.

"Each one knows the ties which bind him to his fellow–creatures best," he answered. "Though it is greatly to be mourned that colour, and property, and tongue, and l'arning should make so wide a difference in those who, after all, are but the children of one father! Howsomever," he continued, by a transition not a little characteristic of the pursuits and feelings of the man, "as this is a business in which there is much more likelihood of a fight than need for a sermon, it is best to be prepared for what may follow—— Hush! there is a movement below; it is an equal chance that we are seen."

"The family is stirring;" cried Ellen with a tremor in her voice that announced nearly as much terror at the approach of her friends, as she had before manifested at the presence of her enemies. "Go, Paul, leave me. You, at least, must not be seen!"

"If I leave you, Ellen, in this desert before I see you safe in the care of old Ishmael, at least, may I never hear the hum of another bee, or, what is worse, fail in sight to line him to his hive!"

"You forget this good old man. He will not leave me. Though I am sure, Paul, we have parted before, where there has been more of a desert than this."

"Never! These Indians may come whooping back, and then where are you! Half way to the Rocky Mountains before a man can fairly strike the line of your flight. What think you, old trapper? How long may it be before these Tetons, as you call them, will be coming for the rest of old Ishmael's goods and chattels?"

"No fear of them," returned the old man again, laughing in his own peculiar and silent manner; "I warrant me the devils will be scampering after their beasts these six hours yet! Listen! you may hear them in the willow bottoms at this very moment; ay, your real Sioux cattle will run like so many long-legged elks. Hist! crouch again into the grass, down with ye both; as I'm a miserable piece of clay, I heard the ticking of a gun-lock!"

The trapper did not allow his companions time to hesitate, but dragging them both after him, he nearly buried his own person in the fog of the prairie, while he was speaking. It was fortunate that the senses of the aged hunter remained so acute, and that he had lost none of his readiness of action. The three were scarcely bowed to the ground, when their ears were saluted with the well-known sharp, short reports of the western rifle, and instantly, the whizzing of the ragged lead was heard, buzzing within a dangerous proximity of their heads.

"Well done, young chips! well done, old block!" whispered Paul, whose spirits no danger nor situation could entirely depress. "As pretty a volley, as one would wish to hear on the wrong end of a rifle! What say, trapper! here is likely to be a three-cornered war. Shall I give 'em as good as they send?"

"Give them nothing, but fair words," returned the other, hastily, "or you are both lost."

"I'm not certain it would much mend the matter, if I were to speak with my tongue instead of the piece," said Paul in a tone half jocular half bitter.

"For the sake of heaven, do not let them hear you!" cried Ellen! "Go, Paul, go; you may easily go!"

Several shots in quick succession, each sending its dangerous messenger, still nearer than the preceding discharge, cut short her speech, no less in prudence than in terror.

"This must end," said the trapper rising with thedignity of one bent only on the importance of his object. "I know not what need ye may have, children, to fear those you should both love and honour, but something must be done to save your lives. A few hours more or less can never be missed from the time of one who has already numbered so many days; therefore I will advance. Here is a clear space around you. Profit by it as you need, and may God bless and prosper each of you, as ye deserve!"

Without waiting for any reply, the trapper walked boldly down the declivity in his front, taking the direction of the encampment, neither quickening his pace in trepidation, nor suffering it to be retarded by fear. The light of the moon fell brighter for a moment on his tall, gaunt form, and served to warn the emigrants of his approach. Indifferent, however, to this unfavourable circumstance, he held his way, silently and steadily towards the copse, until a stern, threatening voice met him with the challenge of——

"Who comes; friend or foe?"

"Friend," was the reply; "one who has lived too long to disturb the close of life with quarrels."

"But not so long as to forget the tricks of his youth," said Ishmael, rearing his huge frame from beneath the slight covering of a low bush, and meeting the trapper, face to face; "old man, you have brought this tribe of red devils upon us, and to-morrow you will be sharing the booty."

"What have you lost?" calmly demanded the trapper.

"Eight as good mares as ever travelled in gears, besides a foal that is worth thirty of the brightest Mexicans that bear the face of the King of Spain. Then the woman has not a cloven hoof for her dairy or her loom, and I believe even the grunters, foot sore as they be, are ploughing the prairie. And now, stranger," he added, dropping the butt of his rifle on the hard earth, with a violence and clatterthat would have intimidated one less firm than the man he addressed, "how many of these creatures, may fall to your lot?"

"Horses have I never craved, nor even used; though few have journeyed over more of the wide lands of America than myself, old and feeble as I seem. But little use is there for a horse among the hills and woods of York——that is, as York was, but as I greatly fear York is no longer——as for woollen covering and cow's milk, I covet no such womanly fashions! The beasts of the field give me food and raiment. No, I crave no cloth better than the skin of a deer, nor any meat richer than his flesh."

The sincere manner of the trapper, as he uttered this simple vindication, was not entirely thrown away on the emigrant, whose dull nature was gradually quickening into a flame, that might speedily have burst forth with dangerous violence. He listened like one who doubted, though not entirely convinced; and he muttered between his teeth the denunciation, with which a moment before he intended to precede the summary vengeance he had certainly meditated.

"This is brave talking," he at length grumbled; "but to my judgment, too lawyer–like, for a straight forward, fair–weather, and foul–weather hunter."

"I claim to be no better than a trapper," the other meekly interrupted.

"Hunter or trapper——There is little difference. I have come, old man, into these districts because I found the law sitting too tight upon me, and am not over fond of neighbours who can't settle a dispute without troubling a justice and twelve men; but I didn't come to be robb'd of my plunder, and then to say thank'ee to the man who did it!"

"He, who ventures far into the prairies, must abide by the ways of its owners."

"Owners!" echoed the sullen squatter, "I am as rightful an owner of the land I stand on, as any governorin all the states! Can you tell me, stranger, where the law or the reason is to be found, which says that one man shall have a section, or a town, or perhaps a county, to his use, and another have to beg for earth to make his grave in. This is not nature, and I deny that it is law. That is, your legal law."

"I cannot say that you are wrong," returned the trapper, whose opinions on this important topic, though drawn from very different premises, were in singular accordance with those of his companion, "and I have often thought and said as much, when and where I have believed my voice could be heard. But your beasts are stolen by them who claim to be masters of all they find in the deserts."

"They had better not dispute that matter with a man who knows better," said the other in a voice of portentous tones, though it seemed as deep and sluggish as he who uttered it. "I call myself a fair trader, and one who gives to his chaps as good as he receives. You saw the Indians?"

"I did——they held me a prisoner, while they stole into your camp."

"It would have been more like a white—man and a christian, to have let me known as much in better season;" retorted Ishmael, casting another ominous side—long glance at the trapper, as if still meditating evil. "I am not much given to call every man I fall in with, cousin, but colour should be something, when christians meet in such a place as this. But what is done, is done, and cannot be mended, by words. Come out of your ambush boys; here is no one but the old man: he has eaten of my bread, and should be a friend; though there is such good reason to suspect him of harbouring with my enemies."

The trapper made no reply to the harsh suspicion which the other did not scruple to utter without the smallest delicacy, notwithstanding the explanationsand denials to which he had just listened. The summons of the unnurtured squatter brought an immediate accession to their party. Four or five of his sons made their appearance from beneath as many covers, where they had been posted under the impression that the figures they had seen, on the swell of the prairie, were a part of the Sioux band. As each man approached, and dropped his rifle into the hollow of his arm, he cast an indolent but inquiring glance at the form of the stranger, though neither of them expressed the least curiosity to know whence he had come or why he was there. This forbearance, however, proceeded only in part, from the sluggishness of their common temper; for long and frequent experience in scenes of a similar character, had taught them the virtue of discretion. The trapper endured their sullen but silent scrutiny with the steadiness of one as practised as themselves, and with the entire composure of innocence. Content with the momentary examination he had made, the eldest of the groupe, who was in truth the delinquent sentinel by whose remissness the wily Mahtoree had so well profited, turned towards his father and said bluntly:

"If this man is all that is left of the party I saw on the upland, yonder, we haven't altogether thrown away our ammunition."

"Asa, you are right;" said the father, turning suddenly on the trapper, as though a lost idea was recalled by the hint of his sluggish son. "How is it, stranger; there were three of you, just now, or there is no virtue in moonlight!"

"If you had seen the Tetons racing across the prairies, like so many black–looking evil–ones, on the heels of your cattle, my friend, it would have been an easy matter to have fancied them a thousand."

"Ay, for a town bred boy or a skeary woman; though, for that matter, there is old Esther yon; she has no more fear of a red–skin than of a suckling cub, or of a wolf pup. I'll warrant ye, had your stealing devils made their push by the light of the sun, the good woman would have been seen smartly at work among them, and the Siouxes would have found she was not given to part with her cheese and her butter without a price. But there'll come a time, stranger, right soon, when justice will have its dues, and that too, without the help of what is called the law. We ar' of a slow breed, it may be said, and it is often said of us; but slow is sure; and there ar' few men, living, who can say they ever struck a blow, that they did not get one as hard in return, from Ishmael Bush."

"Then has Ishmael Bush followed the instinct of the beasts rather than the genuine principle which ought to belong to his kind," returned the stubborn trapper. "I have struck many a blow myself, but never have I felt the same ease of mind that of right belongs to a man who follows his reason, after slaying even a fawn when there was no call for his meat or hide, as I have felt at leaving a Mingo unburied in the woods, when following the trade of open and honest warfare."

"What, you have been a soldier, have you, trapper! I made a forage or two among the Cherokees, when I was a lad myself; and I followed mad Anthony, one season, through the beeches; but there was altogether too much tatooing and regulating among his troops for me; so I left him without calling on the paymaster to settle my arrearages. Though, as Esther afterwards boasted, she had made such use of the pay–ticket, that the States gained no great sum, by the oversight. You have heard of such a man as mad Anthony, if you tarried long among the soldiers."

"I fou't my last battle, as I hope, under his orders," returned the trapper, a gleam of sun–shine shootingfrom his dim eyes, as if the event was recollected with pleasure, and then a sudden shade of sorrow succeeding, as though he felt a secret admonition against dwelling on the violent scenes in which he had so often been an actor. "I was passing from the states on the sea shore into these far regions, when I cross'd the trail of his party, and I fell in, on his rear, just as a looker−on; but when they got to blows, the crack of my rifle was heard among the rest, though to my shame it may be said, I never knew the right of the quarrel as well as a man of threescore and ten should know the reason of his acts afore he takes mortal life, which is a gift he never can return!"

"Come, stranger," said the emigrant, his rugged nature a good deal softened when he found that they had fought on the same side in the wild warfare of the west, "it is of small account, what may be the ground−work of the disturbance, when it's a Christian ag'in a savage. We shall hear more of this horse−stealing to−morrow; to−night we can do no wiser or safer thing than to sleep."

So saying, Ishmael deliberately led the way back towards his rifled encampment, and ushered the man, whose life a few minutes before had been in real jeopardy through his resentment, into the presence of his family. Here, with a very few words of explanation, mingled with scarce but ominous denunciations against the plunderers, he made his wife acquainted with the state of things on the Prairie, and then announced his own determination to compensate himself for his broken rest, by devoting the remainder of the night to sleep.

The trapper gave his ready assent to the measure, and adjusted his gaunt form on the pile of brush that was offered him, with as much composure as a sovereign, could resign himself to sleep in the security of his capital and surrounded by his armed protectors.The old man, did not close his eyes, however, until he had assured himself that Ellen Wade was among the females of the family, and that her relation or lover, whichever he might be, had observed the caution of keeping himself out of view: after which he slept, though with the peculiar watchfulness of one long accustomed to vigilance, even in the hours of deepest night.

CHAPTER VI.

"He is too picked, too spruce, too affected, too odd,

As it were too peregrinate, as I may call it."

The Prairie, Volume 1

—— Shakspeare

The Anglo-American is apt to boast, and not without a show of reason, that his nation may claim a descent more truly honourable than that of any other people whose history is to be credited. Whatever might have been the weaknesses of the original colonists, their virtues have rarely been disputed. If they were superstitious, they were sincerely pious, and, consequently, honest. The descendants of these simple and single-minded provincials have been content to reject the ordinary and artificial means by which honours have been perpetuated in families, and have substituted a standard which brings the individual himself to the ordeal of the public estimation, paying as little deference as may be to those who have gone before him. This forbearance, self-denial, or common sense, or by whatever term it may be thought proper to distinguish the measure, has subjected the nation to the imputation of having an ignoble origin. Were it worth the enquiry, it would be found that more than a just proportion of the renowned names of the mother country are, at this hour, to be found in her ci-devant colonies, and it isa fact well known to the few who have wasted sufficient time to become the masters of so unimportant a subject, that the direct descendants of many a failing line, which the policy of England has seen fit to sustain by collateral supporters, are now discharging the simple duties of citizens in the bosom of our republic. The hive has remained stationary, and they who flutter around the venerable straw are wont to claim the empty distinction of antiquity, regardless alike of the frailty of their tenement and of the enjoyments of the numerous and vigorous swarms that are culling the fresher sweets of a virgin world. But as this is a subject which belongs rather to the politician and historian than to the humble narrator of the home-bred incidents we are about to reveal, we must confine our reflections to such matters as have an immediate relation to the subject of the tale.

Although the citizen of the United States may claim so just an ancestry, he is far from being exempt from the penalties of his fallen race. Like causes are well known to produce like effects. That tribute, which, it would seem nations must ever pay, by way of a weary probation, around the shrine of Ceres before they can be indulged in her fullest favours, is in some measure exacted in America, from the descendant instead of the ancestor. The march of civilization with us, has a strong analogy to that of all coming events, which are known "to cast their shadows before." The gradations of society, from that state which is called refined to that which approaches as near barbarity as connexion with an intelligent people will readily allow, are to be traced from the bosom of the states, where wealth, luxury and the arts are beginning to seat themselves, to those distant, and ever-receding borders which mark the skirts, and announce the approach, of the nation, as moving mists precede the signs of day.

Here, and here only, is to be found that widely spread though far from numerous class which may be at all likened to those who have paved the way for the intellectual progress of nations, in the old world. The resemblance between the American borderer and his European prototype is singular, though not always uniform. Both might be called without restraint; the one being above, the other beyond the reach of the law——brave, because they were inured to dangers——proud, because they were independent, and vindictive, because each was the avenger of his own wrongs. It would be unjust to the borderer to pursue the parallel much farther. He is irreligious, because he has inherited the knowledge that religion does not exist in forms, and his reason rejects a mockery that his conscience does not approve. He is not a knight, because he has not the power to bestow distinctions; and he has not the power, because he is the offspring and not the parent of a system. In what manner these several qualities are exhibited, in some of the most strongly marked of the latter class, will be seen in the course of the ensuing narrative.

Ishmael Bush had passed the whole of a life of more than fifty years on the skirts of society. He boasted that he had never dwelt where he might not safely fell every tree he could view from his own threshold; that the law had rarely been known to enter his clearing, and that his ears had never willingly admitted the sound of a church bell. His exertions seldom exceeded his wants, which were peculiar to his class, and rarely failed of being supplied. He had no respect for any learning except that of the leech; because he was ignorant of the application of any other intelligence, than such as met the senses. His deference to this particular branch of science had induced him to listen to the application of a medical man, whose thirst for natural history had led him to the desire of profiting by the migratorypropensities of the squatter. This gentleman he had cordially received into his family, or rather under his protection, and they had journeyed together, thus far through the prairies, in perfect harmony: Ishmael often felicitating his wife on the possession of a companion, who would be so serviceable in their new abode, wherever it might chance to be, until the family were thoroughly "acclimated." The pursuits of the naturalist frequently led him, however, for days at a time, from the direct line of the route of the squatter, who rarely seemed to have any other guide than the sun. Most men would have deemed themselves fortunate to have been absent on the perilous occasion of the Sioux inroad, as was Obed Bat, (or as he was fond of hearing himself called, Battius) M. D. and fellow of several cis–atlantic learned societies——the adventurous gentleman in question.

Although the sluggish nature of Ishmael was not actually awakened, it was sorely pricked by the liberties which had just been taken with his property. He slept, however, for it was the hour he had allotted to that refreshment, and because he knew how impotent any exertions to recover his effects must prove in the darkness of midnight. He also knew the danger of his present situation too well, to hazard what was left, in pursuit of that which was lost. Much as the inhabitants of the prairies were known to love horses, their attachment to many other articles, still in the possession of the travellers, was equally well understood. It was a common artifice to scatter the herds, and profit by the confusion. But, Mahtoree, had it would seem in this particular, undervalued the acuteness of the man he had assailed. The phlegm with which the squatter learned his loss, has already been seen, and it now remains to exhibit the results of his more matured determinations.

Though the encampment contained many an eyethat was long unclosed, and many an ear that listened greedily to catch the faintest evidence of any new alarm, it lay in deep quiet during the remainder of the night. Silence and fatigue finally performed their accustomed offices, and before the morning all but the sentinels were again buried in sleep. How well these indolent watchers performed their duties, after the assault, has never been known, inasmuch as nothing occurred to confirm or disprove their subsequent vigilance.

Just as day, however, began to dawn, and a gray light was falling from the heavens, on the dusky objects of the plain, the half startled, anxious and yet blooming countenance of Ellen Wade was reared above the confused mass of children, among whom she had clustered on her stolen return to the camp Arising warily she stepped lightly across the recumbent bodies, and proceeded with the same caution to the utmost limits of the defences of Ishmael. Here, she listened, as though she doubted the propriety of venturing further. The pause was only momentary, however; and long before the drowsy eyes of the sentinel, who overlooked the spot where she stood, had time to catch a glimpse of her active form, it had glided along the bottom and stood on the summit of the nearest eminence.

Ellen now listened long and intently to hear some other sound, than the breathing of the morning air, which faintly rustled the herbage at her feet. She was about to turn in disappointment from the inquiry, when the sound of human feet making their way through the matted grass met her ear. Springing eagerly forward, she soon beheld the outlines of a figure advancing up the eminence, on the side opposite to the camp, as though it had caught the view of her own person drawn against the heavens. She had already uttered the name of Paul, and was beginning to speak in the hurried and eager voice withwhich female affection is apt to greet a friend, when, drawing back, the disappointed girl closed her salutation by coldly adding:

"I did not expect, Doctor, to meet you at this unusual hour."

"All hours and all seasons are alike, my good Ellen, to the genuine lover of nature"——returned a small, slightly made, but exceedingly active man, dressed in an odd mixture of cloth and skins, a little past the middle age, who advanced directly to her side, with the familiarity of an old acquaintance; "and he who does not know how to find things to admire by this gray light, is ignorant of a large portion of the blessings he enjoys."

"Very true," said Ellen, suddenly recollecting the necessity of accounting for her own appearance abroad at that unseasonable hour, "I know many who think the earth has a pleasanter look in the night, than when seen by the brightest sunshine."

"Ah! Their organs of sight must be too convex. But the man who wishes to study the active habits of the feline race, or the variety, albinos, must be stirring at this hour. I dare say, there are men who prefer even looking at objects by twilight, for the simple reason, that they see better at that time of the day."

"And is this the cause why you are so much abroad in the night?"

"I am abroad at night, my good girl, because the earth in its diurnal revolutions leaves the light of the sun but half the time on any given meridian, and because what I have to do cannot be performed in twelve or fifteen consecutive hours. Now have I been off two days from the family, in search of a plant, that is known to exist on the tributaries of La Platte, without seeing even a blade of grass that is not already enumerated and classed."

"You have been unfortunate, Doctor, but——"

"Unfortunate!" echoed the little man, sideling nigher to his companion, and producing his tablets with an air in which exultation struggled, strangely, with an affectation of self abasement. "No, no, Ellen, I am any thing but unfortunate. Unless, indeed a man may be so called, whose fortune is made, whose fame may be said to be established for ever, whose name will go down to posterity with that of Buffon——Buffon! a mere compiler; one who flourishes on the foundation of other men's labours. No; pari passu with Solander, who bought his knowledge with pain and privations!"

"Have you discovered a mine, Doctor Bat?"——

"More than a mine; a treasure coined, and fit for instant use, girl——Listen! I was making the angle necessary to intersect the line of your uncle's march, after my fruitless search, when I heard sounds like the explosion produced by fire arms——"

"Yes," exclaimed Ellen eagerly, "we had an alarm——"

"And thought I was lost," continued the man of science, too much bent on his own ideas, to understand her interruption. "Little danger of that. I made my own base, knew the length of the perpendicular by calculation, and to draw the hypothenuse had nothing to do but to work my angle. I supposed the guns were fired for my benefit, and changed my course for the sounds——not that I think the senses more accurate, or even as accurate as a mathematical calculation, but I feared, that some of the children might need my services."

"They are all happily——"

"Listen;" interrupted the other, already forgetting his affected anxiety for his patients, in the greater importance of the present subject. "I had crossed a large tract of prairie——for sound is conveyed far where there is little obstruction——when I heard the trampling of feet, as though bisons were beating theearth. Then I caught a distant view of a herd of quadrupeds, rushing up and down the swells——animals, which would have still remained unknown and undescribed, had it not been for a most felicitous accident! One, and he a noble specimen of the whole, was running a little apart from the rest. The herd made an inclination in my direction, in which the solitary animal coincided, and this brought him within fifty yards of where I stood. I profited by the opportunity, and by the aid of my steel and taper, I wrote his description on the spot. I would have given a thousand dollars, Ellen, for a single shot from the rifle of one of the boys!"

"You carry a pistol, Doctor, why didn't you use it?" said the half inattentive girl, anxiously examining the prairie, but still lingering where she stood, quite willing to be detained.

"Ay, but it carries itself nothing but the most minute particles of lead, adapted to the destruction of the larger insects and reptiles. No, I did better than to attempt waging a war, in which I could not be the victor. I recorded the event; noting each particular with the precision necessary to science. You shall hear, Ellen; for you are a good and improving girl, and by retaining what you learn in this way, may yet be of great service to learning, should any accident occur to me. Indeed, my worthy Ellen, mine is a pursuit, which has its dangers as well as that of the warrior. This very night," he continued, glancing his eye, involuntarily behind him, "this awful night, has the principle of life, itself, been in great danger of extinction!"

"By what?"

"By the monster I have discovered. It approached me often, and ever as I receded, it continued to advance. I believe nothing but the little lamp, I carried, was my protector. I kept it between us, whilst I wrote, making it serve the double purposeof a luminary and a shield. But you shall hear the character of the beast, and you may then judge of the risk we promoters of science run in behalf of mankind."

The naturalist now raised his tablets to the heavens and disposed himself to read as well as he could, by the dim light they yet shed upon the plain; premising with saying——

"Listen, girl, and you shall hear, with what a treasure it has been my happy lot to enrich the pages of natural history!"

"Is it then a creature of your forming," said Ellen, turning away from her fruitless examination, with a sudden lighting of her sprightly blue eyes, that shewed she knew how to play with the foible of her learned companion.

"Is the power to give life to inanimate matter the gift of man? I would it were! You should speedily see a Historia naturalis Americana, that would put the sneering imitators of the Frenchman de Buffon to shame! A great improvement might be made in the formation of all quadrupeds in particular; especially those, in which velocity is a virtue. Two of the inferior limbs should be on the principle of the lever; wheels, perhaps, as they are now formed; though I have not yet determined whether the improvement might be better applied to the anterior or posterior members, inasmuch as I am yet to learn whether dragging or shoving requires the greatest muscular exertion. A natural exudation of the animal might assist in overcoming the friction, and a powerful momentum be obtained. But all this is hopeless——at least for the present!"——he added, with a slight sigh, raising his tablets again to the light and reading aloud; "Oct. 6, 1805, that's merely the date, which I dare say you know better than I——mem. Quadruped; seen by star–light, and by the aid of apocket–lamp, in the prairies of North America——see Journal for Latitude and Meridian. Genus——unknown: therefore named after the discoverer, and from the happy coincidence of being seen in the evening——Vespertilio Horribilis, Americanus. Dimensions (by estimation)——Greatest length, eleven feet; height, six feet; head, erect; nostrils, expansive: eyes, expressive and fierce; teeth, serrated and abundant; tail, horizontal, waving and slightly feline; feet, large and hairy; talons, long, curvated, dangerous; ears, inconspicuous; horns, elongated, diverging and formidable; colour, plumbeous–ashy with fiery spots; voice, sonorous, martial and appalling; habits, gregarious, carnivorous, fierce and fearless. There," exclaimed Obed, when he had ended this sententious but comprehensive description, "there is an animal , which will be likely to dispute with the lion his title to be called the king of the beasts!"

"I know not the meaning of all you have said, Doctor Battius," returned the quick–witted girl, who understood the weakness of the philosopher, and often indulged him with a title he loved so well to hear, "but I shall think it dangerous to venture far from the camp, if such monsters are prowling over the prairies."

"You may well call it prowling," returned the naturalist, nestling still closer to her side, and dropping his voice to such low and perhaps undignified tones of confidence as possibly conveyed a meaning still more pointed than he had intended. "I have never before experienced such a trial of the nervous system; there was a moment I acknowledge, when the fortiter in re faltered before so terrible an enemy; but the love of natural science bore me up, and brought me off in triumph!"

"You speak a language so different from that we use in Tennessee," said Ellen, struggling to conceal her laughter, "that I hardly know whether I understand your meaning. If I am right, you wish to say you were a little chicken–hearted."

"An absurd simile drawn from an ignorance of the formation of the biped. The heart of a chicken has a just proportion to its other organs, and the domestic fowl is, in a state of nature, a gallant bird. "Ellen," he added with a countenance so solemn as to produce an impression on the attentive girl, "I was pursued, hunted, and in a danger that I scorn to dwell on——what's that?"

Ellen started; for the earnestness and simple sincerity of her companion's manner had produced a certain degree of credulity even on her buoyant mind. Looking in the direction indicated by the Doctor, she beheld, in fact, a beast coursing over the prairie, and making a straight and rapid approach to the very spot they occupied. The day was not yet far enough advanced to enable her to distinguish its form and character, though enough was discernible to induce her to imagine it a fierce and savage animal.

"It comes, it comes!" exclaimed the Doctor, fumbling, by a sort of instinct, for his tablets, while he fairly tottered on his feet under the powerful efforts he made to maintain his ground. "Now, Ellen, has fortune given me an opportunity to correct the errors made by star–light,——hold,——ashy–plumbeous, ——no ears,——horns, excessive."——His quivering voice and shaking hand were both arrested by a roar, or rather a shriek from the beast, that was sufficiently terrific to appal even a stouter heart than that of the naturalist. The cries of the animal passed over the prairie in strange and savage cadences, and then succeeded a deep and solemn silence, that was only broken by a heart–felt and uncontrolled fit of merriment from the more musical voice of Ellen Wade. In the mean time the naturalist stood like a statue ofamazement, permitting a well–grown ass, against whose approach he no longer offered his boasted shield of light, to smell about his person, without comment or hindrance.

"It is your own ass!" cried Ellen, the instant she found breath for words; "your own patient, hard working, hack!"

The Doctor rolled his eyes wildly from the beast to the speaker, and from the speaker to the beast; but gave no audible expression of his wonder.

"Do you refuse to know an animal that has laboured so long in your service!" continued the still laughing girl. "A beast, that I have heard you say a thousand times, has served you well, and whom you loved like a brother!"

"Asinus domesticus!" ejaculated the Doctor, drawing his breath like one who had been near suffocation. "There is no doubt of the genus; and I will always maintain that the animal is not of the species equus. This is undeniably Asinus himself, Ellen Wade; but this is not the Vespertilio horribilis of the prairies! Very different animals, I can assure you, young woman, and differently characterised in every important particular. That, carnivorous," he continued, glancing his eye at the open page of his tablets; "this, granivorous; habits, fierce, dangerous; habits, patient, abstemious; ears, inconspicuous; ears, elongated; horns, diverging, etc. horns, none!"

He was interrupted by another burst of merriment from Ellen, which served, in some measure, to recall him to his recollection.

"The image of the Vespertilio was on the retina," the astounded enquirer into the secrets of nature observed, in a manner that seemed a little apologetic, "and I was silly enough to mistake my own faithful beast for the monster? Though even now I greatly marvel to see the animal running at large!"

Ellen then proceeded to explain, in detail, the history of the attack and its results. She described, with an accuracy that might have raised suspicions of her own movements in the mind of one less simple than her auditor, the manner in which the beasts burst out of the encampment and the headlong speed with which they had dispersed themselves over the open plain. Although she forbore to say as much in terms, she so managed as to present before the eyes of her listener the strong probability of his having mistaken the frightened drove for savage beasts, and then terminated her account by a lamentation for their loss, and some very natural remarks on the helpless condition in which it had left the family. The naturalist listened in silent wonder, neither interrupting her narrative nor suffering a single exclamation of surprise to escape him. The keen−eyed girl, however, saw that as she proceeded, the important leaf was torn from the tablets, in a manner which shewed that their owner had got rid of his delusion at the same instant. From that moment the world has heard no more of the Vespertilio horribilis Americanus, and the natural sciences have irretrievably lost an important link in that great animated chain which is said to connect earth and heaven, and in which man is thought to be so

69

familiarly complicated with the monkey.

When Dr. Batt was put in full possession of all the circumstances of the inroad, his concern immediately took a different direction. He had left sundry folios, and certain boxes well stored with botanical specimens and defunct animals, under the good keeping of Ishmael, and it immediately struck his acute mind, that marauders as subtle as the Siouxes would never neglect the opportunity to despoil him of these treasures. Nothing that Ellen could say to the contrary served to appease his apprehensions, and, consequently, they separated; he to relieve his doubtsand fears together, and she to glide, as swiftly and silently as she had just before passed it, into the still and solitary tent.

CHAPTER VII.

"What, fifty of my followers, at a clap!"

—— Lear

The day had now fairly opened on the seemingly interminable waste of the prairie. The entrance of Obed at such a moment into the camp, accompanied as it was by vociferous lamentations over his anticipated loss, did not fail to rouse the drowsy family of the squatter. Ishmael and his sons, together with the forbidding–looking brother of his wife, were all speedily afoot; and then, as the sun began to shed his light on the place, they became gradually apprised of the extent of their loss.

Ishmael looked round upon the motionless and heavily loaded vehicles with his teeth firmly compressed, cast a glance at the amazed and helpless groupe of children, which clustered around their sullen but despondent mother, and walked out upon the open land, as if he found the air of the encampment too confined to breathe in. He was followed by several of the men, who were his attentive observers watching the dark expression of his eye as the index of their own future movements. The whole proceeded in profound and moody silence to the summit of the nearest swell, whence they could command an almost boundless view of the naked plains. Here nothing was visible but a solitary buffaloe, that gleaned a meagre subsistence from the decaying herbage, at no great distance, and the ass of the physician, who profited by his freedom to enjoy a richer meal than common.

"Yonder is one of the creatures left by the villains to mock us," said Ishmael, glancing his eye towards the latter, "and that the meanest of the stock. This is a hard country to make a crop in, boys; and yet food must be found to fill so many hungry mouths."

"The rifle is better than the hoe, in such a place as this," returned the eldest of his sons, kicking the hard and thirsty soil on which he stood, with an air of fierce scorn. "It is good for such as they who make their dinner better on beggars' beans than on homminy. A crow would shed tears if forced to fly across the district."

"What say you, trapper;" returned the father, showing the slight impression his powerful heel had made on the compact earth, and laughing with frightful ferocity. "Is this the quality of land a man would choose who never troubles the county clerk with title deeds!"

"There is richer soil in the bottoms," returned the old man calmly, "and you have passed millions of acres to get to this dreary spot, where he who loves to till the 'arth might have received bushels in return for pints, and that too at the cost of no very grievous labour. If you have come in search of land, you have journeyed hundreds of miles too far, or as many leagues too little."

"There is then a better choice towards the other Ocean?" demanded the squatter, pointing in the direction of the Pacific.

"There is, and I have seen it all;" was the answer of the other, who dropped his rifle to the earth, and stood leaning on its barrel, like one who recalled the scenes he had witnessed with melancholy pleasure. "I have seen the waters of the two seas! On one of them was I born, and raised to be a lad like yonder tumbling boy. America has grown, my men, since the days of my youth, to be a country largerthan I once had thought the world itself to be. Near seventy years I dwelt in York, province and state together——You've been in York, 'tis like?"

"Not I——not I; I never visited the towns; but often have heard the place you speak of named. 'Tis a wide clearing there, I reckon——"

"Too wide! too wide! They scourge the very 'arth with their axes. Such hills and hunting-grounds as I have seen stripped of the gifts of the Lord, without remorse or shame! I tarried till the mouths of my hounds were deafened by the blows of the chopper, and then I came west in search of quiet. It was a grievous journey that I made; a grievous toil to pass through falling timber and breathe the thick air of smoky clearings, week after week, as I did! 'Tis a far country too, that state of York from this!"

"It lies ag'in the outer edge of old Kentuck, I reckon; though what the distance may be I never knew."

"A gull would have to fan a thousand miles of air, to find the eastern sea. And yet it is no mighty reach to hunt across, when shade and game are plenty! The time has been when I followed the deer in the mountains of the Delaware and Hudson, and took the beaver on the streams of the upper lakes, in the same season: but my eye was quick and certain at that day, and my limbs were like the legs of a moose! The dam of Hector," he added, dropping his look kindly to the aged hound that crouched at his feet, "was then a pup, and apt to open on the game the moment she struck the scent. She gave me a deal of trouble, that slut, she did."

"Your hound is old, stranger, and a rap on the head would prove a mercy to the beast."

"The dog is like his master," returned the trapper, without appearing to heed the brutal advice the other gave, "and will number his days, when his work amongst the game is over, and not before. Tomy eye things seem ordered to meet each other in this creation. 'Tis not the swiftest running deer that always throws off the hounds, nor the biggest arm that holds the truest rifle. Look around you, men; what will the Yankee Choppers say, when they have cut their path from the eastern to the western waters, and find that a hand, which can lay the 'arth bare at a blow, has been here and swept the country, in very mockery of their wickedness. They will turn on their tracks like a fox that doubles, and then the rank smell of their own footsteps will show them the madness of their waste. Howsomever, these are thoughts that are more likely to rise in him who has seen the folly of eighty seasons, than to teach wisdom to men still bent on the pleasures of their kind! You have need yet, of a stirring time, if you think to escape the craft and hatred of the burnt–wood Indians. They claim to be the lawful owners of this country, and seldom leave a white more than the skin he boasts of, when once they get the power, as they always have the will, to do him harm."

"Old man," said Ishmael sternly, "to which people do you belong? You have the colour and speech of a Christian, while it seems that your heart is with the red–skins."

"To me there is little difference in nations. The people I loved most are scattered as the sands of the dry river beds fly before the fall hurricanes, and life is too short to make use and custom with strangers, as one can do with such as he has dwelt amongst for years. Still am I a man without the cross of Indian blood; and what is due from a warrior to his nation, is owing by me to the people of the states; though little need have they, with their militia and their armed boats, of help from a single arm of fourscore."

"Since you own your kin, I may ask a simple question. Where are the Siouxes who have stolen my cattle?"

"Where is the herd of buffaloes, which was chased by the panther across this plain, no later than the morning of yesterday! It is as hard——"

"Friend," said Dr. Battius, who had hitherto been an attentive listener, but who now felt a sudden impulse to mingle in the discourse, "I am grieved when I find a venator or hunter, of your experience and observation, following the current of vulgar error. The animal you describe is in truth a species of the bos ferus (or bos sylvestris, as he has been happily called by the poets), but, though of close affinity, is altogether distinct from the common bubulus. Bison is the better word, and I would suggest the necessity of adopting it in future, when you shall have occasion to allude to the species."

"Bison or buffaloe, it makes but little matter. The creatur' is the same, call it by what name you will, and——"

"Pardon me, venerable venator; as classification is the very soul of the natural sciences, the animal or vegetable must, of necessity, be characterised by the peculiarities of its species, which is always indicated by the name——"

"Friend," said the trapper, a little positively, "would the tail of a beaver make the worse dinner, for calling it a mink; or could you eat of the wolf with relish, because some bookish man had given it the name of venison?"

As these questions were put with no little earnestness and some spirit, there was every probability that a hot discussion would have succeeded between the two, of whom one was so purely practical and the other so much given to theory, had not Ishmael seen fit to terminate the dispute, by bringing into view a subject that was much more important to his own immediate interests.

"Beavers' tails and minks' flesh may do to talk about before a maple fire and a quiet hearth," interruptedthe squatter, without the smallest deference to the interested feelings of the disputants; "but there is something more than foreign words, or words of any sort, now needed. Tell me, trapper; where are your Siouxes skulking?"

"It would be as easy to tell you the colours of the hawk that is floating beneath yonder white cloud! When a red−skin strikes his blow, he is not apt to wait until he is paid for the evil deed in lead."

"Will the beggarly savages believe they have enough when they find themselves master of all the stock?"

"Natur' is much the same, let it be covered by what coloured skin it may. Do you ever find your longings after riches less when you have made a good crop, than before you were master of a kernel of corn? If you do, you differ from what the experience of a long life tells me is the common cravings of man."

"Speak plainly, old stranger," said the squatter, striking the butt of his rifle heavily on the earth, his dull capacity finding no pleasure in a discourse that was conducted in such obscure allusions; "I have asked a simple question, and one I know well that you can answer."

"You are right, you are right. I can answer, for I have too often seen the disposition of my kind to mistake it, when evil is stirring. When the Siouxes have gathered in the beasts, and have made sure that you are not upon their heels, they will be back nibbling like hungry wolves to take the bait they have left: or it may be, they'll shew the temper of the great bears, that are found at the falls of the Long River, and strike at once with the paw, without stopping to nose their prey."

"You have then seen, the animals you mention!" exclaimed Dr. Battius, who had now been thrownout of the conversation quite as long as his impatience could well brook, and who approached the subject with his tablets ready opened, as a book of reference. "Can you tell me if what you encountered was of the species, ursus horribilis——with the ears, rounded——front, arquated——eyes——destitute of the remarkable supplemental lid——with six incisores, one false, and four perfect molares——"

"Trapper, go on," interrupted Ishmael; "you believe we shall see more of the robbers."

"Nay——nay——I do not call them robbers, for it is the usage of their people, and what may be called the prairie law."

"I have come five hundred miles to find a place where no man can ding the words of the law in my ears," said Ishmael, fiercely, "and I am not in a humour to stand quietly at a bar, while a red-skin sits in judgment. I tell you, trapper, if another Sioux is seen prowling around my camp, wherever it may be, he shall feel the contents of old Kentuck," slapping his rifle, in a manner that could not be easily misconstrued, "though he wore the medal of Washington, himself; I call the man a robber who takes that which is not his own."

"The Teton, and the Pawnee, and the Konza, and men of a dozen other tribes, claim to own these naked fields."

"Natur' gives them the lie in their teeth. The air, the water and the ground, are all free gifts to man, and no one has the power to portion them out in parcels. Man must drink, and breathe, and walk ——and therefore each has a right to his perfect share of 'arth. Why do not the surveyors of the states set their compasses and run their lines over our heads as well as beneath our feet? Why do they not cover their shining sheep-skins with big words, giving to the land-holder, or perhaps he should becalled air-holder, so many rods of heaven, with the use of such a star for a boundary-mark, and such a cloud to turn a mill!"

As the squatter uttered his wild conceit, he laughed from the very bottom of his chest in scorn. The deriding but frightful merriment passed from the mouth of one of his ponderous sons to that of the other, until it had made the circuit of the whole family.

"Come, trapper," continued Ishmael in a tone of better humour, like a man who feels that he has triumphed, "neither of us, I reckon, has ever had much to do with title-deeds, or county clerks, or blazed trees; therefore we will not waste words on fooleries. You ar' a man that has tarried long in this clearing, and now I ask your opinion, face to face, without fear or favour, if you had the lead in my business, what would you do?"

75

The old man hesitated, and seemed to give the required advice with deep reluctance. As every eye, however, was fastened on him, and whichever way he turned his face, he encountered a look riveted on the lineaments of his own working countenance, he answered in a low, melancholy tone——

"I have seen too much mortal blood poured out in empty quarrels, to wish ever to hear an angry rifle again. Ten weary years have I sojourned alone on these naked plains, waiting for my hour to come, and not a blow have I struck, ag'in an enemy more humanized than the grizzly bear."

"Ursus horribilis," muttered the Doctor.

The speaker paused at the sound of the other's voice, but perceiving it was no more than a sort of mental ejaculation, he continued in the same strain——

"More humanized than the grizzly bear, or the panther of the Rocky Mountains; unless the beaver, which is a wise and knowing animal, may be soreckoned. What would I advise? Even the female buffaloe will fight for her young!"

"It never then shall be said, that Ishmael Bush has less kindness for his children than the bear for her cubs!"

"And yet this is but a naked spot for a dozen men to make head in, ag'in five hundred."

"Ay, it is so," returned the squatter, glancing his eye towards his humble camp; "but something might be done, with the wagons and the cotton-wood."

The trapper shook his head incredulously, and pointed across the rolling plain in the direction of the west, as he answered——

"A rifle would send a bullet from these hills into your very sleeping-cabins; nay, arrows from the thicket in your rear would keep you all burrowed, like so many prairie dogs: it wouldn't do, it wouldn't do. Three long miles from this spot is a place, where as I have often thought in passing across the desert, a stand might be made for days and weeks together, if there were hearts and hands ready to engage in the bloody work."

Another low, deriding laugh passed among the young men, announcing, in a manner sufficiently intelligible, their readiness to undertake a task even more arduous. The squatter himself eagerly seized the hint which had been so reluctantly extorted from the trapper, who by some singular process of reasoning had evidently persuaded himself that it was his duty to be strictly neutral. A few direct and pertinent inquiries served to obtain the little additional information that was necessary, in order to make the contemplated movement, and then Ishmael, who was, on emergencies, as terrifically energetic, as he was sluggish in common, set about effecting his object without delay.

Notwithstanding the industry and zeal of all engaged, the task however, was one of great labour and difficulty. The loaded vehicles were to be drawn, by hand, across a wide distance of plain, without track or guide of any sort, except that which the trapper furnished by communicating his knowledge of the cardinal points of the compass. In accomplishing this object, the gigantic strength of the men was taxed to the utmost, nor were the females or the children spared a heavy proportion of the toil. While the sons distributed themselves about the heavily loaded wagons, and drew them by main strength up the neighbouring swell, their mother and Ellen, surrounded by the amazed groupe of little ones, followed slowly in the rear, bending under the weight of such different articles as were suited to their several strengths.

Ishmael himself superintended and directed the whole, occasionally applying his colossal shoulder to some lagging vehicle, until he saw that the chief difficulty, that of gaining the level of their intended route, was accomplished. Then he pointed out the required course, cautioning his sons to proceed in such a manner that they should not lose the advantage they had with so much labour obtained, and beckoning to the brother of his wife, they returned together to the empty camp.

Throughout the whole of this movement, which occupied an hour of time, the trapper had stood apart, leaning on his rifle, with the aged hound slumbering at his feet, a silent but attentive observer of all that passed. Occasionally, a smile lighted his hard, muscular, but wasted features, like a gleam of sunshine flitting across a naked ragged ruin, and betrayed the momentary pleasure he found in witnessing from time to time the vast power the youths discovered. Then, as the train drew slowly up the ascent, a cloud of thought and sorrow threw all intothe shade again, leaving the expression of his countenance in its usual state of quiet melancholy gravity. As vehicle after vehicle left the place of the encampment, he noted the change, with increasing attention; seldom failing to cast an inquiring look at the little neglected tent, which with its proper wagon, still remained, as before, solitary and apparently forgotten. The summons of Ishmael to his gloomy associate, had however, as it would now seem, this hitherto neglected portion of his effects for its object.

First casting a cautious and suspicious glance on every side of him, the squatter and his companion advanced to the little wagon, and caused it to enter within the folds of the cloth, much in the same manner that it had been extricated the preceding evening. They both then disappeared behind the drapery, and many moments of suspense succeeded, during which the old man, secretly urged by a burning desire to know the meaning of so much mystery, insensibly drew nigher to the place, until he stood within a few yards of the proscribed spot. The agitation of the cloth betrayed the nature of the occupation of those whom it concealed, though their work was conducted in the most rigid silence. It would appear that long practice had made each of the two acquainted with his particular duty, for neither sign nor direction of any sort was necessary from Ishmael, in order to apprise his surly associate of the manner in which he was to proceed. In less time than has been consumed in relating it, the interior portion of the arrangement was completed, when the men re−appeared without the tent. Too busy with his occupation to heed the presence of the trapper, Ishmael began to release the folds of the cloth from the ground, and to dispose of them in such a manner around the vehicle as to form a sweeping train to the new form the little pavilion had now assumed. The arched rooftrembled with the occasional movement of the light vehicle, which, it was now apparent, once more supported its secret burden. Just as the work was ended the scowling eye of Ishmael's assistant caught a glimpse of the figure of the attentive observer of their movements. Dropping the shaft, which he had already lifted from the ground preparatory to occupying the place that was usually filled by an animal less reasoning and perhaps less dangerous than himself, he bluntly exclaimed——

"I am a fool, as you often say! But look for yourself: if that man is not an enemy, I will disgrace father and mother, call myself an Indian, and go hunt with the Siouxes!"

The cloud as it is about to discharge the subtle lightning is not more dark nor threatening, than was the look with which Ishmael greeted the intruder. He turned his head on every side of him, as if seeking some engine sufficiently terrible to annihilate the offending trapper at a blow; and then, possibly recollecting the further occasion he might have for his counsel, he forced himself to say, with an appearance of moderation that nearly choked him——

"Stranger, I did believe this prying into the concerns of others was the business of women in the towns and settlements, and not the manner in which men, who are used to live where each has room for himself, deal with the secrets of their neighbours. To what lawyer or sheriff do you calculate to sell your news?"

"I hold but little discourse except with one; and then chiefly of my own affairs," returned the old man, without the least observable apprehension, and pointing imposingly upward; "a judge; and judge of all. Little does he need knowledge from my hands, and but little will your wish to keep any thing secret from him profit you, even in this desert."

The mounting tempers of his unnurtured listenerswere rebuked by the simple, solemn manner of the trapper. Ishmael stood sullen and thoughtful; while his companion stole a furtive and involuntary glance at the placid sky, which spread so wide and blue above his head, as if he expected to see the Almighty eye itself beaming from the heavenly vault. But impressions of a serious character are seldom lasting on minds long indulged in forgetfulness. The hesitation of the squatter was consequently of very short duration. The language, however, as well as the firm and collected air of the speaker, were the means of preventing much subsequent abuse, if not violence.

"It would be shewing more of the kindness of a friend and comrade," Ishmael returned, in a tone sufficiently sullen to betray his humour, though it was no longer threatening, "had your shoulder been put to the wheel of one of yonder wagons, instead of edging itself in here, where none are wanted but such as are invited."

"I can put the little strength that is left me," returned the trapper, "to this, as well as to another of your loads."

"Do you take us for boys!" exclaimed Ishmael, laughing, half in ferocity and half in derision, applying his powerful strength at the same time to the little vehicle, which rolled over the grass with as much seeming facility as though it were drawn by its usual team.

The trapper paused, and followed the departing wagon with his eye, marvelling greatly as to the nature of its concealed contents, until it had also gained the summit of the eminence, and in its turn disappeared behind the swell of the land. Then he turned to gaze at the desolation of the scene around him. The absence of human forms would have scarce created a sensation in the bosom of one so long accustomed to solitude, had not the site of the deserted camp furnished such strong memorials of its recent visiters, and as the old man was quick to detect, of their waste also. He cast his eye upwards, with a significant shake of the head, at the vacant spot in the heavens, which had so lately been filled by the branches of those trees that now lay stripped of their verdure, worthless and deserted logs, at his feet."

"Ay!" he muttered to himself, "I might have know'd it! I might have know'd it! often have I seen the same before, and yet I brought them to the spot myself, and have now sent them to the only neighbourhood of their kind, within many long leagues of the spot where I stand. This is man's wish, and pride, and waste, and sinfulness! He tames the beasts of the field to feed his idle wants, and having robbed the brutes of their natural food, he teaches them to strip the 'arth of its trees to quiet their hunger."

A rustling in the low bushes that still grew for some distance, along the swale, that formed the thicket on which the camp of Ishmael had rested, caught his ear at the moment and cut short the soliloquy. The habits of so many years spent in the wilderness, caused the old man to bring his rifle to a poise, with something like the activity and promptitude of his youth; but suddenly recovering his recollection, he dropped it into the hollow of his arm again, and resumed his air of melancholy resignation.

"Come forth, come forth!" he said aloud; "be ye bird or be ye beast——ye are safe from these old hands. I have eaten and I have drunk; why should I take life, when my wants call for no such sacrifice. It will not be long afore the birds will peck at eyes that shall not see them, and perhaps light on my very bones; for if things like these are only made to perish, why am I to expect to live for ever! Come forth——come forth; ye are safe from harm, at these weak hands."

"Thank you for the good word, old trapper," cried Paul Hover, springing actively forward from his place of concealment. "There was an air about you, when you threw forward the muzzle of the piece, that I did not like; for it seemed to say that you were master of all the rest of the motions."

"You are right! you are right!" cried the trapper, laughing with inward self complacency, at the recollection of his former skill. "The day has been, when few men knew the virtues of a long rifle, like this I carry, better than myself, old and useless as I now seem. You are right, young man; and the time was, when it was dangerous to move a leaf, within ear–shot of my stand, or," he added, dropping his voice and looking serious, "for a Red Mingo to show even an eyeball from his ambushment. You have heard of the Red Mingos?"

"I have heard of minks," said Paul, taking the old man by the arm, and gently urging him towards the thicket as he spoke, while at the same time he cast quick and uneasy glances behind him, in order to make sure he was not observed. "Of your common black minks; but of none of any other colour."

"Lord! lord!" continued the trapper, shaking his head, and still laughing in his deep but quiet mannan; "the boy mistakes a brute for a man! Though, a Mingo is little better than a beast; or, for that matter, he is worse, when rum and opportunity are placed before his eyes. There was that accursed Huron from the upper lakes, that I knocked from his perch, among the rocks in the hills, back of the Hori——"

His voice was lost in the thicket, into which he had suffered himself to be led by Paul, while speaking; too much occupied by thoughts which dwelt onscenes and acts that had taken place half a century earlier in the history of the country, to offer the smallest resistance.

CHAPTER VIII.

"Now they are clapper–clawing one another; I'll go look on. That dissembling abominable varlet, Diomed, has got that same scurvy, doting, foolish young knave in his helm."

—— Troilus and Cressida

It is necessary, in order that the thread of the narrative should not be spun to a length which might fatigue the reader, that he should imagine a week to have intervened between the scene with which the preceding chapter closed, and the events with which it is our intention to resume its relation in this. The season was on the point of changing its character; the verdure of summer giving place more rapidly to the brown and party–coloured livery of the fall. The heavens were clothed in driving clouds, piled in vast masses one above the other, which whirled violently in the gusts; opening, occasionally, to admit transient glimpses of the bright and glorious sight of the heavens dwelling in a magnificence, by far too grand and durable to be disturbed by the fitful efforts of the lower world. Beneath, the wind swept across the wild and naked prairies, with a violence that is seldom witnessed in any section of the continent less open. It would have been easy to have imagined, in the ages of fable, that the god of the winds had permitted his subordinate agents to escape from their den, and that they now rioted, in wantonness, across wastes, where neither tree, nor work of man, nor mountain, nor obstacle of any sort opposed itself to their gambols.

Though nakedness might, as usual, be given as the pervading character of the spot, whither it is now necessary to transfer the scene of the tale, it was not entirely without the signs of human life. Amid the monotonous rolling of the prairie, a single naked and ragged rock arose on the margin of a little water–course, which found its way, after winding a vast distance through the plains, into one of the numerous tributaries of the Father of Rivers. A swale of low land lay near the base of the eminence, and as it was still fringed with a thicket of alders and sumack, it bore the signs of having once nurtured a feeble growth of wood. The trees themselves had been transferred, however, to the summit and crags of the neighbouring rocks. It was on this little elevation that the signs of man were to be found, to which the allusion just made applies.

Seen from beneath, they presented no more than a breast–work of logs and stones, intermingled in such a manner as to save all unnecessary labour; of a few low roofs made of bark and boughs of trees; of an occasional barrier, constructed like the defences on the summit, and placed on such points of the acclivity as were easier of approach than the general face of the eminence, and of a little dwelling of cloth, perched on the apex of a small pyramid, that shot up on one angle of the rock, the white covering of which glimmered from a distance like a spot of snow——or to make the simile more suitable to the rest of the subject, like a spotless and carefully guarded standard, which was to be protected by the dearest blood of those who defended the citadel beneath. It is hardly necessary to add, that this rude and characteristic fortress was the place where Ishmael Bush had taken refuge, after the robbery of his flocks and herds.

On the day to which the narrative is advanced; the squatter was to be seen standing near the base ofthese very rocks, leaning on his rifle, and regarding the sterile soil that

82

The Prairie, Volume 1

supported him with a look in which contempt and disappointment were strongly blended.

"'Tis time to change our natur's," he observed to the brother of his wife, who was rarely far from his elbow; "and to become ruminators, instead of people used to the fare of Christians and free men. I reckon, Abiram, you could glean a living among the grasshoppers; you ar' an active man, and might outrun the nimblest skipper of them all."

"The country will never do," returned the other, who relished but little the forced humour of his kinsman; "and it is well to remember that a lazy traveller makes a long journey."

"Would you have me draw a cart at my heels, across this desert, for weeks; ay, months!" retorted Ishmael, who, like all of his class, could labour with incredible efforts on emergencies, but who too seldom exerted continued industry, on any occasion, to brook a proposal that offered so little repose. "It may do for your people, who live in settlements, to hasten on to their houses. But, thank Heaven, my farm is too big for its owner ever to want a resting–place!"

"Since you like the plantation, then, you have only to make your crop!"

"That is easier said than done, on this corner of the estate. I tell you, Abiram, there is need of moving for more reasons than one. You know I'm a man that very seldom enters into a bargain; but who always fulfils his agreements better than your dealers in wordy contracts written on rags of paper. If there's one mile, there ar' a hundred still needed to make up the distance for which you have my honour."

As he spoke, the squatter glanced his eye upward at the little tenement of cloth which crowned thesummit of his ragged fortress. The look was understood and answered by the other, and by some secret influence, which operated either through their interests or feelings, it served to re–establish that harmony between them, which had just been threatened with something very like a momentary breach.

"I know it, and feel it in every bone of my body. But I remember the reason, why I have set myself on this accursed journey too well, to forget the distance between me and the end. Neither you nor I will ever be the better for what we have done, unless we thoroughly finish what is so well begun. Ay; that is the doctrine of the whole world, I judge: I heard a travelling preacher, who was skirting it down the Ohio, a time since, say, if a man should live up to the faith for a hundred years and then fall from his work a single day, he would find the settlement was to be made for the finishing blow that he had put to his job, and that all the bad and none of the good would come into the final account."

"And you believed what the hungry hypocrite preached!"

"Who said that I believed it!" retorted Abiram with a bullying look, that betrayed how much his fears had dwelt on the subject he affected to despise. "Is it believing to tell what a roguish——And yet, Ishmael, the man might have been honest after all! He told us that the world was, in truth, no better than a desert, and that there was but one hand that could lead the most learned man through all its windings of good and evil. Now, if this be true of the whole world, it may be true of a part."

"Abiram, out with your grievances like a man," interrupted the squatter, with a hoarse, taunting laugh. "You want to pray. But of what use will it be, according to your own doctrine, to serve God five minutes and the devil an hour. Harkee, friend; I'm not much of a husbandman, but this I know tomy cost; that to make a right good crop, even on the richest bottom, there must be hard labour; and your snufflers often liken the 'arth to a field of corn, and the men, who live on it, to its yield. Now I tell you, Abiram, that you are no better than a thistle or a mullin; yea, ye ar' wood of too open a pore to be good even to burn!"

The malign glance which shot from the scowling eye of Abiram, announced the angry character of his feelings, but as the furtive look quailed, almost immediately, before the unmoved, steady countenance of the squatter, it also betrayed how much the bolder spirit of the latter had obtained the mastery over his craven nature.

Content with his ascendency, which was too apparent, and had been too often exerted on similar occasions, to leave him in any doubt of its extent, Ishmael coolly continued the discourse, by adverting more directly to his future plans.

"You will own the justice at any rate of paying every one in kind," he said; "I have been robbed of my stock, and I have a scheme to make myself as good as before, by taking hoof for hoof; or for that matter, when a man is put to the trouble of bargaining for both sides, he is a fool if he dont pay himself something in the way of commission."

As the squatter made this declaration in a loud and decided tone, which was a little excited by the humour of the moment, four or five of his lounging sons, who had been leaning against the foot of the rock, came forward with the indolent step so common to the whole family.

"I have been calling Ellen Wade, who is on the rock keeping the look–out, to know if there is any thing to be seen," observed the eldest of the young men; "and she shakes her head for an answer. Ellen is sparing of her words, for a woman; and mightbe taught manners, at least, without spoiling any of her uncommon good looks."

Ishmael cast his eye upward to the place, where the offending, but unconscious girl was holding her anxious watch. She was seated at the edge of the uppermost crag, by the side of the little tent, and at least a hundred feet above the level of the plain. Little else was to be distinguished, at that distance, but the outline of her form, her fair hair streaming in the gusts beyond her shoulders, and the steady and seemingly unchangeable look that she had riveted on some remote point of the prairie.

"What is it, Nell?" cried Ishmael, lifting his powerful voice a little above the rushing of the element. "Have you got a glimpse of any thing bigger than one of them burrowing barkers?"

The lips of the attentive Ellen parted; she rose to the utmost height her small stature admitted, seeming still to regard the unknown object; but her voice, if she spoke at all, was not sufficiently loud to be heard amid the roaring of the wind.

"It ar' a fact that the child sees something more uncommon than a buffaloe or a prairie dog!" continued Ishmael. "Why, Nell, girl, ar' ye deaf? Nell, I say;——I hope it is an army of red–skins she has in her eye; for I should mightily relish the chance to pay them for their kindness, under the favour of these logs and rocks!"

As the squatter had accompanied his vaunt with corresponding gestures, and directed his eyes to the circle of his equally confident sons while speaking, he had drawn their gaze from Ellen to himself; but now, when they turned together to note the succeeding movements of their female sentinel, the place which had so lately been occupied by her form was vacant.

"As I am a sinner," exclaimed Asa, usually one of the most phlegmatic of the youths, in a tone of extraordinary excitement, "the girl is blown away by the wind!"

Something like a sensation was exhibited among them, which might have denoted that the influence of the laughing blue eyes, flaxen hair, and glowing cheeks of Ellen, had not been lost on the dull natures of the young men, and looks of dull amazement, mingled slightly with concern, passed from one to the other, as they gazed, in stupid wonder, at the point of the naked rock.

"It might well be!" added another; "she sat on a slivered stone, and I have been thinking of telling her she was in danger for more than an hour."

"Is that a riband of the child, dangling from the corner of the hill below!" cried Ishmael; "ha! who is moving about the tent; have I not told you all——"

"Ellen! 'tis Ellen!" interrupted the whole body of his sons in a breath; and at that instant she re-appeared to put an end to their different surmises, and, to relieve more than one sluggish nature from its unwonted excitement. As Ellen issued from beneath the folds of the tent, she advanced with a light and fearless step to her former giddy stand, and pointed toward the prairie, appearing to speak in an eager and rapid voice to some invisible auditor.

"Nell is mad!" said Asa, half in contempt and yet not a little in concern. "The girl is dreaming with her eyes open; and thinks she sees some of them fierce creatur's, with hard names, with which the Doctor fills her ears."

"Can it be, the child has found a scout of the Siouxes," said Ishmael, bending his look toward the plain; but a low, significant whisper from Abiram drew his eyes quickly upward again, where they were turned just in time to perceive that the cloth of the tent was agitated by a motion very evidentlydifferent from the quivering occasioned by the wind. "Let her, if she dare!" the squatter muttered in his teeth. "Abiram; they know my temper too well to play the prank with me!"

"Look for yourself! if the curtain is not lifted, I can see no better than an owl by daylight."

Ishmael struck the breech of his rifle violently on the earth, and shouted in a voice that might easily have been heard by Ellen, had not her attention still continued rapt on the object which so unaccountably attracted her eyes in the distance.

"Nell!" continued the squatter; "away with you, fool! will you bring down punishment on your own head. Why Nell!——she has forgotten her native speech; let us see if she can understand another language."

Ishmael threw his rifle to his shoulder, and at the next moment it was pointed upward at the summit of the rock. Before time was given for a word of remonstrance, it had sent forth its contents, in its usual streak of bright flame. Ellen started like the frightened chamois, and uttering a piercing scream, she darted into the tent, with a swiftness that left it uncertain whether terror or actual injury had been the penalty of her slight offence.

The action of the squatter was too sudden and unexpected to admit of prevention, but the instant it was done, his sons manifested, in an unequivocal manner, the temper with which they witnessed the desperate measure. Angry and fierce glances were interchanged, and a murmur of disapprobation was uttered by the whole in common.

"What has Ellen done, father," said Asa, with a degree of spirit, which was the more striking from being unusual, "that she should be shot at like a straggling deer or a hungry wolf!"

"Mischief;" deliberately returned the squatter, but with a cool expression of defiance in his eyethat showed how little he was moved by the ill-concealed humour of his children. "Mischief, boy; mischief! take you care that the disorder don't spread."

"It would need a different treatment in a man, than in you screaming girl!"

"Asa, you ar' a man, as you have often boasted; but remember I am your father, and your better."

"I know it well; and what sort of a father!"

"Harkee, boy: I more than half believe that your drowsy head let in the Siouxes. Be modest in your speech, my watchful son, or you may have to answer yet for the mischief

87

your own bad conduct has brought upon us."

"I'll stay no longer to be hectored like a child in petticoats. You talk of law, as if you knew of none, and yet you keep me down, as though I had not life and wants of my own to provide for. I'll stay no longer to be treated like one of your meanest cattle."

"The world is wide, my gallant boy, and there's many a noble plantation on it, without a tenant. Go; you have title deeds sign'd and seal'd to your hand. Few fathers portion their children better than Ishmael Bush; you will say that for me at least, when you get to the end of your journey."

"Look! father, look!" exclaimed several voices at once, as though they seized, with avidity an opportunity to interrupt a dialogue which threatened to become still more violent.

"Look!" repeated Abiram, in a voice which sounded hollow and warning; "If you have time for any thing but quarrels, Ishmael, look!"

The squatter turned slowly from his offending son, and cast an eye upward that still lowered with deep resentment, but which, the instant it caught a view of the object that now attracted the attention of all around him, changed its expression to one of astonishment and dismay.

A female stood on the spot, from which Ellen had been so fearfully expelled. Her person was of the smallest size that is believed to comport with beauty, and which poets and artists have chosen as the beau idéal of feminine loveliness. Her dress was of a dark and glossy silk, and fluttered like gossamer around her form. Long, flowing, and curling tresses of hair, still blacker and more shining than her robe, fell at times about her shoulders, completely enveloping the whole of her delicate bust in their ringlets; or at others streaming long and waving in the wind. The elevation at which she stood prevented a close examination of the lineaments of a countenance which, however, it might be seen was youthful, speaking, and, at the moment of her unlooked-for appearance, chanrged with powerful emotion. So young, indeed, did this fair and fragile being appear, that it might be doubted whether the age of childhood was entirely passed. One small and exquisitely moulded hand was pressed on her heart, while with the other she made an impressive gesture, which seemed to invite Ishmael, if any further violence was meditated, to direct it against her bosom.

The silent wonder, with which the groupe of borderers gazed upward at so extraordinary a spectacle, was only interrupted as the person of Ellen was seen emerging with marked timidity from the tent, as if equally urged, by apprehensions in behalf of herself and the fears which she felt on account of her companion, to remain concealed and to advance. She spoke, but her words were unheard by those below, and unheeded by her to whom they were addressed. The latter, however, as if content with the offer she had made of herself as the most proper victim to the resentment of Ishmael, now calmly retired, and the spot she had so lately occupied became vacant, leaving a sort of stupid impression on the spectators beneath, not unlike that which it might be supposed would have been created had they just been gazing at some supernatural vision.

More than a minute of profound silence succeeded, during which the sons of Ishmael still continued gazing at the naked rock in stupid wonder. Then, as eye met eye, an expression of novel intelligence passed from one to the other, indicating that to them, at least, the appearance of this extraordinary tenant of the pavilion was as unexpected as it was incomprehensible. At length Asa, in right of his years, and moved by the still rankling impulse of his recent quarrel, took on himself the office of interrogator. Instead, however, of braving the resentment of his father, of whose fierce nature, when aroused, he had had too frequent evidence to excite it wantonly, he turned upon the cowering person of Abiram, observing with a sneer——

"This then is the beast you were bringing into the prairies for a decoy! I know you to be a man who seldom troubles truth, when any thing worse may answer, but I never knew you to outdo yourself so thoroughly before. The newspapers of Kentuck have called you a dealer in black flesh a hundred times, but little did they reckon that you drove the trade into white families."

"Who is a kidnapper!" demanded Abiram with a blustering show of resentment. "Am I to be called to account for every lie they put in print throughout the states! Look to your own family, boy; look to yourselves. The very stumps of Kentucky and Tennessee cry out ag'in ye! Ay, my tonguey gentleman, I have seen father and mother and three children, yourself for one, published on the logs and stubs of the settlements, with dollars enough for reward to have made an honest man rich, for——"

He was interrupted by a back–handed but violent blow on the mouth, that caused him to totter, andwhich left the impression of its weight in the starting blood and swelling lips.

"Asa," said the father, advancing with a portion of that dignity with which the hand of Nature seems to have invested the parental character, "you have struck the brother of your mother!"

"I have struck the abuser of the whole family," returned the angry youth; "and, unless he teaches his tongue a wiser language, he had better part with it altogether as the unruly member. I'm no great performer with the knife, but, on an occasion, could make out, myself, to cut off a slande——"

"Boy, twice have you forgotten yourself to–day. Be careful that it does not happen the third time. When the law of the land is weak, it is right the law of nature should be strong. You understand me, Asa; and you know me. As for you, Abiram, the child has done you wrong, and it is my place to see you righted. Remember; I tell you justice shall be done; it is enough. But you have said hard things ag'in me and my family. If the hounds of the law have put their bills on the trees and stumps of the clearings, it was for no act of dishonesty as you know, but because we maintain the rule that the 'arth is common property. No, Abiram; could I wash my hands of things done by your advice, as easily as I can of the things done by the whisperings of the devil, my sleep would be quieter at night, and none who bear my name need blush to hear it mentioned. Peace, Asa, and you too man; enough has been said. Let us all think well before any thing is added, that may make what is already so bad still more bitter."

Ishmael waved his hand with authority as he ended, and turned away with the air of one who felt assured, that those he had addressed would not have the temerity to dispute his commands. Asa evidently struggled with himself to compel the requiredobedience, but his heavy nature quietly sunk into its ordinary repose, and he soon appeared again the being he really was; dangerous, only, at moments, and one whose passions were too sluggish to be long maintained at the point of ferocity. Not so with Abiram. While there was an appearance of a personal conflict, between him and his colossal nephew, his mien had expressed the infallible evidences of engrossing apprehension, but now, that the authority as well as gigantic strength of the father were interposed between him and his assailant, his countenance changed from paleness to a livid hue, that bespoke how deeply the injury he had received rankled in his breast. Like Asa, however, he acquiesced in the decision of the squatter, and the appearance, at least, of harmony was restored again among a set of beings, who were restrained by no obligations more powerful than the frail web of authority with which Ishmael had been able to envelope his restless children.

One effect of the quarrel had been to divert the thoughts of the young men from their recent visiter. With the dispute that succeeded the disappearance of the fair stranger, all recollection of her existence appeared to have vanished. A few ominous and secret conferences it is true were held apart, during which the direction of the eyes of the different speakers betrayed their subject; but these threatening symptoms soon disappeared, and the whole party was again seen broken into its usual, listless, silent and lounging groupes.

"I will go upon the rock, boys, and look abroad for the savages," said Ishmael shortly after, advancing towards them with a mien which he intended should be conciliating at the same time that it was absolute. "If there is nothing to fear, we will go out on the plain; the day is too good to be lost inwords, like women in the towns wrangling over their tea and sugared cakes."

Without waiting for approbation or dissent, the squatter then advanced to the base of the rock, which formed a sort of perpendicular wall near twenty feet high around the whole acclivity. Ishmael, however, directed his footsteps to a point where an ascent might be made through a narrow cleft, which he had taken the precaution to fortify with a breast–work of cotton–wood logs, and which, in its turn, was defended by a chevaux–de–frise of the branches of the same tree. Here an armed man was usually kept, as at the key of the whole position, and here one of the young men now stood, indolently leaning against the rock, ready to protect the pass, if it should prove necessary, until the whole party could be mustered at the several points of defence.

From this place the squatter found the ascent still difficult, partly by nature and partly by artificial impediments, until he reached a sort of terrace, or to speak more properly the plain of the elevation, where he had established the huts in which the whole family dwelt. These tenements were, as already mentioned, of that class which are so often seen on the borders, and such as belonged to the infancy of architecture; being simply formed of logs, bark, and poles. The area on which they stood contained several hundred square feet, and was sufficiently elevated above the plain greatly to lessen if not to remove all danger from Indian missiles. Here Ishmael believed he might leave his infants in comparative security, under the protection of their spirited mother, and here he now found Esther engaged at her ordinary domestic employments, surrounded by her daughters, and lifting her voice, in the tones of declamatory censure, as one or another of the idle fry incurred her displeasure, and far too much engrossedwith the tempest of her own conversation to know any thing of the violent scene which had been passing among the party below.

"A fine windy place you have chosen for the camp, Ishmael!" she commenced or rather continued, by merely diverting the attack from a sobbing girl of ten, at her elbow, to her husband. "My word! if I haven't to count the young ones every ten minutes, to see they are not flying away among the buzzards or the ducks. Why do ye all keep hovering round the rock, like lolloping reptiles in the spring, when the heavens are beginning to be alive with birds, man! D'ye think mouths can be filled, and hunger satisfied, by laziness and sleep!"

"You'll have your say, Eester;" said the husband, using the provincial pronunciation of America for the name, and regarding his noisy companions, with a look of habitual tolerance rather than of affection. "But the birds you shall have, if your own tongue don't frighten them to take too high a flight. Ay, woman," he continued, standing on the very spot whence he had so rudely banished Ellen, which he had by this time gained, "and buffaloe too, if my eye can tell the animal at the distance of a Spanish league."

"Come down; come down, and be doing, instead of talking. A talking man is no better than a barking dog. Nell shall hang out the cloth, if any of the red-skins show themselves, in time to give you notice. But, Ishmael, what have you been killing, my man; for it was your rifle I heard a few minutes agone, unless I have lost my skill in sounds."

"Poh! 'twas to frighten the hawk you see sailing above the rock."

"Hawk, indeed! at your time of day to be shooting at hawks and buzzards, with eighteen open mouths to feed. Look at the bee, and at the beaver, my good man, and learn to be a provider. Why, Ishmael! I believe my soul," she continued, droppingthe tow she was twisting on a distaff, "the man is in that tent ag'in! More than half his time is spent about the worthless, good-for-nothing——"

The sudden re–appearance of her husband closed the mouth of the wife; and, as the former descended to the place where Esther had resumed her employment, she was content to grumble forth her dissatisfaction, instead of expressing it in more audible terms.

The dialogue that now took place between the affectionate pair was sufficiently succinct and expressive. The woman was at first a little brief and sullen in her answers, but care for her family soon rendered her more complaisant. As the purport of the conversation was merely an engagement to hunt during the remainder of the day, in order to provide the chief necessary of life, we shall not stop to record it.

With this resolution, then, the squatter descended to the plain and divided his force into two parts, one of which was to remain as a guard with the fortress, and the other to accompany him to the field. He warily included Asa and Abiram in his own party, well knowing that no authority, short of his own, was competent to repress the fierce disposition of his headlong son, if fairly awakened. When these arrangements were completed, the hunters sallied forth, separating at no great distance from the rock, in order to form a circle about the distant herd of buffaloes.

CHAPTER IX.

"Priscian a little scratch'd;

'Twill serve."

—— Love's Labour Lost

Having made the reader acquainted with the manner in which Ishmael Bush had disposed of his family, under circumstances that might have proved so embarrassing to most other men, we shall again shift the scene a few short miles from the place last described, preserving, however, the due and natural succession of time. At the very moment that the squatter and his sons departed in the manner mentioned in the preceding chapter, two men were intently occupied in a swale that lay along the borders of a little run, just out of cannon–shot from the encampment, discussing the merits of a savoury bison's hump, that had been prepared for their palates with the utmost attention to the particular merits of that description of food. The choice morsel had been judiciously separated from the adjoining and less worthy parts of the beast, and, enveloped in the hairy coating provided by nature, it had duly undergone the heat of the customary subterraneous oven, and was now laid before its proprietors in all the culinary glory of the prairies. So far as richness, delicacy and wildness of flavour, and substantial nourishment were concerned, the viand might well have claimed a decided superiority over the meretricious cookery and laboured compounds of the most renowned restaurateur; though the service of the dainty was certainly achieved in a manner far from artificial. It would appear that the two fortunate mortals, to whose happy lot it fell to enjoy a meal in which health and appetite lent so keen a relish to the exquisite food of the American deserts, were farfrom being insensible of the advantage they possessed.

The one to whose knowledge in the culinary art the other was indebted for his banquet, seemed the least disposed of the two to profit by his own skill. He eat, it is true, and with a relish; but it was always with the moderation with which age is apt to temper the appetite. No such restraint, however, was imposed on the inclination of his companion. In the very flower of his days and in the fullest vigour of manhood, the homage that he paid to the work of his more aged friend's hands was of the most profound and engrossing character. As one delicious morsel succeeded another he rolled his eyes towards his companion, and seemed to express that gratitude which he had not speech to utter, in looks of the most benignant nature.

"Cut more into the heart of it, lad," said the trapper, for it was the venerable inhabitant of those vast wastes, who had served the bee–hunter with the banquet in question; "cut more into the centre of the piece; there you will find the genuine riches of natur'; and that without need from spices, or any of your biting mustard to give it a foreign relish."

"If I had but a cup of metheglin," said Paul, stopping to perform the necessary operation of breathing, "I should swear this was the strongest meal that was ever placed before the mouth of man!"

"Ay, ay, well you may call it strong!" returned the other laughing after his peculiar manner, in pure satisfaction at witnessing the infinite contentment of his companion; "strong it is, and strong it makes him who eats it! Here, Hector," tossing his patient hound, who was watching his eye with a wistful look, a portion of the meat, "you have need of strength, my friend, in your old days as well as your master. Now, lad, there is a dog that has eaten and slept wiser and better, ay, and that of richer food, than any king of them all! and why? because he has used and not abused the gifts of his Maker. He was made a hound; and like a hound has he feasted. Them did He create men; but they have eaten like famished wolves! A good and prudent dog has Hector proved, and never have I found one of his breed false in nose or friendship. Do you know the difference between the cookery of the wilderness and that which is found in the settlements? No; I see plainly you don't, by your appetite; then I will tell you. The one follows man, the other natur'. One thinks he can add to the gifts of the Creator, while the other is humble enough to enjoy them; therein lies the secret."

"I tell you, trapper," said Paul, who was very little edified by the morality with which his associate saw fit to season their repast, "that, every day while we are in this place, and they are likely to be many, I will shoot a buffaloe and you shall cook his hump!"

"I cannot say that, I cannot say that. The beast is good, take him in what part you will, and it was to be food for man that he was fashioned; but I cannot say that I will be a witness and a helper to the waste of killing one daily."

"The devil a bit of waste shall there be, old man. If they all turn out as good as this, I will engage to eat them clean myself, even to the hoofs——how now, who comes here! some one with a long nose I will answer; and one that has led him on a true scent, if he is following the trail of a dinner."

The individual who had interrupted the conversation, and who had elicited the foregoing remark of Paul, was seen advancing along the margin of the run, with a deliberate pace, in a direct line for the two revellers. As there was nothing formidable nor hostile in his appearance, the bee–hunter, instead of suspending his operations, rather increased his efforts,in a manner which would seem to imply that he doubted whether the hump would suffice for the proper entertainment of all who were now likely to partake of the delicious morsel. With the trapper, however, the case was different. His more tempered appetite was already satisfied, and he faced the new comer with a look of cordiality, that plainly evinced how very opportune he considered his arrival.

"Come on, friend," he said waving his hand, as he observed the stranger to pause a moment, apparently in doubt. "Come on, I say: if hunger be your guide, it has led you to a fitting place. Here is meat, and this youth can give you corn, parch'd till it be whiter than the upland snow; come on, without fear. We are not ravenous beasts, eating of each other, but Christian men, receiving thankfully that which the Lord hath seen fit to give."

"Venerable hunter," returned the Doctor, for it was no other than the naturalist on one of his daily exploring expeditions, who approached, "I rejoice greatly at this happy meeting; we are lovers of the same pursuits, and should be friends."

"Lord, lord!" said the old man laughing, without much deference to the rules of decorum, in the philosopher's very face, "it is the man who wanted to make me believe that a name could change the natur' of a beast! Come, friend; you are welcome, though your notions are a little blinded with reading too many books. Sit ye down, and after eating of this morsel, tell me, if you can, the name of the creatur' that has bestowed on you its flesh for a meal?"

The eyes of Doctor Battius (for we deem it decorous to give the good man the appellation he most preferred) the eyes of Dr. Battius sufficiently denoted the satisfaction with which he listened to this proposal. The exercise he had taken, and the sharpnessof the wind, had proved excellent stimulants, and Paul himself had hardly been in better plight to do credit to the trapper's cookery, than was the lover of nature, when the grateful sounds of the invitation met his ears. Indulging in a small laugh, which his exertions to repress reduced nearly to a simper, he took the indicated seat by the old man's side, and made the customary dispositions to commence his meal without further ceremony.

"I should be ashamed of my profession," he said, swallowing a morsel of the hump with evident delight, slily endeavouring at the same time to distinguish the peculiarities of the singed and defaced skin, "I ought to be ashamed of my profession were there beast or bird on the continent of America that I could not tell by some one of the many evidences which science has enlisted in her cause. This——then ——the food is nutritious and savoury——a mouthful of your corn, friend, if you please?"

Paul, who continued eating with increasing industry, looking askaunt not unlike a dog when engaged in the same agreeable pursuit, threw him his pouch, without deeming it at all necessary to suspend his own labours.

"You were saying, friend, that you have many ways of telling the creatur'?"——observed the attentive trapper.

"Many; very many and infallible. Now, the animals that are carnivorous are known by their incisores."

"Their what!" demanded the trapper.

"The teeth with which nature has furnished them for defence, and in order to tear their food. Again——"

"Look you then for the teeth of this creatur'," interrupted the trapper, who was bent on convincing a man who had presumed to enter into competition with himself, in matters pertaining to the wilds, of gross ignorance; "turn the piece round and find your inside–overs."

The Doctor complied, and of course without success; though he profited by the occasion to take another fruitless glance at the wrinkled hide.

"Well, friend, do you find the things you need, before you can pronounce the creatur' a duck or a salmon?"

"I apprehend the entire animal is not here?"

"You may well say as much," cried Paul, who was now compelled to pause from pure repletion; "I will answer for some pounds of the fellow, weighed by the truest steel–yards west of the Alleghanies. Still you may make out to keep soul and body together, with what is left," reluctantly eyeing a piece large enough to dine twenty men, which he felt compelled to abandon from satiety; "cut in nigher to the heart, as the old man says, and you will find the riches of the piece."

"The heart!" exclaimed the Doctor, inwardly delighted to learn there was a distinct part to be submitted to his inspection. "Ay, let me see the organ ——it will at once determine the character of the animal——certes this is not the cor——ay, sure enough it is——the animal must be of the order belluæ, from its obese habits!"

He was interrupted by a long and hearty, but still noiseless fit of merriment, from the trapper, which was considered so ill–timed by the offended naturalist, as to produce an instant cessation of speech, if not a stagnation in his ideas.

"Listen to his beasts' habits and belly orders," said the old man, delighted, with the evident embarrassment of his rival; "and then he says it is not the core! Why, man, you are farther from the truth than you are from the settlements, with all your bookish larning and hard words; which I have once for all, said cannot be understood by any tribe or nation east of the Rocky Mountains. Beastly habits or no beastly habits, the creatur's are to be seen cropping the prairies, by tens of thousands, and the piece in your hand is the core of as juicy a buffaloe–hump as stomach need ever crave!"

"My aged companion," said Obed, struggling to keep down a rising irascibility, that he conceived would ill comport with the dignity of his character, "your system is erroneous from the premises to the conclusion, and your classification so faulty, as utterly to confound the distinctions of science. The buffaloe is not gifted with a hump at all. Nor is his flesh savoury and wholesome, as I must acknowledge it would seem the subject before us may well be characterized——"

"There I'm dead against you, and clearly with the trapper," interrupted Paul Hover. "The man who denies that buffaloe beef is good, should scorn to eat it!"

The Doctor, whose observation of the bee–hunter had hitherto been exceedingly cursory, stared at the new speaker with a look which denoted something like recognition.

"The principal characteristics of your countenance, friend," he said, "are familiar; either you, or some other specimen of your class, is known to me."

"I am the man you met in the woods east of the big river, and whom you tried to persuade to line a yellow hornet to his nest: as if my eye was not too true to mistake any other animal for a honey–bee, in a clear day! we tarried together a week, as you may remember; you at your toads and lizards, and I at my high–holes and hollow trees. And a good job we made of it, between us! I filled my tubs with the sweetest honey I ever sent to the settlements, besides housing a dozen hives; and your bag was near burstingwith a crawling museum. I never was bold enough to put the question to your face, stranger, but I reckon you are a keeper of curiosities?"

"Ay! that is another of their wanton wickednesses!" exclaimed the trapper. "They slay the buck, and the moose, and the wild cat and all the beasts that range the woods, and after stuffing them with worthless rags, and placing eyes of glass into their heads, they set them up to be stared at, and call them the creatur's of the Lord; as if any mortal effigy could equal the works of his hand!"

"I know you well," returned the Doctor, on whom the plaint of the old man produced no visible impression. "I know you," offering his hand cordially to Paul; "it was a prolific week, as my herbal and catalogues shall one day prove to the world. Ay, I remember you well, young man. You are of the class, mammalia; order, primates; genus, homo; species, Kentucky." Then, after pausing an instant to smile complacently at his own humour, the naturalist proceeded. "Since our separation, I have journeyed far, having entered into a compactum or agreement with a certain man, named Ishmael——"

"Bush!" interrupted the impatient and reckless Paul. "By the Lord, trapper, this is the very blood–letter that Ellen told me of!"

"Then Nelly has not done me credit for what I trust I deserve;" returned the single–minded Doctor, "for I am not of the phlebotomizing school at all; greatly preferring the practice which purifies the blood instead of abstracting it."

"It was a blunder of mine, good stranger; the girl called you a skilful man."

"Therein she may have exceeded my merits," Dr. Battius continued, bowing with sufficient meekness. "But Ellen is a good, and a kind, and a spirited girl, too. A kind and a sweet girl I have ever found Nelly Wade to be!"

"The devil you have!" cried Paul, dropping the morsel he was sucking, from sheer reluctance to abandon the grateful hump, and casting a fierce and direct look into the very teeth of the unconscious physician. "I reckon, stranger, you have a mind to bag Ellen too!"

"The riches of the whole vegetable and animal world united, would not tempt me to harm a hair of her head! I love the child, with what may be called amor naturalis——or rather paternus——The affection of a father."

"Ay——that indeed is more befitting the difference in your years," Paul coolly rejoined, stretching forth his hand to regain the rejected morsel. "You would be no better than a drone at your time of day, with a young hive to feed and swarm."

"Yes, there is reason, because there is natur', in what he says," observed the trapper: "But, friend, you have said you were a dweller in the camp of one Ishmael Bush?"

"True; it is, as you know, in virtue of a compactum——"

"I know but little of the virtue of packing, though I follow trapping, in my old age, for a livelihood. They tell me that skins are well kept, in the new fashion, but it is long since I have left off killing more than I need for food and garments. I was an eye-witness, myself, of the manner in which the Siouxes broke into your encampment, and drove off the cattle; stripping the poor man you call Ishmael of his smallest hoofs, counting even the cloven feet."

"Asinus excepted;" muttered the Doctor, who by this time was very coolly discussing his portion of the hump, in utter forgetfulness of all its scientific attributes. "Asinus domesticus Americanus excepted."

"I am glad to hear that so many of them are saved, though I know not the value of the animals youname; which is nothing uncommon, seeing how long it is that I have been out of the settlements. But can you tell me, friend, what the traveller carries under the white cloth, he guards with teeth as sharp as a wolf that quarrels for the carcass the hunter has left?"

"You've heard of it!" exclaimed the other, dropping the morsel he was conveying to his mouth, in manifest surprise.

"Nay, I have heard nothing; but I have seen the cloth, and had like to have been bitten for no greater crime than wishing to know what it covered."

"Bitten! then after all the animal must be carnivorous! It is too tranquil for the ursus horridus; if it were the canis latrans, the voice would betray it. Nor would Nelly Wade be so familiar with any of the genus, feræ. Venerable hunter! the solitary animal confined in that wagon by day, and in the tent at night, has occasioned me more perplexity of mind than the whole catalogue of quadrupeds besides: and for this plain reason; I did not know how to class it."

"You think it a ravenous beast?"

"I know it to be a quadruped: your own danger proves it to be carnivorous."

During this broken explanation, Paul Hover had sat silent and thoughtful, regarding each speaker with eyes of deep attention. But, as if suddenly moved by the confident manner of the Doctor, the latter had scarcely time to utter his positive assertion, before the young man bluntly demanded——

"And pray, friend, what may you call a quadruped?"

"A vagary of nature, wherein she has displayed less of her infinite wisdom than is usual. Could rotary levers be substituted for two of the limbs, agreeably to the improvement in my new order of phalangacrura, which might be rendered into thevernacular as lever–legged, there would be a delightful perfection and harmony in the construction. But, as the quadruped is now formed, I call it a mere vagary of nature; no other than a vagary."

"Harkee, stranger! in Kentucky we are but small dealers in dictionaries. Vagary is as hard a word to turn into English as quadruped".

"A quadruped is an animal with four legs——a beast."

"A beast! Do you then reckon that Ishmael Bush travels with a beast caged in that little wagon?"

"I know it, and lend me your ear——not literally, friend," observing Paul to start and look surprised, "but figuratively through its functions, and you shall hear. I have already made known that in virtue of a compactum, I journey with the aforesaid Ishmael Bush; but though I am bound to perform certain duties while the journey lasts, there is no condition which says that the said journey shall be sempiternum, or eternal. Now, though this region may scarcely be said to be wedded to science, being to all intents a virgin territory as respects the inquirer into natural history, still it is greatly destitute of the treasures of the vegetable kingdom. I should therefore have tarried some hundreds of miles more to the eastward, were it not for the inward propensity that I feel to have the beast in question inspected and suitably described and classed. For that matter," he continued, dropping his voice, like one who imparts an important secret, "I am not without hopes of persuading Ishmael to let me dissect it."

"You have seen the creature?"

"Not with the organs of sight; but with much more infallible instruments of vision: the conclusions of reason, and the deductions of scientific premises. I have watched the habits of the animal, young man; and can fearlessly pronounce, by evidence that would be thrown away on ordinary observers, that it is of vast dimensions, inactive, possibly torpid, of voracious appetite, and, as it now appears by the direct testimony of this venerable hunter, ferocious and carnivorous!"

"I should be better pleased, stranger," said Paul, on whom the Doctor's description was making a very sensible impression, "to be sure the creature was a beast at all."

"As to that, if I wanted evidence of a fact, which is abundantly apparent by the habits of the animal, I have the word of Ishmael, himself. A reason can be given for my smallest deductions. I am not troubled, young man, with a vulgar and idle curiosity, but all my aspirations after knowledge, as I humbly believe, are, first, for the advancement of learning, and secondly, for the benefit of my fellow-creatures. I pined greatly in secret to know the contents of the tent, which Ishmael guarded so carefully, and which he had covenanted that I should swear, (jurare per deos) not to approach nigher than a defined number of cubits, for a definite period of time. Your jusjurandum, or oath, is a serious matter, and not to be dealt in lightly; but, as my expedition depended on complying, I consented to the act, reserving to myself at all times the power of distant observation. It is now some ten days since Ishmael, pitying the state in which he saw me, a humble lover of science, imparted the fact that the vehicle contained a beast, which he was carrying into the prairies as a decoy, by which he intends to entrap others of the same genus, or perhaps species. Since then, my task has been reduced simply to watch the habits of the animal, and to record the results. When we reach a certain distance where these beasts are said to abound, I am to have the liberal examination of the specimen."

Paul continued to listen, in the most profound silence, until the Doctor concluded his singular butcharacteristic explanation; then the incredulous bee-hunter shook his head, and saw fit to reply, by saying——

"Stranger, old Ishmael has burrowed you in the very bottom of a hollow tree, where your eyes will be of no more use than the sting of a drone. I, too, know something of that very wagon, and I may say that I have lined the squatter down into a flat lie. Harkee, friend; do you think a girl, like Ellen Wade, would become the companion of a wild beast?"

"Why not! why not!" repeated the naturalist; "Nelly has a taste for learning, and often listens with pleasure to the treasures that I am sometimes compelled to scatter in this desert. Why should she not study the habits of any animal, even though it were a rhinoceros!"

"Softly, softly," returned the equally positive, and, though less scientific, certainly, on this subject, better instructed bee–hunter; "Ellen is a girl of spirit, and one too that knows her own mind, or I'm much mistaken; but with all her courage and brave looks, she is no better than a woman after all. Haven't I often had the girl, crying——"

"You are an acquaintance, then, of Nelly's?"

"The devil a bit. But I know a woman is a woman; and all the books in Kentucky couldn't make Ellen Wade go into a tent alone with a ravenous beast!"

"It seems to me," the trapper calmly observed, "that there is something dark and hidden in this matter. I am a witness that the traveller likes none to look into the tent, and I have a proof more sure than what either of you can lay claim to, that the wagon does not carry the cage of a beast. Here is Hector, come of a breed with noses as true and faithful as a hand that is all–powerful has made any of their kind, and had there been a beas in theplace, the hound would long since have told it to his master."

"Do you pretend to oppose a dog to a man! brutality to learning! instinct to reason!" exclaimed the Doctor in some heat. "In what manner, pray, can a hound distinguish the habits, species, or even the genus of an animal, like reasoning, learned, scientific, triumphant man!"

"In what manner?" coolly repeated the veteran woodsman. "Listen; and if you believe that a schoolmaster can make a quicker wit than the Lord, you shall be made to see how much you're mistaken. Do you not hear something move in the brake? it has been cracking the twigs these five minutes. Now tell me what the creatur' is?"

"I hope nothing ferocious!" exclaimed the Doctor, starting, for he still retained a lively impression of his rencounter with the vespertilio horribilis. "You have rifles, friends;

would it not be prudent to prime them, for my fowling–piece is little to be depended on."

"There may be reason in what he says," returned the trapper, smiling, and so far complying as to take his piece from the place where it had lain during the repast, and raising its muzzle in the air. "Now tell me the name of the creatur'?"

"It exceeds the limits of earthly knowledge! Buffon himself could not tell whether the animal was a quadruped, or of the order, serpens! a sheep, or a tiger!"

"Then was your buffoon a fool to my Hector! Here; pup! What is it, dog? Shall we run it down, pup——or shall we let it pass?"

The hound, which had already manifested to the experienced trapper, by the tremulous motion of his ears, his consciousness of the proximity of a strange animal, now lifted his head from his fore paws and slightly parted his lips, as if about to shew the remnants of his teeth. But, suddenly abandoning his hostile purpose, he snuffed the air a moment, gaped heavily, shook himself, and then peaceably resumed his former recumbent attitude.

"Now Doctor," cried the trapper, triumphantly, "I am well convinced there is neither game nor ravenous beast in the thicket; and that I call substantial knowledge to a man who is too old to be a spendthrift of his strength, and yet who would not wish to be a meal for a panther!"

The dog interrupted his master by a loud growl, but still kept his head crouched to the earth.

"It is a man!" exclaimed the trapper, rising. "It is a man, if I am a judge of the creatur's ways. There is but little said atwixt the hound and me, but we seldom make a blunder!"

Paul Hover sprang to his feet like lightning, and, throwing forward his rifle, he cried in a voice of menace——

"Come forward, if a friend; if an enemy, stand ready for the worst!"

"A friend, a white man, and I hope a Christian," returned a voice from the thicket; which opened at the same instant, and at the next, the speaker himself made his appearance.

CHAPTER X.

"Go apart, Adam, and thou shalt hear How he will shake me up."

———— As you like it

It is well known, that even long before the immense regions of Louisiana changed their masters for the second, and, as it is to be hoped for the lasttime, its unguarded territory was by no means safe from the inroads of white adventurers. The semibarbarous hunters from the Canadas, the same description of population, a little more enlightened, from the States, and the metiffs or half–breeds, who claimed to be ranked in the class of white men, were scattered among the different Indian tribes, or gleaned a scanty livelihood in solitude, amid the haunts of the beaver and the bison; or, to adopt the popular nomenclature of the country————of the buffaloe.*

It was, therefore, no unusual thing for strangers to encounter each other in the endless wastes of the west. By signs, which an unpractised eye would pass unobserved, these borderers knew when one of his fellows was in his vicinity, and he avoided or approached the intruder as best comported with his feelings or his interests. Generally, these interviews were pacific; for the whites had a common enemy to dread, in the ancient and perhaps more lawful occupants of the country; but instances were not rare, in which jealousy and cupidity had caused them to terminate in scenes of the most violent and ruthless treachery. The meeting of two hunters on the American desert, as we find it convenient sometimes to call this region, was consequently, somewhat in the suspicious and wary manner in which two vessels draw together in a sea that is known to be infested with pirates. While neither party is willing to betray its weakness, by exhibiting distrust, neither is disposed to commit itself by any acts of confidence, from which it may be difficult to recede.

Such was, in some degree, the character of the present interview. The stranger drew nigh, deliberately; keeping his eyes steadily fastened on themovements of the other party, while he purposely created little difficulties to impede an approach which might prove too hasty. On the other hand, Paul stood playing with the lock of his rifle, too proud to let it appear that three men could manifest any apprehension of a solitary individual, and yet too prudent to omit, entirely, the customary precautions. The principal reason of the marked difference, which the two legitimate proprietors of the banquet made in the receptions of their guests, was to be explained by the entire difference which existed in their respective appearances.

While the exterior of the naturalist was decidedly pacific, not to say abstracted, that of the new comer, was distinguished by an air of vigour, and a front and step which it would not have been difficult to have at once pronounced to be military.

He wore a forage–cap of fine blue cloth, from which depended a soiled tassel in gold, and which was nearly buried in a mass of exuberant, curling, jet–black hair. Around his throat he had negligently fastened a stock of black silk. His body was enveloped in a hunting–shirt of dark green, trimmed with the yellow fringes and ornaments that were sometimes seen among the border–troops of the Confederacy. Beneath this, however, were visible the collar and lappells of a jacket, similar in colour and cloth to the cap. His lower limbs were protected by buckskin leggings, and his feet by the ordinary Indian moccasins. A richly ornamented, and exceedingly dangerous straight dirk, was stuck in a sash of red silk–net work; another girdle or rather belt of uncoloured leather contained a pair of the smallest sized pistols, in holsters nicely made to fit, and across his shoulder was thrown a short, heavy, military rifle; its horn and pouch occupying the usual places beneath his arms. At his back he bore a knapsack, which was marked by the well known initialsthat have since gained for the government of the United States, the good–humoured and quaint appellation of Uncle Sam.

"I come in amity," the stranger said, like one too much accustomed to the sight of arms to be startled at the ludicrously belligerent attitude which Dr. Battius had seen fit to assume. "I come as a friend; and am one whose pursuits and wishes will not at all interfere with your own."

"Harkee, stranger," said Paul Hover, bluntly; "do you understand lining a bee from this open place into a wood, distant, perhaps, a dozen miles."

"The bee is a bird I have never been compelled to seek," returned the other, laughing; "though I have, too, been something of a fowler in my time."

"I thought as much," exclaimed Paul, thrusting forth his hand frankly, and with the true freedom of manner that marks an American borderer. "Let us cross fingers. You and I will never quarrel about the comb, since you set such little store by the honey. And, now, if your stomach has an empty corner, and you know how to relish a genuine dew-drop when it falls into your very mouth, there lies the exact morsel to put into it. Try it, stranger; and having tried it, if you dont call it as snug a fit as you have made since——How long ar' you from the settlements, pray?"

"'Tis many weeks, and I fear it may be as many more, before I can return. I will, however, gladly profit by your invitation, for I have fasted since the rising of yesterday's sun, and I know too well the merits of a bison's hump to reject the food."

"Ah! you're acquainted with the dish! Well, therein you have the advantage of me, in setting out, though I think, I may say we could now, start on equal ground. I should be the happiest fellow, between Kentucky and the Rocky Mountains, if I had a snug cabin, near some old wood that was filled with hollow trees, just such a hump every day as that for dinner, a load of fresh straw for hives, and little El——"

"Little what?" demanded the stranger, evidently amused with the communicative and frank disposition of the bee-hunter.

"Something that I shall have one day, and which concerns nobody so much as myself;" returned Paul, picking the flint of his rifle, and beginning very cavalierly to whistle an air well known on the waters of the Mississippi.

During this preliminary discourse the stranger had taken his seat by the side of the hump, and was already making a serious inroad on its relics. Dr. Battius, however, watched his movements with a jealousy, still more striking than the cordial reception which the open-hearted Paul had just exhibited.

But the doubts or rather apprehensions of the naturalist were of a character altogether different from the confidence of the bee-hunter. He had been struck with the stranger's using the legitimate, instead of the perverted name of the animal off which he was making his repast; and as he had been among the foremost himself to profit by the removal of the impediments which the policy of Spain had placed in the way of all explorers of her Trans-Atlantic dominions, whether bent on the purposes of commerce, or, like himself, on the more laudable pursuits of science, he had a sufficiency of every-day philosophy to feel that the same motives, which had so powerfully urged himself to his present undertaking, might produce a like result on the mind of some other student of nature. Here, then, was the prospect of an alarming rivalry, which bade fair to strip him of at least a moiety of the just rewards of all his labours, privations and dangers. Under these views of his character, therefore, it is not at all surprising that the native meekness of the naturalist'sdisposition was a little disturbed, and that he watched the proceedings of the other with such a degree of vigilance as he believed best suited to detect his sinister designs.

"This is truly a delicious repast," observed the unconscious young stranger, for both young and handsome he was fairly entitled to be considered; "either hunger has given a peculiar relish to the viand, or the bison may lay claim to be the finest of the ox family!"

"Naturalists, sir, are apt, when they speak familiarly, to give the cow the credit of the genus," said Dr. Battius, swelling with his secret distrust, and clearing his throat, before speaking, much in the manner that a duellist examines the point of the weapon he is about to plunge into the body of his foe. "The figure is more perfect; as the bos, meaning the ox, is unable to perpetuate his kind; and the bos, in its most extended meaning, or vacca, is altogether the nobler animal of the two."

The Doctor uttered this opinion with a certain air, which he intended should express his readiness to come, at once, to any of the numerous points of difference which he doubted not existed between them; and he now awaited the blow of his antagonist, intending that his next thrust should be still more vigorous. But the young stranger appeared much better disposed to partake of the good cheer, with which he had been so providentially provided, than to take up the cudgels of argument on this, or on any other of the knotty points which are so apt to furnish the lovers of science with the materials of a mental joust.

"I dare say you are very right, sir," he replied, with a most provoking indifference to the importance of the points he conceded. "I dare say you are quite right; and that vacca would have been the better word."

"Pardon me, sir; you are giving a very wrong construction to my language, if you suppose I include, without many and particular qualifications, the bibulus Americanus, in the family of the vacca. For, as you well know, sir——or, as I presume I should say, Doctor——you have the medical diploma, no doubt?——"

"You give me credit for an honour I can lay no claim to," interrupted the other.

"An under–graduate!——or perhaps your degrees have been taken in some other of the liberal sciences?"

"Still wrong, I do assure you."

"Surely, young man, you have not entered on this important——I may say, this awful service, without some evidence of your fitness for the task! Some commission by which you can assert an authority to proceed, or by which you may claim an affinity and a communion with your fellow–workers in the same beneficent pursuits!"

"I know not by what means, or for what purposes, you have made yourself master of my objects!" exclaimed the youth, reddening and rising with a quickness which manifested how little he regarded the grosser appetites, when a subject nearer his heart was approached. "Still, sir, your language is incomprehensible. That pursuit, which in another might perhaps be justly called beneficent, is, in me, a dear and cherished duty; though why a commission should be demanded or needed is, I confess, no less a subject of surprise."

"It is customary to be provided with such a document," returned the Doctor, gravely; "and, on all suitable occasions to produce it, in order that congenial and friendly minds may, at once, reject unworthy suspicions, and stepping over, what may be called the elements of discourse, come at once to those points which are desiderata to both."

"It is a strange request!" the youth muttered, turning his dark, frowning eye from one to the other, as if examining the characters of his companions, with a view to weigh their physical powers. Then, putting his hand into his bosom, he drew forth a small box, and extending it with an air of dignity towards the Doctor, he continued——"You will find by this, sir, that I have some right to travel in a country which is now the property of the American States."

"What have we here!" exclaimed the naturalist, opening the folds of a large parchment. "Why, this is the sign–manual of the philosopher, Jefferson! The seal of state! Countersigned by the minister of war! Why this is a commission creating Duncan Uncas Middleton a captain of artillery!"

"Of whom? of whom?" repeated the trapper, who had sat regarding the stranger, during the whole discourse, with eyes that seemed greedily to devour each lineament. "How is the name? did you call him Uncas?——Uncas! Was it Uncas?"

"Such is my name," returned the youth, a little naughtily. "It is the appellation of a native chief, that both my uncle and myself bear with pride; for it is the memorial of an important service done my family by a warrior in the old wars of the provinces."

"Uncas! did ye call him Uncas?" repeated the trapper, approaching the youth and parting the dark curls which clustered over his broad brow, without the slightest resistance on the part of their wondering owner. "Ah! my eyes are old, and not so keen as when I was a warrior myself; but I can see the look of the father in the son! I saw it when he first came nigh; but so many things have since passed before my failing sight, that I could not name the place where I had met his likeness! Tell me, lad; by what name is your father known?"

"He was an officer of the States in the war of the revolution, of my own name of course; my mother's brother was called Duncan Uncas Heyward."

"Still Uncas! still Uncas!" echoed the other, trembling with eagerness. "And his father?"

"Was called the same, without the appellation of the native chief. It was to him, and to my grandmother, that the service of which I have just spoken was rendered."

"I know'd it! I know'd it!" shouted the old man, in his tremulous voice, his rigid features working powerfully, as if the names the other mentioned awakened some long dormant emotions, connected with the events of an anterior age. "I know'd it! son or grandson, it is all the same; it is the blood, and 'tis the look! Tell me, is he they call'd Duncan, without the Uncas——is he living!"

The young man shook his head sorrowfully, as he replied in the negative.

"He died full of days and of honours. Beloved, happy and bestowing happiness?"

"Full of days!" repeated the trapper, looking down at his own meagre, but still muscular hands. "Ah! he liv'd in the settlements, and was wise only after their fashions. But you have often seen him; and you have heard him discourse of Uncas, and of the wilderness?"

"Often! he was then an officer of the king; but when the war took place between the crown and her colonies, my grandfather did not forget his birth-place, but threw off the empty allegiance of names, and was true to his proper country; he fought on the side of liberty."

"There was reason in it; and what is better, there was natur'! Come, sit ye down beside me lad; sit ye down, and tell me of what your grand'ther used to speak, when his mind dwelt on the wonders of the wilderness."

The youth smiled, no less at the importunity than at the interest manifested by the old man; but as he found there was no longer the least appearance of any violence being contemplated, he unhesitatingly complied.

"Give it all to the trapper by rule, and by figures of speech;" said Paul, very coolly taking his seat on the other side of the young soldier. "It is the fashion of old age to relish these ancient traditions, and, for that matter, I can say that I don't dislike to listen to them myself."

Middleton smiled again, and perhaps with a slight air of derision; but good-naturedly turning to the trapper, he continued——

"It is a long, and might prove a painful story Bloodshed and all the horrors of Indian cruelty and of Indian warfare, are fearfully mingled in the narrative."

"Ay, give it all to us, stranger," continued Paul; "we are used to these matters in Kentuck, and, I must say, I think a story none the worse for having a few scalps in it!"

"But he told you of Uncas, did he!" resumed the trapper, without regarding the slight interruptions of the bee-hunter, which amounted to no more than a sort of by-play. "And, what thought he and said ne of the lad, in his parlour, with the comforts and ease of the settlements at his elbow?"

"I doubt not he used a language similar to that he would have adopted in the woods, and had he stood face to face, with his friend——"

"Did he call the savage his friend; the poor, naked, painted warrior? he was not too proud then to call the Indian his friend?"

"He even boasted of the connexion; and as you have already heard, bestowed a name on his firstborn, which is likely to be handed down as an heir loom among the rest of his descendants."

"It was well done! like a man: ay! and like a Christian, too! He used to say the Delaware was swift of foot——did he remember that?"

"As the antelope! Indeed, he often spoke of him by the appellation of Le Cerf Agile, a name he had obtained by his activity."

"And bold, and fearless, lad!" continued the trapper looking up into the eyes of his companion, with a wistfulness that bespoke the delight he received in listening to the praises of one, whom it was so very evident, he had once tenderly loved.

"Brave as a blooded hound! Without fear! He always quoted Uncas and his father, who from his wisdom was called the Great Serpent, as models of heroism and constancy."

"He did them justice! he did them justice! Truer men, were not to be found in any tribe or nation, be their skins of what colour they might. I see your grand'ther was just, and did his duty, too, by his offspring! 'Twas a perilous time he had of it, among them hills, and nobly did he play his own part! Tell me lad, or officer, I should say,——since officer you be ——was this all?"

"Certainly not; it was, as I have said, a fearful tale, full of moving incidents, and the memories both of my grandfather and of my grandmother——"

"Ah!" exclaimed the trapper, tossing a hand into the air as his whole countenance lighted with the recollections the name revived. "They called her Alice! Elsie or Alice; 'tis all the same. A laughing, playful child she was, when happy; and tender and weeping in her misery! Her hair was shining and yellow, as the coat of the young fawn, and her skin clearer than the purest water that drips from the rock. Well do I remember her! I remember her right well!"

"The lip of the youth slightly curled, and he regardedthe old man with an expression, which might easily have been construed into a declaration that such were not his own recollections of his venerable and revered ancestor, though it would seem he did not think it necessary to say as much in words. He was content to answer:——

"They both retained impressions of the dangers they had passed, by far too vivid easily to lose the recollection of any of their fellow-actors."

The trapper looked aside, and seemed to struggle with some deeply innate feeling; then, turning again towards his companion, though his honest eyes no longer dwelt with the same open interest, as before, on the countenance of the other, he continued——

"Did he tell you of them all? Were they all red-skins, but himself and the daughters of Munro?"

"No. There was a white man associated with the Delawares. A scout of the English army, but a native of the provinces."

"A drunken, worthless vagabond, like most of his colour who harbour with the savages, I warrant you!"

"Old man, your gray hairs should caution you against slander. The man, I speak of, was of great simplicity of mind, but of sterling worth. Unlike most of those who live a border life, he united the better, instead of the worst qualities, of the two people. He was a man endowed with the choicest and perhaps rarest gift of nature; that of distinguishing good from evil. His virtues were those of simplicity, because such were the fruits of his habits, as were indeed his very prejudices. In courage he was the equal of his red associates; in warlike skill, being better instructed, their superior. 'In short, he was a noble shoot from the stock of human nature, which never could attain its proper elevation and importance, for no other reason, than because it grew in the forest:' such, old hunter, were the very words of my grandfather, when speaking of the man you imagine so worthless!"

The eyes of the trapper had sunk to the earth, as the stranger delivered this character of the subject of their discourse in the ardent tones of generous youth. He played with the ears of his hound; fingered his own rustic garment, and opened and shut the pan of his rifle, with hands that trembled in a manner that would have implied their total unfitness to wield the weapon. When the other had concluded he hoarsely added——

"Your grand'ther didn't then entirely forget the white man!"

"So far from that, there are already three among us, who have also names derived from that scout."

"A name, did you say?" exclaimed the old man, starting; "what, the name of the solitary, unl'arned hunter? Do the great, and the rich, and the honoured, and, what is better still, the just, do they bear his very, actual, name?"

"It is borne by my brother, and by two of my cousins, whatever may be their titles to be described by the terms you have mentioned."

"Do you mean the actual name itself; spelt with the very same letters, beginning with an N and ending with an L?"

"Exactly the same," the youth smilingly replied. "No, no, we have forgotten nothing that was his. I have at this moment a dog brushing a deer, not far from this, who is come of a hound that very scout sent as a present after his friends, and which was of the stock he always used himself: a truer breed, in nose and foot, is not to be found in the wide Union."

"Hector!" said the old man, struggling to conquer an emotion that nearly suffocated him, and speaking to his hound in the sort of tones he would have used to a child, "do ye hear that, pup! your kin andblood are in the prairie! A name——it is wonderful ——it is very wonderful!"

Nature could endure no more. Overcome by a flood of unusual and extraordinary sensations, and stimulated by tender and long dormant recollections, strangely and unexpectedly revived, the old man had just self–command enough to add, in a voice that was hollow and unnatural, through the efforts he made to command it——

"Boy, I am that scout; a warrior once, a miserable trapper now!" when the tears broke, over his wasted cheeks, out of fountains that had long been dried, and, sinking his face between his knees, he covered it decently with his buckskin garment, and sobbed aloud.

The spectacle produced correspondent emotions in his companions. Paul Hover had actually swallowed each syllable of the discourse as they fell alternately from the different speakers, his feelings keeping equal pace with the increasing interest of the scene. Unused to such strange sensations, he was turning his face on every side of him, to avoid he knew not what, until he saw the tears and heard the sobs of the old man, when he sprang to his feet, end grappling his guest fiercely by the throat, he demanded by what authority he had made his aged companion weep. A flash of recollection crossing his brain at the same instant, he released his hold, and stretching forth an arm in the very wantonness of his gratification, he seized the Doctor by the hair, which instantly revealed its artificial formation, by cleaving to his hand, leaving the white and shining poll of the naturalist with a covering no warmer than the skin.

"What think you of that, Mr. Bug–gatherer!" he rather shouted than cried; "is not this a strange bee to line into his hole!"

" 'Tis remarkable! wonderful! edifying!" returnedthe lover of nature, good–humouredly recovering his wig, with twinkling eyes and a husky voice. "'Tis rare and commendable! Though I doubt not in the exact order of causes and effects."

With this sudden outbreaking, however, the commotion instantly subsided; the three spectators clustering around the trapper with a species of awe, at beholding the tears of one so aged.

"It must be so, or how could he be so familiar with a history that is little known beyond my own family;" at length the youth observed, not ashamed to acknowledge how much he had been affected, by unequivocally drying his own eyes.

"True!" echoed Paul; "if you want any more evidence I will swear to it! I know every word of it myself to be true as the gospel!"

"And yet we had long supposed him dead!" continued the soldier. "My grandfather had filled his days with honour, and he had believed him the junior of the two."

"It is not often that youth has an opportunity of thus looking down on the weakness of age!" the trapper observed, raising his head, and looking around him with composure and dignity. "That I am still here, young man, is the pleasure of the Lord, who has spared me until I have seen fourscore long and laborious years, for his own secret ends. That I am the man I say, you need not doubt; for why should I go to my grave with so cheap a lie in my mouth?"

"I do not hesitate to believe; I only marvel that it should be so! But why do I find you, venerable and excellent friend of my parents, in these wastes, so far from the comforts and safety of the lower country?"

"I have come into these plains to escape the sound of the axe; for here surely the chopper can never follow! But I may put the like question to yourself. Are you of the party which the Stateshave sent into their new purchase, to look after the natur' of the bargain they have made?"

"I am not, Lewis is making his way up the river, some hundreds of miles from this. I come on a private adventure."

"Though it is no cause of wonder, that a man whose strength and eyes have failed him as a hunter, should be seen nigh the haunts of the beaver, using a trap instead of a rifle, it is strange that one so young and prosperous, and bearing the commission of the Great Father, should be moving among the prairies, without even a camp–colourman to do his biddings!"

"You would think my reasons sufficient did you know them, as know them you shall if you are disposed to listen to my story. I think you all honest, and men who would rather aid than betray one bent on a worthy object."

"Come, then, and tell us at your leisure," said the trapper, seating himself, and beckoning to the youth to follow his example. The latter willingly complied, and after Paul and the Doctor had disposed of themselves to their several likings, the new comer entered into a narrative of the singular reasons which had led him so far into the deserts.

CHAPTER XI.

"So foul a sky clears not without a storm."

The Prairie, Volume 1

—— King John

In the mean time the industrious and irreclaimable hours continued their labours. The sun, which had been struggling through such masses of vapour throughout the day, fell slowly into a streak of clear sky, and thence sunk gloriously into the gloomy wastes, as he is wont to settle into the waters of the ocean. The vast herds which had been grazing among the wild pastures of the prairies, gradually disappeared, and the endless flocks of aquatic birds, that were pursuing their customary annual journey from the virgin lakes of the north towards the gulf of Mexico, ceased to fan that air, which had now become loaded with dew and vapour. In short, the shadows of night fell upon the rock, adding the mantle of darkness to the other dreary accompaniments of the place.

As the light began to fail, Esther collected her younger children at her side, and placing herself on a projecting point of her insulated fortress, she sat patiently awaiting the return of the hunters. Ellen Wade was at no great distance, seeming to keep a little aloof from the anxious circle, as if willing to mark the distinction which existed in their characters.

"Your uncle is, and always will be a dull calculator, Nell," observed the mother, after a long pause in a conversation that had turned on the labours of the day; "a lazy hand at figures and foreknowledge is that said Ishmael Bush! Here he sat lolloping about the rock from light till noon, doing nothing but scheme——scheme——scheme——with seven as noble boys at his elbows as woman ever gave to man; and what's the upshot! why, night is setting in, and his needful work not yet ended."

"It is not prudent, certainly, aunt," Ellen replied, with a vacancy in her air, that proved how little she knew what she was saying; "and it is setting a very bad example to his sons."

"Hoity, toity, girl! who has reared you up as a judge over your elders, ay, and your betters, too! I should like to see the man on the whole frontier who sets a more honest example to his children than this same Ishmael Bush! Show me, if you can, MissFault–finder, but not fault–mender, a set of boys who will, on occasion, sooner chop a piece of logging and dress it for the crop, than my own children; though I say it myself, who, perhaps, should be silent; or a cradler that knows better how to lead a gang of hands through a field of wheat, leaving a cleaner stubble in his track, than my own good man! Then, as a father, he is as generous as a lord; for his sons have only to name the spot where they would like to pitch, and he gives 'em a deed of the plantation, and no charge for papers is ever made!"

As the wife of the squatter concluded, she raised a hollow, taunting laugh, that was echoed from the mouths of several juvenile imitators, whom she was training to a life as shiftless and lawless as her own; but which, notwithstanding its uncertainty was not without its secret charms.

"Holloa! old Eester;" shouted the well-known voice of her husband, from the plain beneath; "'ar you keeping your junketts, while we are finding you in venison and buffaloe beef! Come down——come down, old girl, with all your young; and lend us a hand to carry up the meat——why, what a frolic you ar' in, woman! Come down, come down, for the boys are at hand, and we have work here for double your number."

Ishmael might have spared his lungs more than a moiety of the effort they were compelled to make in order that he should be heard. He had hardly uttered the name of his wife, before the whole of the crouching circle rose in a body, and tumbling over each other, they precipitated themselves down the dangerous passes of the rock with ungovernable impatience. Esther followed the young fry with a more measured gait; nor did Ellen deem it wise, or rather discreet, to remain behind. Consequently the whole were soon assembled at the base of their citadel, on the open plain.

Here the squatter was found, staggering under the weight of a fine fat buck, attended by one or two of his younger sons. Abiram quickly appeared, and before many minutes had elapsed most of the hunters dropped in, singly and in pairs, each man bringing with him some fruits of his prowess in the field.

"The plain is free from red-skins, to-night at least," said Ishmael, after the bustle of reception had a little subsided; "for I have scoured the prairie for many long miles, on my own feet, and I call myself a judge of the print of an Indian moccasin. So, old woman, you can give us a few steaks of the venison, and then we will sleep on the day's work."

"I'll not swear there are no savages near us," said Abiram. "I too, know something of the trail of a red-skin, and unless my eyes have lost some of their sight, I would swear, boldly, that there ar' Indians at hand. But wait till Asa comes in. He pass'd the spot where I found the marks, and the boy knows something of such matters too."

"Ay, the boy knows too much of many things," returned Ishmael, gloomily. "It will be better for him when he thinks he knows less. But what matters it, Hetty, if all the Sioux tribes, west of the big river, are within a mile of us; they will find it no easy matter to scale this rock, in the teeth of ten bold men."

"Call 'em twelve, at once, Ishmael; call 'em twelve!" cried his termagant assistant. "For if your moth–gathering, bug–hunting friend, can be counted a man, I beg you will set me down as two. I will not turn my back to him, with the rifle or the shot–gun, and for courage!——the yearling heifer, that them skulking devils the Tetons stole, was the biggest coward among us all; and after her came your drivelling Doctor. Ah! Ishmael, you rarely attempt a regular trade but you come out the loser; and this man, I reckon, is the hardest bargain among themall! Would you think it, the fellow ordered me a blister around my mouth, because I complained of a pain in the foot!"

"It is a pity, Eester," her husband coolly answered, "that you did not take it; I reckon it would have done you considerable good. But, boys, if it should turn out as Abiram thinks, that there are Indians near us, we may have to scamper up the rock, and lose our suppers after all. Therefore we will make sure of the game, and talk over the performances of the Doctor when we have nothing better to do."

The hint was taken, and in a few minutes, the exposed situation in which the family was collected, was exchanged for the more secure elevation of the rock. Here Esther busied herself, working and scolding, with equal industry, until the repast was prepared, when she summoned her husband to his meal in a voice as sonorous as that with which the Imaun reminds the Faithful of a more important duty.

When each had assumed his proper and customary place around the smoking viands, the squatter set the example by beginning to partake of a delicious venison steak, prepared like the hump of the bison, with a skill that rather increased than concealed its natural properties. A painter would gladly have seized the moment, to transfer the wild and characteristic scene to the canvass.

The reader will remember that the citadel of Ishmael stood insulated, lofty, ragged, and nearly inaccessible. A bright flashing fire that was burning on the centre of its summit, and around which the busy groupe was clustered, lent it the appearance of some tall Pharos placed in the centre of the deserts, to light such adventurers as wandered through their broad wastes. The flashing flame gleamed from one sun–burnt countenance to another, exhibiting everyvariety of expression, from the juvenile simplicity of the children, mingled as it was with a shade of the wildness peculiar to their semi–barbarous lives, to the dull and immovable apathy that dwelt on the features of the squatter, when unexcited. Occasionally a gust of wind would fan the embers, and, as a brighter light shot upwards, the little solitary tent was seen as it were suspended in the gloom of the upper air. All beyond was enveloped, as usual at that hour, in an impenetrable body of darkness.

"It is unaccountable that Asa should choose to be out of the way at such a time as this," Esther pettishly observed. "When all is finished and to–rights, we shall have the boy coming up, grumbling for his meal, and hungry as a bear after his winter's nap. His stomach is as true as the best clock in Kentucky, and seldom wants winding up to tell the time, whether of day or night. A desperate eater is Asa, when a–hungered, by a little work!"

Ishmael looked sternly around the circle of his silent sons, as if to see whether any among them would presume to say aught in favour of the absent delinquent. But now, when no exciting causes existed to arouse their slumbering tempers, it seemed to be too great an effort to enter on the defence of their rebellious brother. Abiram, however, who since the pacification, either felt, or affected to feel, a more generous interest in his late adversary, saw fit to express an anxiety, to which the others were strangers——

"It will be well if the boy has escaped the Tetons!" he muttered. "I should be sorry to have Asa, who is one of the stoutest of our party, both in heart and hand, fall into the power of the red–devils."

"Look to yourself, Abriam; and spare your breath, if you can use it only to frighten the woman and her huddling girls. You have whitened the faceof Ellen Wade, already; who looks as pale as if she was staring to–day at the very Indians you name, when I was forced to speak to her through the rifle, because I couldn't reach her ears with my tongue. How was it, Nell! you have never given the reason of your deafness?"

The colour of Ellen's cheek changed as suddenly as the squatter's piece had flashed on the occasion to which he alluded, the burning glow suffusing her features, until it even mantled her throat with its fine healthful tinge. She hung her head abashed, but did not seem to think it necessary to reply.

Ishmael, too sluggish to pursue the subject, or content with the pointed allusion he had just made, rose from his seat on the rock, and stretching his heavy frame, like a well–fed and fattened ox, he announced his intention to sleep. Among a race who lived chiefly for the indulgence of the natural wants, such a declaration could not fail of meeting with sympathetic dispositions. One after another disappeared, each seeking his or her rude dormitory, and, before many minutes, Esther, who by this time had scolded the younger fry to sleep, found herself, if we except the usual watchman below, in solitary possession of the naked rock.

Whatever less valuable fruits had been produced, in this uneducated woman by her migratory habits, the great principle of female nature was too deeply rooted ever to be entirely eradicated. Of a powerful, not to say fierce temperament, her passions were violent and difficult to be smothered. But, however she might and did abuse the accidental prerogatives of her situation, her love for her offspring, while it often slumbered, could never be said to become extinct. She liked not the protracted absence of Asa. Too fearless herself to have hesitated an instant on her own account about crossing the dark abyss, into which she now sat looking with longing eyes, herbusy imagination, in obedience to this inextinguishable sentiment, began to conjure nameless evils on account of her son. It might be true, as Abiram had hinted, that he had become a captive to some of the tribes who were hunting the buffaloe in that vicinity, or even a still more dreadful calamity might have befallen. So thought the mother, while silence and darkness lent their aid to the secret impulses of nature.

Agitated by these reflections, which put sleep at defiance, Esther continued at her post, listening with that sort of acuteness which is termed instinct, in the animals a few degrees below her in the scale of intelligence, for any of those noises which might indicate the approach of footsteps. At length, her wishes had an appearance of being realized, for the long desired sounds were distinctly audible, and presently she distinguished the dim form of a man, at the base of the rock.

"Now, Asa, richly do you deserve to be left with an earthen bed this blessed night!" the woman began to mutter, with a revolution in her feelings, that will not be surprising to those who have made the contradictions that give variety to the human character a study. "And a hard one I've a mind it shall be! Why Abner; Abner; you Abner, do you sleep? Let me not see you dare to open the hole, till I get down. I will know who it is that wishes to disturb a peaceable, ay, and an honest family too, at such a time in the night as this!"

"Woman!" exclaimed a voice, that intended to bluster, while the speaker was manifestly a little apprehensive of the consequences; "Woman, I forbid you on pain of the law to project any of your infernal missiles. I am a citizen and a freeholder, and, a graduate of two universities; and I stand upon my rights! Beware of malice prepense, of chance medleyand of manslaughter. It is I——your amicus; a friend and inmate. I——Dr. Obed Battius."

"Who!" demanded Esther, in a voice that nearly refused to convey her words to the ears of the anxious listener beneath. "Did you say it was not Asa?"

"Nay, I am neither Asa, nor Absalom, nor any of the Hebrew princes; but Obed, the root and stock of them all. Have I not said, woman, that you keep one in attendance who is entitled to a peaceable as well as an honourable admission. Do you take me for an animal of the class amphibia, and that I can play with my lungs as a blacksmith does with his bellows!"

The naturalist might have expended his breath much longer, without producing any desirable result, had Esther been his only auditor. Disappointed and alarmed, the woman had already sought her pallet, and was preparing, with a sort of desperate indifference, to compose herself to sleep. Abner, the sentinel below, however, had been aroused from an exceedingly equivocal situation, by the outcry; and as he had now regained sufficient consciousness to recognize the voice of the physician, the latter was admitted, with the least possible delay. Dr. Battius bustled through the narrow entrance, with an air of singular impatience, and was already beginning to mount the difficult ascent, when catching a view of the porter, he paused, to observe with an air that he intended should be impressively admonitory——

"Abner, there are dangerous symptoms of somnolency about thee! It is sufficiently exhibited in the tendency to hiation, and may prove dangerous not only to yourself, but to all thy father's family!"

"You never made a greater mistake, Doctor," returned the youth, gaping like an indolent lion, "I haven't a symptom, as you call it, about any part of me; and as to father and the children, I reckon the small-pox and the measles have been thoroughly through the breed these many months ago."

Content with his brief admonition, the naturalist had surmounted half the difficulties of the ascent before the deliberate Abner had ended his justification. On the summit, Obed fully expected to encounter Esther, of whose linguacious powers, he had too often been furnished with the most sinister proofs, and of which he stood in an awe too salutary to covet a repetition of her attacks. The reader can foresee that he was to be agreeably disappointed. Treading lightly, and looking timidly over his shoulder, as if he apprehended a shower of something, even more formidable than words, the Doctor proceeded to the place which had been allotted to himself in the general disposition of the dormitories.

Instead of sleeping, the worthy naturalist sat ruminating over what he had both seen and heard that day, until the tossing and mutterings which proceeded from the cabin of Esther, who was his nearest neighbour, advertised him of the wakeful situation of its inmate. Perceiving the necessity of doing something to disarm this female Cerberus, before his own purpose could be accomplished, the Doctor, reluctant as he was to encounter her tongue, found himself compelled to invite a colloquial communication.

"You appear not to sleep, my very kind and worthy Mrs. Bush," he said, determined to commence his applications with a plaster that was usually found to adhere; "you appear to rest badly, my excellent hostess; can I administer to your ailings?"

"What would you give me, man," grumbled Esther. "A blister to make me sleep?"

"Say rather a cataplasm. But if you are in pain, here are some cordial drops, which taken in a glass of my own cogniac will give you rest, if I know aught of the materia medica."

The Doctor, as he very well knew, had assailed Esther on her weak side; and, as he doubted not of the acceptability of his prescription, he sat himself at work, without unnecessary delay, to prepare it. When he made his offering, it was received in a snappish and threatening manner, but swallowed with a facility that sufficiently proclaimed how much it was relished by the patient. The woman muttered her thanks, and her leech reseated himself in silence, to await the operation of the dose. In less than half an hour the breathing of Esther became so profound, and as the Doctor himself might have termed it, so very abstracted, that had he not known how easy it was to ascribe this new instance of somnolency to the powerful dose of opium with which he had garnished the brandy, he might have seen reason to distrust his own prescription. With the sleep of the restless woman, the stillness became profound and general.

Then it was that Dr. Battius saw fit to arise, with the silence and caution of the midnight robber, and to steal out of his own cabin, or rather kennel, for it deserved no better name, towards the adjoining dormitories. Here he took time to assure himself that all his neighbours were buried in deep sleep. Once advised of this important fact, he hesitated no longer, but commenced the difficult ascent which led to the upper pinnacle of the rock. His advance, though abundantly guarded, was not entirely noiseless; but while he was felicitating himself on having successfully effected his object, and he was in the very act of placing his foot on the highest ledge, a hand was laid upon the skirts of his coat, which as effectually put an end to his advance, as though the gigantic strength of Ishmael himself had pinned him to the earth.

"Is there sickness in the tent," whispered a softvoice in his very ear, "that Dr. Battius is called to visit it at such an hour?"

So soon as the heart of the naturalist had returned from its hasty expedition into his throat, as one less skilled than Dr. Battius in the formation of the animal would have been apt to have accounted for the extraordinary sensation with which he received this unlooked–for interruption, he found resolution to reply; using, as much in terror as in prudence, the same precaution in the indulgence of his voice.

"My worthy Nelly! I am greatly rejoiced to find it is no other than thee! Hist! child, hist! Should Ishmael gain a knowledge of our plans, he would not hesitate to cast us both from off this rock, upon the plain beneath. Hist! Nelly, hist!"

As the Doctor delivered his injunctions between the intervals of his ascent, by the time they were concluded, both he and his auditor had gained the upper level.

"And now, Dr. Battius," the girl gravely demanded, "may I know the reason why you have run so great a risk of flying from this place, without wings, and at the certain expense of your neck?"

"Nothing shall be concealed from thee, my worthy and trusty Nelly——but are you certain that Ishmael will not awake?"

"No fear of him; he will sleep until the sun scorches his eye–lids. The danger is from my aunt."

"Esther sleepeth!" the Doctor sententiously replied. "Ellen, you have been watching on this rock to–day?"

"I was ordered to do so."

"And you have seen the bison, and the antelope, and the wolf, and the deer, as usual; animals of the orders, pecora, belluæ and feræ."

"I have seen the creatures you named in English; but I know nothing of the Indian languages."

"There is still an order that I have not named, which you have also seen. The primates——is it not true?"

"I cannot say. I know no animal by that name."

"Nay, Ellen, you confer with a friend. Of the genus, homo, child?"

"Whatever else I may have had in view, I have not seen the vespertilio horribi——"

"Hush, Nelly, thy vivacity will betray us! Tell me, girl, have you not seen certain bipeds, called men, wandering about the prairies?"

"Surely. My uncle and his sons have been hunting the buffaloe, since the sun began to fall."

"I must speak in the vernacular, to be comprehended! Ellen, I would say of the species, Kentucky."

Though Ellen reddened like the rose, her blushes were happily concealed by the darkness. She hesitated an instant, and then summoned sufficient spirit, to say, decidedly——

"If you wish to speak in parables, Doctor Battius, you must find another listener. Put your questions plainly in English, and I will answer them honestly in the same tongue."

"I have been journeying in this desert, as thou knowest, Nelly, in quest of animals that have been hidden from the eyes of science, until now. Among others, I have discovered a primates, of the genus, homo; species, Kentucky; which I term, Paul——"

"Hist, for the sake of mercy!" said Ellen—— "speak lower, Doctor; or we shall be heard."

"Hover; by profession a collector of the apes or bee," continued the other. "Do I use the vernacular now,——am I understood?"

"Perfectly, perfectly," returned the agitated girl, breathing with difficulty, in her surprise. "But what of him? did he tell you to mount this rock——he knows nothing, himself; for the oath I gave my uncle, has shut my mouth."

"Ay, but there is one, that has taken no oath, who has revealed all. I would that the mantle which is wrapped around the mysteries of nature, were as effectually withdrawn from its hidden treasures! Ellen! Ellen! the man with whom I have unwittingly formed a compactum or agreement is sadly forgetful of the obligations of honesty! Thy uncle, child."

"You mean Ishmael Bush, my father's brother's widow's husband," returned the offended girl, a little proudly.——"Indeed, indeed, it is cruel to reproach me with a tie that chance has formed, and which I would rejoice so much to break for ever!"

The humbled Ellen could utter no more, but sinking on a projection of the rock, she began to sob in a manner that rendered their situation doubly critical. The Doctor muttered a few words, which he intended as an apologetic explanation, but before he had time to complete his laboured vindication, she arose and said with great decision——

"I did not come here to pass my time in foolish tears, nor you to try to stop them. What then has brought you hither?"

"I must see the inmate of that tent."

"You know what it contains?"

"I am taught to believe I do; and I bear a letter, which I must deliver with my own hands. If the animal prove a quadruped, Ishmael is a true man—— if a biped, fledged or unfledged, I care not, he is false, and our compactum at an end!"

Ellen made a sign for the Doctor to remain where he was, and to be silent. She then glided into the tent, where she continued many minutes, that proved exceedingly weary and anxious to the expectant without, but the instant she returned, she took him by the arm, and together they entered beneath the folds of the mysterious cloth.

CHAPTER XII.

"Pray God the Duke of York excuse himself!"

—— King Henry VI.

The mustering of the borderers on the following morning was silent, sullen, and gloomy. The repast of that hour was wanting in the inharmonious accompaniment with which Esther ordinarily enlivened their meals; for the effects of the powerful opiate the Doctor had administered, still muddled her usually quick intellects. The young men brooded over the absence of their elder brother, and the brows of Ishmael himself were sternly knit, as he cast his scowling eyes from one to the other, like a man who was preparing to meet and to repel an expected assault on his authority. In the midst of this family distrust, Ellen and her midnight confederate, the naturalist, took their usual places among the children, without awakening suspicion or exciting comment. The only apparent fruits of the adventure in which they had been engaged, were occasional upliftings of the eyes, on the part of the Doctor, which were mistaken by the observers for some of his scientific contemplations of the heavens, but which, in reality, were no other than furtive glances at the fluttering walls of the proscribed tent.

At length the squatter, who had waited in vain for some more decided manifestation of the expected rising among his sons, resolved to make a demonstration of his own intentions.

127

"Asa shall account to me for this undutiful conduct!" he coolly observed. "Here has the live-long night gone by, and he out-lying on the prairie, when his hand and his rifle might both have been wanted in a brush with the Siouxes, for any right he had to know the contrary."

"Spare your breath, good man;" retorted his wife, "be saving of your breath; for you may have to call long enough for the boy before he will answer!"

"It ar' a fact, that some men be so womanish, as to let the young master the old! But, you, old Esther, should know better than to think such will ever be the nature of things in the family of Ishmael Bush."

"Ah! you are a hectorer with the boys, when need calls! I know it well, Ishmael; and one of your sons have you driven from you, by your temper; and that, too, at a time when he is most wanted."

"Father," said Abner, whose sluggish nature had gradually been stimulating itself to the exertion of taking so bold a stand, "the boys and I have pretty generally concluded to go out on the search of Asa. We are disagreeable about his 'camping on the prairie, instead of coming in to his own bed, as we all know he would like to do——"

"Pshaw!" muttered Abiram; "the boy has killed a buck; or perhaps a buffaloe; and he is sleeping by the carcass to keep off the wolves, till day; we shall soon see him, or hear him bawling for help to bring in his load."

" 'Tis little help that a son of mine will call for, to shoulder a buck or to quarter your wild-beef!" returned the mother, "And you, Abiram, to say such an uncertain thing! you, who said yourself that the red-skins had been prowling around this place no later than the yesterday——"

"I!" exclaimed her brother, hastily, as if anxious to retract an error; "I said it then, and I say it now; and so you will find it to be. The Tetons are in our neighbourhood, and happy will it prove for the boy if he is well shut of them."

"It seems to me," said Dr. Battius, speaking withthe sort of deliberation and dignity one is apt to use after having thoroughly ripened his opinions by sufficient reflection, "it seems to me, a man but little skilled in the signs and tokens of Indian warfare, especially as practised in these remote plains, but one, who I may say without vanity has some insight into the mysteries of nature——it seems, then, to me, thus humbly qualified, that when doubts exist in a matter of such moment, it would always be the wisest course to appease them."

"No more of your doctoring for me!" cried the grum Esther; "no more of your quiddities in a healthy family, say I! Here was I doing well, only a little out of sorts with over instructing the young, and you dos'd me with a drug that still hangs about my tongue, like a pound weight on a humming–bird's wing?"

"Is the medicine out?" drily demanded Ishmael: "it must be a rare doser that, if it gives a heavy feel to the tongue of old Eester!"

"Friend," continued the Doctor, waving his hand for the angry wife to maintain the peace, "that it cannot perform all that is said of it, the very charge of good Mrs. Bush is a sufficient proof. But to speak of the absent Asa. There is doubt as to his fate, and there is a proposition to solve it. Now, in the natural sciences truth is always a desideratum; and I confess it would seem to be equally so in the present case, which may be called a vacuum where, according to the laws of physic, there should exist some pretty palpable proofs of materiality."

"Dont mind him, dont mind him," cried Esther, observing that the rest of his auditors listened with an attention, which might proceed, equally, from acquiescence in his proposal or ignorance of its meaning. "There is a drug in every word he utters."

"Dr. Battius wishes to say," Ellen modestly interposed, "that as some of us think Asa is in danger,and some think otherwise, the whole family might pass an hour or two in looking for him."

"Does he?" interrupted the woman, "then Dr. Battius has more sense in him that I believed! She is right, Ishmael; and what she says, shall be done. I will shoulder a rifle myself; and woe betide the red–skin that crosses my path! I have pulled a trigger before to–day; ay, and heard an Indian yell, too, to my sorrow."

The spirit of Esther diffused itself, like the stimulus which attends a victorious war–cry, among her indolent sons. They arose in a body, and declared their determination to second so bold a resolution. Ishmael prudently yielded to an impulse he could not resist, and in a few minutes the woman appeared, shouldering her arms, prepared to lead forth, in person, such of her descendants as chose to follow in her train.

"Let them stay with the children that please, she said, "and them follow me, who ar' not chicken–hearted!"

"Abiram, it will not do to leave the huts without some guard," Ishmael whispered, glancing his eye upward.

The man whom he addressed started, and betrayed extraordinary eagerness in his reply.

"I will tarry and watch the camp."

A dozen voices were instantly raised in objections to this proposal. He was wanted to point out the places where the hostile tracks had been seen, and his termagant sister openly scouted at the idea, as unworthy of his manhood. The reluctant Abiram was compelled to yield, and Ishmael made a new disposition for the defence of the place; which was admitted, by every one, to be all–important to their security and comfort.

He offered the post of commandant to Dr. Battius, who, however, peremptorily and somewhathaughtily, declined the doubtful honour; exchanging looks of singular intelligence with Ellen, as he did so. In this dilemma the squatter was obliged to constitute the girl herself castellain; taking care, however, in deputing this important trust, to omit no words of caution and instruction. When this preliminary point was settled, the young men proceeded to arrange certain means of defence, and signals of alarm, that were adapted to the weakness and character of the garrison. Several masses of rock were drawn to the edge of the upper level, and so placed as to leave it at the discretion of the feeble Ellen and her associates, to cast them or not, as they might choose, on the heads of any invaders, who would, of necessity, be obliged to mount the eminence by the difficult and narrow passage already so often mentioned. In addition to this formidable obstruction, the barriers were strengthened and rendered nearly impassable. Smaller missiles, that might be hurled even by the hands of the younger children, but which would prove, from the elevation of the place, exceedingly dangerous, were provided in profusion. A pile of dried leaves and splinters were placed, as a beacon, on the upper rock, and then, even in the jealous judgment of the squatter, the post was deemed competent to maintain a creditable siege.

The moment the rock was thought to be in a state of sufficient security, the party who composed what might be called the sortie, sallied forth on their anxious expedition. The advance was led by Esther in person, who, attired in a dress half masculine, and bearing a weapon like the rest, seemed no unfit leader for the groupe of wildly clad frontier–men, that followed leisurely in her rear.

"Now, Abiram!" cried the Amazon, in a voice that was cracked and harsh, for the simple reason of being used too often on a strained and unnatural key, "Now, Abiram, run with your nose low; show yourselfa hound of the true breed, and do some credit to your training. You it was that saw the prints of the Indian moccasin, and it behoves you, to let others be as wise as yourself. Come; come to the front, man; and give us a bold lead."

The brother, who appeared at all times to stand in salutary awe of his sister's authority, complied; though it was with a reluctance so evident, as to excite sneers, even among the unobservant and indolent sons of the squatter. Ishmael, himself, moved among his tall children, like one who expected nothing from the search, and who was indifferent alike to its success or failure. In this manner the party proceeded until their distant fortress had sunk so low, as to present an object no larger nor more distinct than a hazy point, on the margin of the prairie. Hitherto their progress had been silent and somewhat rapid, for as swell after swell was mounted and passed, without varying, or discovering a living object to enliven the monotony of the view, even the tongue of Esther was hushed in increasing anxiety. Here, however, Ishmael chose to pause, and casting the butt of his rifle from his shoulder to the ground, he observed——

"This is enough. Buffaloe signs, and deer signs, ar' plenty; but where ar' the Indian footsteps that you have seen, Abiram?"

"Still farther to the west," returned the other, pointing in the direction he named. "This was the spot, where I struck the tracks of the buck, I killed; it was after I took the deer, that I fell upon the Teton trail."

"And a bloody piece of work you made of it, man;" cried the squatter, pointing tauntingly to the soiled garments of his kinsman, and then directing the attention of the spectators to his own, by the way of a triumphant contrast. "Here have I cut the throat of two lively does, and a scampering fawn,without spot or stain; while you, blundering dog as you ar', you have made as much work for Eester and her girls, as though butchering was your regular calling. Come boys; I say it is enough. I am too old not to know the signs of the frontiers, and no Indian has been here, since the last fall of water. Follow me; and I will make a turn that shall give us at least the beef of a fallow cow for our trouble."

"Follow me!" echoed Esther, stepping undauntedly forward. "I am leader to–day, and I will be followed. For who so proper, let me know, as a mother, to head a search for her lost child?"

Ishmael regarded his intractable mate with a smile of indulgent pity. Observing that she had already struck out a path for herself, different both from that of Abiram and the one he had seen fit to choose, and being unwilling to draw the cord of authority too tight, just at that moment, he again sullenly submitted to her will. But Dr. Battius, who had hitherto been a silent and thoughtful attendant on the woman, now saw fit to raise his feeble voice in the way of remonstrance.

"I agree with thy partner in life, worthy and gentle Mrs. Bush," he said, "in believing that some ignis fatuus of the imagination has deceived Abiram, in the signs or symptoms of which he has spoken."

"Symptoms, yourself!" interrupted the termagant. "This is no time for bookish words, nor is this a place to stop and swallow medicines. If you are a–leg–weary, say so, as a plain–speaking man should; then seat yourself on the prairie, like a hound that is foot–sore, and take your natural rest."

"I accord in the opinion," the naturalist calmly replied, complying, literally, with the opinion of the deriding Esther, by taking his seat, very coolly, by the side of an indigenous shrub; the examination of which he commenced, on the instant, in order that science might not lose any of its just and important dues. "I honour your excellent advice, Mistress Esther, as you may perceive. Go thou in quest of thy offspring; while I tarry here, in pursuit of that which is better; viz. an insight into the arcana of nature's volume."

The woman answered with a hollow, unnatural, and scornful laugh, and even her heavy sons, as they slowly passed the seat of the already abstracted naturalist, did not disdain to manifest their contempt in significant smiles. In a few minutes the train had mounted the nearest eminence, and, as it turned the rounded acclivity, the Doctor was left to pursue his profitable investigations in entire solitude.

Another half–hour passed, during which Esther continued to advance, on her seemingly fruitless search. Her pauses, however, were becoming frequent, and her looks wandering and uncertain, when footsteps were heard clattering through the bottom, and at the next instant a buck was seen to bound up the ascent, and to dart from before their eyes, in the direction of the naturalist. So sudden and unlooked for had been the passage of the animal, and so much had he been favoured by the shape of the ground, that before any one of the foresters had time to bring his rifle to his shoulder, it was already far beyond the range of a bullet.

"Look out for the wolf!" shouted Abner, shaking his head in vexation, at being a single moment too late. "A wolf's skin will be no bad gift in a winter's night; ay, yonder the hungry devil comes!"

"Hold!" cried Ishmael, knocking up the levelled weapon of his too eager son. " 'Tis not a wolf; but a hound of thorough blood and bottom. Ha! we have hunters nigh: there ar' two of them!"

He was still speaking when the animals in question came leaping on the track of the deer, striving with noble ardour to outdo each other. One was an aged dog, whose strength seemed to be sustained purelyby his generous emulation, and the other a pup, that gambolled even while he pressed most warmly on the chase. They both ran, however, with clean and powerful leaps, carrying their noses high, like animals of the most keen and subtle scent. They had passed; and in another minute they would have been running open–mouthed with the deer in view, had not the younger dog suddenly bounded from the course and uttered a cry of surprise. His aged companion stopped also, and returned panting and exhausted to the place, where the other was whirling around in swift, and apparently in mad evolutions, circling the spot in his own footsteps, and continuing his outcry, in a short, snappish barking. But, when the elder hound had reached the spot, he seated himself, and lifting his nose high into the air, he raised a long, loud, and wailing howl.

"It must be a strong scent," said Abner, who had been, with the rest of the family, an admiring observer of the movements of the dogs, "that can break off two such creaturs' so suddenly from their trail."

"Murder them!" cried Abiram; "I'll swear to the old hound; 'tis the dog of the trapper, whom we now know to be our mortal enemy."

Though the brother of Esther gave such hostile advice, he appeared in no way ready to put it in execution himself. The surprise, which had taken possession of the whole party, exhibited itself in his own vacant, wondering stare, as strongly as in any of the admiring visages by whom he was surrounded. His denunciation, therefore, notwithstanding its dire import, was disregarded; and the dogs were left to obey the impulses of their mysterious instinct, without let or hindrance.

It was long before any of the spectators broke the silence; but the squatter, at length, so far recollected his authority, as to take on himself the right to control the movements of his children.

"Come away, boys; come away, and leave the hounds to sing their tunes for their own amusement," Ishmael said, in his coldest manner. "I scorn to take the life of a beast, because its master has pitch'd himself too nigh my clearing; come away, boys, come away; we have enough of our own work before us, without turning aside to do that of the whole neighbourhood."

"Come not away!" cried Esther, in tones that sounded like the admonitions of some Sybil. "I say, come not away, my children. There is a meaning and a warning in this; and as I am a woman and a mother, will I know the truth of it all!"

So saying, the awakened wife of the squatter brandished her weapon, with an air that was not without its wild and secret influence, and led the way towards the spot where the dogs still remained, filling the air with their long–drawn and piteous complaints. The whole party followed in her steps, some too indolent to oppose, others obedient to her will, and all more or less excited by the uncommon character of the scene.

"Tell me, you Abner——Abiram——Ishmael!" the woman cried, standing over a spot where the earth was trampled and beaten, and plainly sprinkled with blood; "tell me, you who ar' hunters! what sort of animal has here met his death? Speak! Ye ar' men, and used to the signs of the plains, all of ye; is it the blood of wolf or panther?"

"A buffaloe——and a noble and powerful creatur' has it been!" returned the squatter, who looked down calmly on the fatal signs which so strangely affected his wife. "Here are the marks of the spot where he has struck his hoofs into the earth, in the death-struggle; and yonder he has plunged and torn the ground with his horns. Ay, a buffaloe bull of wonderful strength and courage has he been!"

"And who has slain him?" continued Esther,"man! where, then, are the offals? Wolves! They devour not the hide! Tell me, ye men and hunters, is this the blood of a beast?"

"The creatur' has plunged over the hillock," said Abner, who had proceeded a short distance beyond the rest of the party. "Ah! there you will find it, in yon swale of alders. Look! a thousand carrion birds, ar' hovering, this very moment, above the carcass."

"The animal has still life in him," returned the squatter, "or the buzzards would settle upon their prey! By the action of the dogs it must be something ravenous; I reckon it is the white bear from the upper falls. They are said to cling desperately to life!"

"Ay, let us go back," said Abiram; "there may be danger, and there can be no good in attacking a ravenous beast. Remember, Ishmael, 'twill be a risky job, and one of small profit!"

The young men smiled at this new proof of the well known pusillanimity of their too sensitive uncle. The oldest even proceeded so far as to express his contempt, by bluntly saying——

"It will do to cage with the other animal we carry; then we may go back double-handed into the settlements, and set up for showmen, around the court-houses and gaols of Kentucky."

The dark, threatening frown, which gathered on the brow of his father, admonished the young man to forbear. Exchanging looks that were half rebellious with his brethren, he saw fit to be silent. But instead of observing the caution recommended by Abiram, they proceeded in a body, until they again came to a halt within a few yards of the matted cover of the thicket.

The scene had now, indeed, become wild and striking enough to have produced a powerful effect on minds better prepared, than those of the unnurturedfamily of the squatter, to resist the impressions of such an exciting spectacle. The heavens were, as usual at the season, covered with dark, driving clouds, beneath which interminable flocks of aquatic birds were again on the wing, holding their toilsome and heavy way towards the distant waters of the south. The wind had risen, and was once more sweeping over the prairie in gusts, which it was often vain to oppose; and then again the blasts would seem to mount into the upper air, as if to sport with the drifting vapour, whirling and rolling vast masses of the dusky and ragged volumes over each other, in a terrific and yet grand disorder. Above the little brake, the flocks of birds still held their flight, circling with heavy wings about the spot, struggling at times against the torrent of wind, and then favoured by their position and height, making bold swoops upon the thicket, away from which, however, they never failed to sail, screaming in terror, as if apprised, either by sight or instinct, that the hour of their voracious dominion had not yet fully arrived.

Ishmael stood for many minutes, with his wife and children clustered together, in an amazement, with which awe was singularly mingled, gazing in death–like stillness on the imposing sight. The voice of Esther at length broke the charm, and reminded the spectators of the necessity of resolving their doubts in some manner more worthy of their manhood, than by a dull and inactive observation.

"Call in the dogs!" she said; "call in the hounds, and put them into the thicket; there ar' men enough of ye, if ye have not lost the spirit with which I know ye were born, to tame the tempers of all the bears west of the big river. Call in the dogs, I say, you Enoch! Abner! Gabriel! has wonder made ye deaf as well as dumb?"

One of the young men complied; and having succeeded in detaching the hounds from the place,around which, until then, they had not ceased to hover, he led them down to the margin of the thicket.

"Put them in, boy; put them in," continued the woman; "and you, Ishmael and Abiram, if anything wicked or hurtful comes forth, show them the use of your rifles, like frontier–men. If ye ar' wanting in spirit, before the eyes of my children will I put ye both to shame!"

The youths who, until now, had detained the hounds, let slip the thongs of skin, by which they had been held, and urged them to the attack by their voices. But, it would seem, that the elder dog was restrained by some extraordinary sensation, or that he was much too experienced to attempt the rash adventure. After proceeding a few yards to the very verge of the brake, he made a sudden pause, and stood trembling in all his aged limbs, apparently as unable to recede as to advance. The encouraging calls of the young men were disregarded, or only answered by a low and plaintive whining. For a minute the pup also was similarly affected; but less sage, or more easily excited, he was induced at length to leap forward, and finally to dash into the cover. An alarmed and startling howl was heard, and, at the next minute, he broke out of the thicket, and commenced circling the spot, in the same wild and unsteady manner as before.

"Have I a man among my children!" demanded the aroused Esther. "Give me a truer piece than a childish shot-gun, and I will show ye what the courage of a frontier-woman can do."

"Stay mother," exclaimed Abner and Enoch; "if you will see the creatur', let us drive it into view."

This was quite as much as the youths were accustomed to utter, even on more important occasions, but having thus given a pledge of their intentions, they were far from being backward in redeeming it.Preparing their arms with the utmost care, they advanced with steadiness to the brake. Nerves less often tried than those of the young borderers might easily have shrunk before the dangers of so uncertain an undertaking. As they proceeded, the howls of the dogs became more shrill and plaintive. The vultures and buzzards settled so low as to flap the bushes with their heavy wings, and the wind came hoarsely sweeping along the naked prairie, as if the spirits of the air had also descended to witness the approaching development.

There was a breathless moment when the blood of the usually undaunted Esther flowed backward to her heart, as she saw her sons push aside the matted branches of the thicket and bury themselves in its labyrinth. A deep and solemn pause succeeded. Then arose two loud and piercing cries, in quick succession, which were followed by a quiet still more awful and appalling.

"Come back, come back, my children!" cried the woman, the feelings of a mother getting the entire ascendancy in her bosom.

But her voice was hushed, and every faculty seemed frozen with horror, as at that instant the bushes once more parted, and the two adventurers re−appeared, pale, and nearly insensible themselves, and laid at her feet the stiff and motionless body of the lost Asa, with the marks of a violent death but too plainly stamped on every pallid lineament.

The dogs uttered a long and closing howl, and then breaking off together, they disappeared on the forsaken trail of the deer. The flight of birds wheeled upward into the heavens, filling the air with their complaints at having been robbed of a victim which, frightful and disgusting as it was, still bore too much of the impression of humanity to become the prey of their obscene appetites.

CHAPTER XIII.

"A pickaxe, and a spade, a spade,

For,——and a shrouding sheet:

O, a pit of clay for to be made

For such a guest is meet."

—— Song in Hamlet

"Stand back! stand off, the whole of ye!" said Esther hoarsely to the crowd, which pressed too closely on the corpse; "I am his mother, and my right is better than that of ye all! Who has done this! Tell me, Ishmael, Abiram, Abner! open your mouths and your hearts, and let God's truth and no other issue from them. Who has done this bloody deed?"

Her husband made no reply, but stood, leaning on his rifle, looking sadly, but with an unaltered eye, at the mangled remains of his son. Not so the mother, she threw herself on the earth, and receiving the cold and ghastly head of the dead man into her lap, she sat many minutes contemplating those muscular features, on which the death–agony was still horridly impressed, in a silence even more expressive than any language of lamentation could possibly have proved.

The voice of the woman was literally frozen in grief. In vain Ishmael attempted a few words of rude consolation; she neither listened nor answered. Her sons gathered about her in a circle, and expressed, after their uncouth manner, their sympathy in her sorrow, as well as their sense of their own loss, but she motioned them away, impatiently, with her hand. At times her fingers played in the matted hair of the dead, and at others they lightly attempted to smooth the painfully expressive muscles of its ghastly visage, as the hand of the mother is often seen tolinger fondly about the features of her sleeping child. Then starting from their revolting office, her hands would flutter around her, and seem to seek some fruitless remedy against the violent blow, which had thus suddenly destroyed the child in whom she had not only placed her greatest hopes, but so much of her maternal pride. It was while engaged in the latter incomprehensible manner, that the lethargic Abner turned aside, and swallowing the unwonted emotions which were rising in his own throat, he observed——

"Mother means that we should look for the signs, that we may know in what manner Asa has come by his end."

"We owe it to the accursed Siouxes!" answered Ishmael; "Twice have they put me deeply in their debt! The third time, the score shall be cleared!"

But, as if not content with this plausible explanation, and, perhaps, secretly glad to avert their eyes from a spectacle which awakened such extraordinary and unusual sensations in their sluggish bosoms, the sons of the squatter turned away in a body from their mother and the corpse, and proceeded to make the inquiries which they fancied the former had so repeatedly demanded. Ishmael made no objections; but, though he accompanied his children while they proceeded in the investigation, it was more with the appearance of complying with their wishes, at a time when resistance might not be seemly, than with any visible interest in the result. As the borderers, notwithstanding their usual dullness, were well instructed in most things connected with their habits of life, an inquiry, the success of which depended so much on signs and evidences that bore so strong a resemblance to a forest trail, was likely to be conducted with skill and acuteness. Accordingly, they proceeded to the melancholy task with great readiness and intelligence.

Abner and Enoch agreed in their accounts as to the position in which they had found the body. It was seated nearly upright, the back supported by a mass of matted brush, and one hand still grasping a broken twig of the alders. It was most probably owing to the former circumstance that the body had escaped the rapacity of the carrion birds, which had been seen hovering above the thicket, and the latter proved that life had not yet entirely abandoned the hapless victim when he entered the brake. The opinion now became general, that the youth had received his death–wound in the open prairie, and had dragged his enfeebled form into the cover of the thicket for the purpose of concealment. A trail through the bushes confirmed this opinion. It also appeared, on examination, that a desperate struggle had taken place on the very margin of the thicket. This was sufficiently apparent by the trodden branches, the deep impressions on the moist ground, and the lavish flow of blood.

"He has been shot in the open ground and come here for a cover," said Abiram; "these marks would clearly prove it. The boy has been set upon by the savages in a body, and has fou't like a hero as he was, until they have mastered his strength and then drawn him to the bushes."

To this probable opinion there was now but one dissenting voice, that of the slow–minded Ishmael, who demanded that the corpse itself should be examined in order to a more accurate knowledge of its injuries. On examination, it appeared that a rifle bullet had passed directly through the body of the deceased, entering beneath one of his brawny shoulders, and making its exit by the breast. It required some knowledge in gun–shot wounds to decide this delicate point, but the experience of the borderers was quite equal to the scrutiny; and a smile of wild, and certainly of singular satisfaction, passed amongthe sons of Ishmael, when Abner confidently announced that the enemies of Asa had assailed him in the rear.

"It must be so," said the gloomy but attentive squatter. "He was of too good a stock and too well trained, knowingly to turn the weak side to man or beast! Remember, boys, that while the front of manhood is to your enemy, let him be who or what he may, you ar' safe from cowardly surprise.——Why Eester, woman! you ar' getting beside yourself; with picking at the hair and the garments of the child! Little good can you do him now, old girl."

"See!" interrupted Enoch, extricating from the fragments of cloth the morsel of lead which had prostrated the strength of one so powerful, "Here is the very bullet."

Ishmael took it in his hand and eyed it long and closely.

"There's no mistake;" at length he muttered through his compressed teeth. "It is from the pouch of that accursed trapper. Like many of the hunters he has a mark in his mould, in order to know the work his rifle performs; and here you see it plainly ——six little holes, laid crossways."

"I'll swear to it!" cried Abiram, triumphantly. "He shew'd me his private mark, himself, and boasted of the number of deer he had laid upon the prairies with these very bullets! Now, Ishmael, will you believe me when I tell you the old knave is a spy of the red–skins!"

The lead passed from the hand of one to that of another; and unfortunately for the reputation of the old man, several among them remembered also to have seen the aforesaid private bullet–marks, during the curious examination which all had made of his accoutrements. In addition to this wound, however, were many others of a less dangerous nature, all ofwhich were supposed to confirm the supposed guilt of the trapper.

The traces of many different struggles were to be seen, between the spot where the first blood was spilt and the thicket to which it was now generally believed Asa had retreated, as a place of refuge. These were interpreted into so many proofs of the weakness of the murderer, who would have sooner despatched his victim, had not even the dying strength of the youth rendered him formidable to the infirmities of one so old. The danger of drawing some others of the hunters to the spot, by repeated firing, was deemed a sufficient reason for not again resorting to the rifle, after it had performed the important duty of disabling the victim. The weapon of the dead man was not to be found, and had doubtless, together with many other less valuable and lighter articles, that he was accustomed to carry about his person, become a prize to his destroyer.

But what, in addition to the tell–tale bullet, appeared to fix the ruthless deed with peculiar certainty on the trapper, was the accumulated evidence furnished by the trail; which proved, notwithstanding his deadly hurt, that the wounded man had still been able to make a long and desperate resistance to the subsequent efforts of his murderer. Ishmael

141

seemed to press this proof with a singular mixture of sorrow and pride: sorrow, at the loss of a son, whom in their moments of amity he highly valued; and pride, at the courage and power he had manifested to his last and weakest breath.

"He died as a son of mine should die," said the squatter, gleaning a hollow consolation from so unnatural an exultation; "a dread to his enemy to the last, and without help from the law! Come, children; we have first the grave to make, and then to hunt his murderer."

The sons of the squatter set about their melancholy office, in silence and in sadness. An excavation was made in the hard earth, at a great expense of toil and time, and the body was wrapped in such spare vestments as could be collected among the labourers. When these arrangements were completed, Ishmael approached the seemingly unconscious Esther, and announced his intention to inter the dead. She heard him, and quietly relinquished her grasp of the corpse, rising in silence to follow it to its narrow resting place. Here she seated herself again at the head of the grave, watching each movement of the youths with eager and jealous eyes. When a sufficiency of earth was laid upon the senseless clay of Asa, to protect it from injury, Enoch and Abner entered the cavity, and trode it into a solid mass, by the weight of their huge frames, with an appearance of a strange, not to say savage, mixture of care and indifference. This well–known precaution was adopted to prevent the speedy exhumation of the body by some of the carnivorous beasts of the prairie, whose instinct was sure to guide them to the spot. Even the rapacious birds appeared to comprehend the nature of the ceremony, for, mysteriously apprised that the miserable victim was now about to be abandoned by the human race, they once more began to make their airy circuits above the place, screaming, as if to frighten the kinsmen from their labour of caution and love.

Ishmael stood, with folded arms, steadily watching the manner in which this necessary duty was performed, and when the whole was completed, he lifted his cap to his sons, to thank them for their services, with a dignity that would have become one much better nurtured. Throughout the whole of a ceremony, which is ever solemn and admonitory, the squatter had maintained a grave and serious deportment. His vast features were visibly stamped with an expression of deep concern; but at no time did they falter, until he turned his back, as he believed for ever, on the grave of his first–born. Nature was then stirring powerfully within him, and the muscles of his stern visage began to work perceptibly. His children fastened their eyes on his, as if to seek a direction to the strange emotions which were moving their own heavy natures, when the struggle in the bosom of the squatter suddenly ceased, and, taking his wife by the arm, he raised her to her feet as though she had been an infant, saying, in a voice that was perfectly steady, though a nice observer would have discovered that it was kinder than usual——

"Eester, we have now done all that man and woman can do. We raised the boy, and made him such as few others were like, on the frontiers of America; and we have given him a grave. Let us go."

The woman turned her eyes slowly from the fresh earth, and laying her hands on the shoulders of her husband, stood looking him anxiously in the eyes for many moments, before she uttered in a voice, deep, frightful, and nearly choked——

"Ishmael! Ishmael! you parted from the boy in your wrath!"

"May the Lord pardon his sins freely as I have forgiven his worst misdeeds," calmly returned the squatter, "woman, go you back to the rock and read in your bible; a chapter in that book always does you good. You can read, Eester; which is a privilege I never did enjoy."

"Yes, yes," muttered the woman, yielding to his strength, and suffering herself to be led, though with powerful reluctance, from the spot. "I can read; and how have I used the knowledge! But he, Ishmael, he has not the sin of wasted l'arning to answer for. We have spared him that, at least! whether it be in mercy, or in cruelty, I know not."

Her husband made no reply, but continued steadily to lead her in the direction of their temporary abode. When they reached the summit of the swell of land, which they knew was the last spot from which the situation of the grave of Asa could be seen, they all turned, as by common concurrence, to take a farewell view of the place. The little mound itself was not visible; but it was frightfully indicated by the flock of screaming birds which hovered above it. In the opposite direction a low, blue hillock, in the skirts of the horizon, pointed out the place where Esther had left the rest of her young, and served as an attraction to draw her reluctant steps from the last abode of her eldest son. Nature quickened in the bosom of the mother at the sight, and she finally yielded the rights of the dead, to the more urgent claims of the living.

The foregoing occurrences had struck a spark from the stern tempers of a set of beings so singularly moulded in the habits of their uncultivated lives, which served to keep alive among them the dying embers of family affection. United to their parents by ties no stronger than those which use had created, there had been great danger, as Ishmael had foreseen, that the overloaded hive would quickly swarm, and leave him saddled with the difficulties of a young and helpless brood, unsupported by the exertions of those, whom he had already brought to a state of maturity. The spirit of insubordination, which emanated from the unfortunate Asa, had spread among his juniors, and the squatter had been made painfully to remember the time when, in the wantonness of his youth and vigour, he had, reversing the order of the brutes, cast off his own aged and failing parents, to enter into the world unshackled and free. Butthe danger had now abated, for a time at least; and if his authority was not restored with all its former influence, it was visibly admitted to exist, and to maintain its ascendancy a little longer.

It is true that his slow–minded sons, even while they submitted to the impressions of the recent event, had glimmerings of terrible distrusts, as to the manner in which their elder brother had met with his death. There were faint and indistinct images in the minds of two or three of the oldest, which pourtrayed the father himself, as ready to imitate the example of Abraham, without the justification of the sacred authority which commanded the holy man to attempt the revolting office. But then, these images were so transient and so much obscured in intellectual mists, as to leave no very strong impressions, and the tendency of the whole transaction, as we have already said, was rather to strengthen than to weaken the authority of Ishmael.

In this disposition of mind, the party continued their route towards the place whence they had that morning issued on a search which had been crowned with so melancholy a success. The long and fruitless march which they had made under the direction of Abiram, the discovery of the body and its subsequent interment, had so far consumed the day, that by the time their steps were retraced across the broad tract of waste which lay between the grave of Asa and the rock, the sun had fallen far below his meridian altitude. The hill had gradually risen as they approached, like some tower emerging from the bosom of the sea, and when within a mile, the minuter objects that crowned its height came dimly into view.

"It will be a sad meeting for the girls!" said Ishmael, who, from time to time, did not cease to utter something which he intended should be consolatory to the bruised spirit of his stricken partner. "Asa was much regarded by all the young; and seldom failed to bring in from his hunts something that they loved."

"He did; he did;" murmured Esther; "the boy was the pride of the family.——My other children are as nothing to him!"

"Say not so, good woman," returned the father, glancing his eye a little proudly at the athletic train which followed, at no great distance, in the rear. "Say not so, old Eester; for few fathers and mothers have greater reason to be boastful than ourselves."

"Thankful, thankful," muttered the humbled woman, "ye mean thankful; Ishmael!"

"Then thankful let it be, if you like the word better, my good girl,——but what has become of Nelly and the young! The child has forgotten the charge I gave her, and has not only suffered the children to sleep, but, I warrant you, is dreaming of the fields of Tennessee at this very moment. The mind of your niece is mainly fixed on the settlements, I reckon."

"Ay, she is not for us; I said it, and thought it, when I took her, because death had stripped her of all other friends. Death is a sad worker in the bosom of families, Ishmael! Asa had a kind feeling to the child, and they might have come one day into our places, had things been so ordered."

"Nay, she is not gifted for a frontier wife, if this is the manner she is to keep house while the husband is on the hunt. Abner, let off your rifle, that they may know we ar' coming. I fear Nelly and the young ar' asleep."

The young man complied with an alacrity that manifested how gladly he would see the rounded, active figure of Ellen, enlivening the ragged summit of the rock. But the report was succeeded neither by signal nor answer of any sort. For a moment, the whole party stood in suspense, awaiting the result, and then a simultaneous impulse caused the whole to let off their pieces at the same instant, producing a noise which might not fail to reach the ears of all within so short a distance.

"Ah! there they come at last!" cried Abiram, who was usually among the first to seize on any circumstance which promised relief from disagreeable apprehensions.

145

"It is a petticoat fluttering on the line," said Esther, "I put it there myself."

"You ar' right; but now she comes; the jade has been taking her comfort in the tent!"

"It is not so," said Ishmael, whose usually inflexible features were beginning to manifest the uneasiness he violently felt. "It is the tent itself blowing about loosely in the wind. They have loosened the bottom, like silly children as they ar', and unless care s had, the whole will come down!"

The words were scarcely uttered before a hoarse, rushing blast of wind, swept by the spot where they stood, raising the dust into little eddies, in its progress; and then, as if guided by a master hand, it quitted the earth, and mounted in its progress to the precise spot, on which all eyes were just then riveted. The loosened linen felt its influence and tottered; but regained its poise, and, for a moment, it became tranquil. The cloud of leaves next played in circling revolutions around the place, and then descended with the velocity of a swooping hawk, and sailed away into the prairie in long straight lines, like a flight of swallows resting on their expanded wings. They were followed for some distance by the snow–white tent, which, however, soon fell behind the rock, leaving its highest peak as naked as when it lay in the entire solitude of the desert.

"The murderers have been here!" moaned Esther. "My babes! my babes!"

For a moment even Ishmael faltered before the weight of such an unexpected blow. But shaking himself, like an awakened lion, he sprang forward, and pushing aside the impediments of the barrier, as though they had been feathers, he rushed up the ascent with an impetuosity which proved how formidable a sluggish nature may become, when thoroughly aroused.

CHAPTER XIV.

"Whose party do the townsmen yet admit?"

—— King John

In order to preserve an even pace between the incidents of the tale, it becomes necessary to revert to such events as occurred during the ward of Ellen Wade.

For the few first hours, the cares of the honest and warm-hearted girl were confined to the simple offices of satisfying the often-repeated demands which her younger associates made on her time and patience, under the pretences of hunger, thirst, and all the other ceaseless wants of captious and inconsiderate childhood. She had seized a moment from their importunities to steal into the tent, where she was administering to the comforts of one far more deserving of her tenderness, when an outcry, which arose among the children she had left, recalled her to the duties she had momentarily forgotten.

"See, Nelly, see!" exclaimed half a dozen eager voices, as she re-appeared among them, "yonder ar' men; and Phœbe says that they ar' Sioux-Indians!"

Ellen turned her eyes in the direction in which so many arms were already extended, and, to her consternation, beheld the forms of several men, who were advancing, manifestly and swiftly, in a straight line towards the rock. She counted four, but wasunable to make out any thing concerning their characters, except that they were not any of those who of right were entitled to admission into the fortress. It was a fearful moment for Ellen. Looking around, at the juvenile and frightened flock that pressed upon the skirts of her garments, she endeavoured to recall to her confused faculties some one of the many tales of female heroism, with which the history of the western frontier abounded. In one, a stockade had been successfully defended by a single man, supported by three or four women, for days, against the assaults of a hundred enemies. In another, the women alone had been able to protect the children, and less valuable effects of their absent husbands; and a third was not wanting, in which a solitary female had destroyed her sleeping captors and given liberty not only to herself, but to a brood of timid and helpless young. This was the case most nearly assimilated to the situation in which Ellen now found herself; and, with flushing cheeks and kindling eyes, the encouraged girl began to consider of, and to prepare her slender means of defence.

She posted the larger girls at the little levers that were to cast the rocks on the assailants, the smaller were to be used more for shew than any positive service they could perform, while, like any other leader, she was reserved in her own person, as a superintendant and encourager of the whole. When these dispositions were made, she endeavoured to await the issue, with an air of composure, that she intended should inspire her assistants with the confidence necessary to insure their success.

Although Ellen was vastly their superior in that spirit which emanates from moral qualities, she was by no means the equal of the two eldest daughters of Esther, in the not less important military property of insensibility to danger. Reared in all the hardihood of a constantly migrating life, on the skirts ofsociety, where they had become familiarized to the sights and dangers of the wilderness, these girls promised fairly to become, at some future day, no less distinguished than their mother for their daring, and for that singular mixture of good and evil, which, in a wider sphere of action, would probably have enabled the wife of the squatter to enrol her name among the remarkable females of her time. Esther had already, on one occasion, made good the log tenement of Ishmael against an inroad of savages; and on another, she had been left for dead by her enemies, after a defence that with a more civilized foe would have entitled her to the honours and attentions of a liberal capitulation. These facts, and sundry others of a similar nature, had often been recapitulated with a suitable exultation in the presence of her daughters, and the bosoms of the young Amazons were now strangely fluctuating between natural terror and the ambitious wish to do something that might render them worthy of being the children of such a mother. It now appeared that the opportunity for distinction, of this wild and unnatural character, was no longer to be denied them.

The party of strangers was already within a hundred rods of the rock. Either consulting their usual wary method of advancing, or admonished by the threatening attitudes of the two figures, who had thrust forth the barrels of as many old muskets from behind their stone entrenchment, the new comers halted under favour of an inequality in the ground, where a growth of grass thicker than common offered them the advantage of a place of concealment. From this spot they reconnoitred the fortress for several anxious, and to Ellen, apparently interminable minutes. Then one advanced singly, and apparently more in the character of a herald than of an assailant.

"Phœbe, do you fire," and "no, Hetty, you," werebeginning to be heard between the half-frightened and yet eager daughters of the squatter, when Ellen probably saved the advancing stranger from some imminent alarm, if from no greater danger, by exclaiming——

"Lay down the muskets; it is Dr. Battius!"

Her subordinates complied, so far as to withdraw their hands from the locks, though the threatening barrels still maintained their portentous levels. The naturalist, who had advanced with sufficient deliberation to note the smallest hostile demonstration made by the garrison, now raised a white handkerchief on the end of his own fusee, and came within speaking distance of the fortress. Then assuming what he intended should be an imposing and dignified semblance of authority, he blustered forth, in a voice that might have been heard at a much greater distance——

"What, ho! I summon ye all, in the name of the Confederacy of the United Sovereign States of North America, to submit yourselves to the laws."

"Doctor or no Doctor; he is an enemy, Nelly; hear him! hear him! he talks of the law."

"Stop! stay till I hear his answer!" said the nearly breathless Ellen, pushing aside the dangerous weapons which were again pointed in the direction of the shrinking person of the herald.

"I admonish and forewarn ye all," continued the startled Doctor, "that I am a peaceful citizen of the before named Confederacy, a supporter of the Social Compact, and a lover of good order and amity;" then, perceiving that the danger was, at least, temporarily removed, he once more raised his voice to the hostile pitch, and continued——"I charge ye all, therefore, to submit to the laws."

"I thought you were a friend," Ellen replied; "and that you travelled with my uncle, in virtue of an agreement——"

"It is void! I have been deceived in the very premises, and, I hereby pronounce, a certain compactum entered into and concluded between Ishmael Bush, squatter, and Obed Battius, M. D. to be incontinently null and of non–effect. Nay, children, to be null is merely a negative property, and is fraught with no evil to your worthy parent; so lay aside the fire–arms and listen to the admonitions of reason. I declare it vicious——null——abrogated. As for thee, Nelly, my feelings towards thee are kind, and not at all given to hostility; therefore listen to that which I have to utter, nor turn away thine ears in the wantonness of security. Thou knowest the character of the man with whom thou dwellest, young woman, and thou also knowest the danger of being found in evil company. Abandon, then, the trifling advantages of thy situation, and yield the rock peaceably to the will of those who accompany me——a legion, young woman——I do assure you an invincible and powerful legion. Give, therefore, the effects of this lawless and wicked squatter———nay, children, such disregard of human life, is literally destroying the pleasures of all amicable intercourse! Point those dangerous weapons aside, I entreat of you; more for your own sakes, than for mine. Hetty, hast thou forgotten who appeased thine anguish, when thy auricular nerves were tortured by the colds and damps of the naked earth! and thou, Phœbe, ungrateful and forgetful Phœbe, but for this very arm, which you would prostrate with an endless paralysis, thy incisores would still be giving thee pain and sorrow! Lay, then, aside thy weapons, and hearken to the advice of one who has always been thy friend. And now, young woman," still keeping a jealous eye on the musket which the girls had suffered to be diverted a little from their aim. "And now, young woman, for the last, and therefore the most solemn asking: I demand of thee the surrender of this rock, without delay orresistance, in the joint names of power, of justice and of the———" law, he would have added; but recollecting that this ominous word would again provoke the hostility of the squatter's children, he succeeded in swallowing it in good season, and concluded with the less dangerous and more convertible term of "reason."

This extraordinary summons, failed however, of producing the desired effect. It proved utterly unintelligible to his younger listeners, with the exception of the few offensive terms, already sufficiently distinguished, and though Ellen better comprehended the meaning of the herald, she appeared as little moved by his rhetoric as her companions. At those passages which he intended should be tender and affecting, the intelligent girl, though tortured by painfully contending feelings, had even manifested a disposition to laugh, while to the threats she turned an utterly insensible ear.

"I know not the meaning of all you wish to say, Dr. Battius," she quietly replied, when he had ended, "but I am sure if it would teach me to betray my trust, it is what I ought not to hear. I caution you to attempt no violence, for let my wishes be what they may, you see I am surrounded by a force that can easily put me down, and you know, or ought to know, too well the temper of this family, to trifle in such a matter with any of its members, let them be of what sex or age they may."

"I am not entirely ignorant of human character," returned the naturalist, prudently receding a little from the position, which he had, until now, stoutly maintained at the very base of the hill. "But here comes one who may know its secret windings still better than I."

"Ellen! Ellen Wade," cried Paul Hover, who had advanced to his elbow, without betraying any of that sensitiveness on the subject of danger, which had so manifestly discomposed the Doctor; "I didn't expect to find an enemy in you!"

"Nor shall you, when you ask that, which I can grant without treachery and disgrace. You know that my uncle has trusted his family to my care, and shall I so far betray the trust as to let in his bitterest enemies to murder his children, perhaps, and to rob him of the little which the Indians have left?"

"Am I a murderer——is this old man——this officer of the States," pointing to the trapper and his newly discovered friend, both of whom by this time stood at his side, "is either of these likely to do the things you name?"

"What is it then you ask of me?" said Ellen, wringing her hands, in the pain of excessive doubt.

"The beast! nothing more nor less than the squatter's hidden, ravenous, dangerous beast!"

"Excellent young woman," commenced the young stranger, who had so lately joined himself to the party on the prairie——but his mouth was immediately stopped by a significant sign from the trapper, who whispered in his private ear——

"Let the lad be our spokesman. Natur' will work in the bosom of the child, and we shall gain our object all in good time."

"The whole truth is out, Ellen," Paul continued, "and we have lined the squatter into his most secret misdoings. We have come to right the wronged and to free the imprisoned; now, if you are the girl of a true heart, as I have always believed, so far from throwing straws in our way, you will join in the general swarming, and leave old Ishmael and his hive to the bees of his own breed."

"I have sworn a solemn oath——"

"A compactum which is entered into through ignorance, or in duresse, is null in the sight of all good moralists,' cried the Doctor.

"Hush, hush," again the trapper whispered, "leave it all to natur' and the lad!"

"I have sworn in the sight and by the name of Him who is the founder and ruler of all that is good, whether it be in morals or in religion," the agitated Ellen continued, "neither to reveal the contents of that tent, nor to help its prisoner to escape. We are both solemnly, terribly sworn; our lives perhaps have been the gift we received for the promises. It is true you are masters of the secret, but not through any means of ours; nor do I know that I can justify myself, for even being neutral, while you attempt to invade the dwelling of my uncle in such a hostile manner."

"I can prove beyond the power of refutation," the naturalist eagerly exclaimed, "by Paley, Berkeley, ay, even by the immortal Binkerschoek, that a compactum, concluded while one of the parties, be it a state or be it an individual, is in durance——"

"You will ruffle the temper of the child, with such abusive language," said the cautious trapper, "while the lad, if left to human feelings, will bring her down to the meekness of a playful fawn. Ah! you are like myself, little knowing in the natur' of these sorts of hidden kindnesses!"

"Is this the only vow you have taken, Ellen!" Paul continued in a tone which, for the gay, light–hearted bee–hunter, sounded dolorous and reproachful. "Have you sworn only to this! are the words which the squatter says, to be as honey in your mouth, and all other promises like so much useless comb."

The paleness, which had taken possession of the usually cheerful countenance of Ellen, was hid in a bright glow, that was plainly visible even at the distance at which she stood. She hesitated a moment, as if struggling to repress something very like resentment, before she answered with all her native spirit——

"I know not what right any one has to question me about oaths and promises, which can only concern her who has made them, if indeed any of the sort you mention, have ever been made, at all. I shall hold no further discourse with one who thinks so much of himself, and takes advice merely of his own feelings."

"Now, old trapper, do you hear that!" said the unsophisticated bee–hunter, turning abruptly to his aged friend. "The meanest insect that skims the heavens, when it has got its load, flies straight and honestly to its nest or hive, according to its kind; but the ways of a woman's mind, are as knotty as a gnarled oak, and more crooked than the windings of the Mississippi!"

"Nay, nay child," said the trapper, good–naturedly interfering in behalf of the offending Paul, "you are to consider that youth is hasty and not overgiven to thought. But then a promise is a promise, and not to be thrown aside and forgotten, like the hoofs and horns of a buffaloe."

"I thank you for reminding me of my oath," said the still resentful Ellen, biting her pretty nether lip with vexation; "I might else have proved forgetful!"

"Ah! female natur' is awakened in her," said the old man, shaking his head in a manner to show how much he was disappointed in the result, "but it manifests itself against the true spirit!"

"Ellen!" cried the young stranger, who until now, had been an attentive listener to the parley, "since Ellen is the name by which you are known——"

"They often add to it another. I am sometimes called by the name of my father."

"Call her Nelly Wade at once," muttered Paul; "it is her rightful name, and I care not if she keeps it for ever!"

"Wade, I should have added," continued the youth. "You will acknowledge that though bound by no oath myself, I at least have known how to respect those of others. You are a witness yourself that I have foreborne to utter a single call, while I am certain it could reach those ears it would gladden so much. Permit me then to ascend the rock, singly; I promise a perfect indemnity to your kinsman, against any injury his effects may sustain."

Ellen seemed to hesitate, but catching a glimpse of Paul, who stood leaning proudly on his rifle, whistling, with an appearance of the utmost indifference the air of a boating song, she recovered her recollection in time to answer:

"I have been left the captain of the rock, while my uncle and his sons hunt, and captain will I remain, till he returns to receive back the charge."

"This is wasting moments that will not soon return, and neglecting an opportunity that may never occur again," the young soldier gravely remarked.

"The sun is beginning to fall already, and many minutes cannot elapse before the squatter and his savage brood will be returning to their huts."

Doctor Battius cast an anxious glance behind him, and took up the discourse by saying——

"Perfection is always found in maturity, whether it be in the animal or the intellectual world. Reflection is the mother of wisdom, and wisdom the parent of success. I propose that we retire to a discreet distance from this impregnable position, and there hold a convocation or council to deliberate on what manner we may sit down regularly before the place, or perhaps by postponing the siege to another season gain the aid of auxiliaries from the inhabited countries, and thus secure the dignity of the laws from any danger of a repulse."

"A storm would be better," the soldier smilingly answered, measuring the height and scanning all its difficulties with a deliberate eye; "'twould be but a broken arm or a bruised head at the most."

"Then have at it!" shouted the impetuous bee-hunter, making a spring that at once put him out of danger from a shot, by carrying him beneath the projecting ledge on which the garrison was posted; "now do your worst, young devils of a wicked breed; you have but a moment to work all your mischief in!"

"Paul! rash Paul!" shrieked Ellen, "another step and the rocks will crush you! they hang but by a thread, and these girls are ready and willing to let them fall!"

"Then drive the accursed swarm from the hive, for scale the rock I will, though I find it covered with hornets."

"Let her if she dare!" tauntingly cried the eldest of the girls, brandishing a musket with a mien and resolution that would have done credit to her Amazonian dam——"I know you, Nelly Wade; you are with the lawyers in your heart, and if you come a foot nigher, you shall have frontier punishment. Put in another pry, girls; in with it. I should like to see the man of them all that dare come up into the camp of Ishmael Bush, without asking leave of his children!"

"Stir not, Paul, for your life keep beneath the rock!"——

Ellen was interrupted by the same bright vision, which on the preceding day had stayed another scarcely less portentous tumult, by exhibiting itself on the same giddy height where it was now seen.

"In the name of Him, who commandeth all, I implore you to pause——both you, who so madly incur the risk, and you, who so rashly offer to take that which you never can return!" said a sweet, imploring voice, in a slightly foreign accent, that instantly drew all eyes upward.

"Inez, Inez!" cried the officer, "do I again see you! mine shall you now be, though a million devils were posted on this rock. Push up, my brave woods man, and give room for another!"

The sudden appearance of the figure from the tent had created a momentary stupor among the defendants of the rock, which might, with suitable forbearance have been happily improved; but startled by the voice of Middleton, the surprised Phœbe discharged her musket at the female, scarcely knowing whether she aimed at the life of a mortal or at some being which belonged to another world. Ellen uttered a cry of horror, and then sprang after her alarmed or wounded friend, she knew not which, into the tent.

During this moment of dangerous bye–play, the sounds of a serious attack were very distinctly audible beneath. Paul had profited by the commotion over his head to change his place so far as to make room for Middleton. The latter had been followed by the naturalist, who, in a state of mental aberration produced by the report of the musket, had instinctively rushed towards the rocks for a cover. The trapper remained where he was last seen, an unmoved but close observer of these several proceedings. Though averse to enter into actual hostilities, the old man was, however, far from being useless. Favoured by his position, he was enabled to apprise his friends beneath of the movements of those who plotted their destruction above, and to advise and control their advance accordingly.

In the mean time the children of Esther were true to the spirit they had inherited from their redoubtable mother. The instant they found themselves delivered from the presence of Ellen and her unknown companion, they bestowed an undivided attention on their more masculine and certainly more dangerous assailants, who by this time had made a completelodgment among the crags of the citadel. The repeated summons to surrender, which Paul uttered in a voice that he intended should strike terror to their young bosoms, were as little heeded as were the calls of the trapper to abandon a resistance, which might prove fatal to some among them without offering the smallest probability of eventual success. Encouraging each other to persevere, they poised the fragments of rocks, prepared the lighter missiles for immediate service, and thrust forward the barrels of the muskets with a business–like air, and a coolness that would have done credit to men long practised in the dangers of warfare.

"Keep under the ledge," said the trapper, pointing out to Paul the manner in which he should proceed; "keep in your foot more, lad——ah! you see the warning was not amiss! had the stone struck it, the bees would miss their companion for many a month. Now, namesake of my friend; Uncas, in name and spirit! now, if you have the activity of Le Cerf Agile, now you may make a far leap to the right, and gain good twenty feet of height, without danger. Beware the bush——beware the bush! 'twill prove a treacherous hold! Ah! he has done it; safely and bravely has he done it! Your turn comes next, friend, that follows the fruits of natur'. Push you to the left, and you will divide the attention of the children. Nay, girls, fire——my old ears are used to the whistling of lead; and little reason have I to prove a doe–heart with fourscore years on my back." He shook his head with a melancholy smile, but without flinching in a muscle, as the bullet which the exasperated Hetty fired, passed innocently at no great distance from the spot where he stood. "It is safer keeping in your track than dodging when a weak finger pulls the trigger," he continued; "but it is a solemn sight to witness how much human natur' is inclined to evil, in one so young! Well done, myman of beasts and plants! Another such leap, and you may laugh at all the squatter's bars and walls. The Doctor has got his temper up! I see it in his eye, and something good will now come of him! Keep closer, man——keep closer."

The trapper, though he was not deceived as to the state of Dr. Battius' mind, was, however, greatly in error as to the exciting cause. While imitating the movements of his companions and toiling his way upward, with the utmost caution, and not without great inward tribulation of spirit, the eye of the naturalist had caught a glimpse of an unknown plant, a few yards above his head, and in a situation more than commonly exposed to the missiles which the girls were unceasingly hurling in the direction of the assailants. Forgetting, in an instant, every thing but the glory of being the first to give this jewel to the catalogues of science, he sprang upward at the prize, with the avidity with which the sparrow darts upon the butterfly. The rocks, which instantly came thundering down, announced that he was seen, and for a moment, as his form was concealed in the cloud of dust and fragments which followed the furious descent, the trapper gave him up for lost; but the next instant he was seen safely seated in a cavity, formed by some of the projecting stones which had yielded to the shock, holding triumphantly in his hand the captured stem, which he was already devouring with delighted, and certainly not unskilful eyes. Paul profited by the opportunity. Turning his course with the quickness of thought, he also sprang to the post which Obed thus securely occupied, and unceremoniously making a footstool of his shoulder as the latter stooped over his treasure, he bounded through the breach left by the fallen rock, and gained the level. He was followed by Middleton, who joined him in seizing and disarming the girls. In this manner a bloodless and complete victory was obtained over that citadel which Ishmael had vainly flattered himself might prove impregnable, for the short period of his absence.

CHAPTER XV.

"So smile the heavens upon this holy act,

That after–hours with sorrow chide us not!"

—— Shakspeare

It is proper that the course of the narrative should be stayed, while we revert to those causes, which have brought in their train of consequences, the singular contest just related. The interruption must necessarily be as brief as we hope it may prove satisfactory to that class of readers, who require that no gap should be left by those who assume the office of historians, for their own fertile imaginations to fill.

Among the troops sent by the government of the Confederacy to take possession of its newly acquired territory in the west, was a detachment led by the young soldier who has become so busy an actor in the scenes of our legend. The mild and indolent descendants of the ancient colonists received their new compatriots without distrust, well knowing that the transfer raised them from the condition of subjects, to the more enviable distinction of citizens in a government of laws. The new rulers exercised their functions with discretion and wielded their delegated authority without offence. In such a novel intermixture, however, of men born and nurtured in freedom, and the compliant minions of absolute power, the catholic and the protestant, the active and the indolent, some little time was necessary to blend the discrepant elements of society. In attaining so desirable an end, woman was made to perform her accustomed and grateful office. The barriers of prejudiceand religion were broken through by the irresistible power of the master–passion, and family unions ere long began to cement the political tie which had made a forced conjunction between people so opposite in their habits, their educations, and their opinions.

Middleton was among the first, of the new possessors of the soil, who became captive to the charms of a Louisianian lady. In the immediate vicinity of the post he had been directed to occupy, dwelt the chief of one of those ancient colonial families, which had been content to slumber for ages amid the ease, indolence and wealth of the Spanish provinces. He was an officer of the crown, and had been induced to remove from the Floridas, among the French of the adjoining province, by a rich succession of which he had become the inheritor. The name of Don Augustin de Certavallos was scarcely known beyond the limits of the little town in which he resided, though he found a secret pleasure himself in pointing it out, in large scrolls of musty documents, to an only child, as enrolled among the former heroes and grandees of old and of new Spain. This fact, so important to himself and of so little moment to any body else, was the principal reason, that while his more vivacious Gallic neighbours were not slow to open a frank communion with their visiters, he chose to keep aloof, seemingly content with the society of his daughter, who was a girl just emerging from the condition of childhood into that of a woman.

The curiosity of the youthful Inez, however, was not so entirely inactive. She had not heard the martial music of the garrison, melting on the evening air, nor seen the strange banner, which fluttered over the heights that rose at no great distance from her father's extensive grounds, without experiencing some of those secret impulses which are thought to distinguish her sex. Natural timidity, and that retiring andperhaps peculiar lassitude, which forms the very groundwork of female fascination in the tropical provinces of Spain, held her in their seemingly indissoluble bonds; and it is more than probable, that had not an accident occurred in which Middleton was of some personal service to her father, so long a time would have elapsed before they met, that another direction might have been given to the wishes of one who was just of an age to be alive to all the power of youth and beauty.

Providence——or if that imposing word is too just to be classical, fate——had otherwise decreed. The haughty and reserved Don Augustin was by far too observant of the forms of that station on which he so much valued himself, to forget the duties of a gentleman. Gratitude, for the kindness of Middleton, induced him to open his doors to the officers of the garrison, and to admit of a guarded but polite intercourse. Reserve gradually gave way before the propriety and candour of their spirited young leader, and it was not long ere the affluent planter rejoiced as much as his daughter, whenever the well known signal at the gate announced one of these agreeable visits from the commander of the post.

It is unnecessary to dwell on the impression which the charms of Inez produced on the soldier, or to delay the tale in order to write a wire–drawn account of the progressive influence that elegance of deportment, manly beauty, and undivided assiduity and intelligence were likely to produce on the sensitive mind of a romantic, warm–hearted, and secluded girl of sixteen. It is sufficient for our purpose to say that they loved, that the youth was not backward to declare his feelings, that he prevailed with some facility over the scruples of the maiden, and with no little difficulty over the objections of her father, and that before the province of Louisiana had been sixmonths in the possession of the States, the officer of the latter was the affianced husband of the richest heiress on the banks of the Mississippi.

Although we have presumed the reader to be acquainted with the manner in which such results are commonly attained, it is not to be supposed that the triumph of Middleton either over the prejudices of the father or of those of the daughter was achieved entirely without difficulty. Religion formed a stubborn and nearly irremoveable obstacle with both. The devoted young man patiently submitted to a formidable essay, which father Ignatius was deputed to make in order to convert him to the true faith. The effort on the part of the worthy priest was systematic, vigorous, and long sustained. A dozen times (it was at those moments when glimpses of the light, sylphlike form of Inez flitted like some fairy being past the scene of their conferences) the good father fancied he was on the eve of a glorious triumph over infidelity; but all his hopes were frustrated by some unlooked–for opposition on the part of the subject of his pious labours. So long as the assault on his faith was distant and feeble, Middleton, who was no great proficient in polemics, submitted to its effects with the patience and humility of a martyr; but the moment the good father, who felt such concern in his future happiness, was tempted to improve his vantage ground by calling in the aid of some of the peculiar subtilties of his own creed, the young man was too good a soldier not to make head against the hot attack. He came to the contest, it is true, with no weapons more formidable than common sense, and some little knowledge of the habits of his country as contrasted with that of his adversary; but with these homebred implements he never failed to repulse the father with something of the power with which a nervous cudgel−player would deal with a skilful masterof the rapier, setting at nought his passados by the direct and unanswerable arguments of a broken head and a shivered weapon.

Before the controversy was terminated, an inroad of Protestants had come to aid the soldier. The reckless freedom of such among them, as thought only of this life, and the consistent and tempered piety of others, caused the honest priest to look about him, in concern. The influence of example on one hand, and the contamination of too free an intercourse on the other, began to manifest themselves, even in that portion of his own flock, which he had supposed to be too thoroughly folded in spiritual government ever to stray. It was time to turn his thoughts from the offensive, and to prepare his followers to resist the lawless deluge of opinion which threatened to break down the barriers of their faith. Like a wise commander, who finds he has occupied too much ground for the amount of his force, he began to curtail his outworks. The relics were concealed from profane eyes; his people were admonished not to speak of miracles before a race that not only denied their existence, but who had even the desperate hardihood to challenge their proofs, and even the bible itself was once more prohibited, with terrible denunciations, for the triumphant reason that it was liable to be misinterpreted.

In the mean time it became necessary to report to Don Augustin the effects his arguments and prayers had produced on the heretical disposition of the young soldier. No man is prone to confess his weakness at the very moment when circumstances demand the utmost efforts of his strength. By a species of pious fraud, for which no doubt the worthy priest found his absolution in the purity of his motives, he declared that, while no positive change was actually wrought in the mind of Middleton, there was every reason to hope the entering wedge of argument hadbeen driven to its head, and that in consequence an opening was left, through which, it might rationally be hoped, the blessed seeds of a religious fructification would find their way, especially if the subject was left uninterruptedly to enjoy the advantage of Catholic communion.

Don Augustin himself was now seized with the desire of proselyting. Even the soft and amiable Inez thought it would be a glorious consummation of her wishes to be a humble instrument of bringing her lover into the bosom of the true church. The offers of Middleton were promptly accepted, and, while the father looked forward impatiently to the day assigned for the nuptials, as to the pledge of his own success, the daughter thought of it with feelings in which the holy emotions of her faith were blended with the softer sensations of her years and situation.

The sun rose the morning of her nuptials on a day so bright and cloudless, that the sensitive Inez hailed it as a harbinger of her future happiness. Father Ignatius performed the offices of the church, in a little chapel that was attached to the estate of Don Augustin, and long ere the sun had begun to fall, Middleton pressed the blushing and timid young Creole to his bosom, as his acknowledged and unalienable wife. It had pleased the parties to pass the day of the wedding in retirement, dedicating it solely to the best and purest affections, aloof from all the noisy and ordinarily heartless rejoicings of a compelled festivity.

Middleton was returning through the grounds of Don Augustin from a visit of duty to his encampment, at that hour in which the light of the sun begins to melt into the shadows of evening, when a glimpse of a robe, similar to that in which Inez had accompanied him to the altar, caught his eye through the foliage of a retired arbour. He approached thespot with a delicacy that was rather increased than diminished by the claim she had perhaps given him to intrude on her private moments; but the sounds of her soft voice, which was offering up prayers, in which he heard himself named by the dearest of all appellations, overcame his scruples, and induced him to take a position where he might listen without the fear of detection. It was certainly grateful to the feelings of a husband to be able in this manner to lay bare the spotless soul of his wife, and to find that his own image lay enshrined amid its purest and holiest aspirations. His self−esteem was too much flattered not to induce him to overlook the immediate object of the petitioner. While she prayed that she might become the humble instrument of bringing him into the flock of the faithful, she petitioned for forgiveness on her own behalf, if presumption or indifference to the counsel of the church had caused her to set too high a value on her influence, and led her into the dangerous error of hazarding her own soul by espousing a heretic. There was so much of fervent piety, mingled with so strong a burst of natural feeling, so much of the woman blended with the angel in her prayers, that Middleton could have forgiven her, had she termed him a Pagan, for the sweetness and interest with which she petitioned in his favour.

The young man waited until his bride arose from her knees, and then he joined her as though entirely ignorant of what had just occurred.

"It is getting late, my Inez," he said, "and Don Augustin would be apt to reproach you with inattention to your health in being abroad at such an hour. What then am I to do, who am charged with all his authority, and twice his love?"

"Be like him in every thing," she answered, looking up in his face with tears in her eyes, and speaking with a marked emphasis; "in every thing. Imitatemy father, Middleton, and I can ask no more of you."

"Nor for me, Inez? I doubt not that I should be all you can wish, were I to become as good as the worthy and respectable Don Augustin. But you are to make some allowances for the infirmities and habits of a soldier. Now let us go and join this excellent father."

"Not yet," said his bride, gently extricating herself from the arm, that he had thrown around her slight form, while he urged her from the place. "I have still another duty to perform, before I can submit so implicitly to your orders, soldier though you are. I promised the worthy Inesella my faithful nurse, she who, as you heard, has so long been a mother to me, Middleton——I promised her a visit at this hour. It is the last, as she thinks, that she can receive from her own child, and I cannot disappoint her. Go you then to Don Augustin, and in one short hour I will rejoin you.

"Remember it is but an hour!"

"One hour," repeated Inez, as she kissed her hand to him; and then blushing, as if ashamed at her own boldness, she darted from the arbour, and was seen for an instant gliding towards the cottage of her nurse, in which at the next moment she disappeared.

Middleton returned slowly and thoughtfully to the house, often bending his eyes in the direction in which he had last seen his wife, as if he would fain trace her lovely form, in the gloom of the evening, still floating through the vacant space. Don Augustin received him with warmth, and for many minutes his mind was amused by relating to his new kinsman plans for the future. The exclusive old Spaniard listened to his glowing but true account of the prosperity and happiness of those States, of which he had been an ignorant neighbour half his life, partly in wonder, and partly with that sort of incredulity with which one attends to what he fancies are the exaggerated descriptions of a too partial friendship.

In this manner the hour for which Inez had conditioned passed away, much sooner than her husband could have thought possible in her absence. At length his looks began to wander to the clock, and then the minutes were counted, as one rolled by after another, and Inez did not yet appear. The hand had already made half of another circuit around the face of the dial, when Middleton arose and announced his determination to go and offer himself as an escort to the absentee. He found the night dark, and the heavens charged with the threatening vapour, which in that climate was the infallible forerunner of a gust. Stimulated no less by the unpropitious aspect of the skies, than by his secret uneasiness, he quickened his pace, making long and rapid strides in the direction of the cottage of Inesella. Twenty times he stopped, fancying that he caught glimpses of the fairy form of Inez, tripping across the grounds on her return to the mansion–house, and as often he was obliged to resume his course in disappointment. He reached the gate of the cottage, knocked, opened the door, entered, and even stood in the presence of the aged nurse without meeting the person of her whom he sought. She had already left the place on her return to her father's house. Believing that he must have passed her in the darkness, Middleton retraced his steps to meet with another disappointment. Inez had not been seen. Without communicating his intention to any one, the bridegroom proceeded with a palpitating heart to the little sequestered arbour, where he had overheard his bride offering up those petitions for his happiness and conversion. Here, too, he was disappointed; and then all was afloat, in the painful incertitude of doubt and conjecture.

For many hours a secret distrust of the motives of his wife caused Middleton to proceed in the search with delicacy and caution. But as day dawned without restoring her to the arms of her father or her husband, reserve was thrown aside, and her unaccountable absence was loudly proclaimed. The inquiries after the lost Inez were now direct and open; but they proved equally fruitless. No one had seen her or heard of her from the moment that she left the cottage of her nurse.

Day succeeded day, and still no tidings rewarded the search that was immediately instituted, until she was finally given over, by most of her relations and friends, as irretrievably lost.

An event of so extraordinary a character was not likely to be soon forgotten. It excited speculation, gave rise to an infinity of rumours, and not a few inventions. The prevalent opinion, among such of those emigrants who were overrunning the country, as had time in the multitude of their employments to think of any foreign concerns, was the simple and direct conclusion that the absent bride was no more nor less than a felo de se. Father Ignatius had many doubts and much secret compunction of conscience, but like a wise chief he endeavoured to turn the sad event to some account in the impending warfare of faith. Changing his battery, he whispered in the ears of a few of his oldest parishioners, that he had been deceived in the state of Middleton's mind, which he was now compelled to believe was completely stranded on the quicksands of heresy. He began to shew his relics again, and was even heard to allude once more to the delicate and nearly forgotten subject of modern miracles. In consequence of these demonstrations on the part of the venerable priest, it came to be whispered among the faithful, and finally it was adopted, as part ofthe parish creed, that Inez had been translated to heaven.

Don Augustin had all the feelings of a father, but they were smothered in the lassitude of a Creole. Like his spiritual governor he began to think that they had been wrong in consigning one so pure, so young, so lovely, and above all so pious, to the arms of a heretic, and he was fain to believe that the calamity, which had befallen his age, was a judgment on his presumption and want of adherence to established forms. It is true, that as the whispers of the congregation came to his ears, he found present consolation in their belief, but then nature was too powerful, and had too strong a hold of the old man's heart, not to give rise to the rebellious thought that the succession of his daughter to the heavenly inheritance was a little premature.

But Middleton, the lover, the husband, the bride-groom——Middleton was nearly crushed by the weight of the unexpected and terrible blow. Educated himself under the dominion of a simple and rational faith, in which nothing is attempted to be concealed from the believers, he could have no other apprehensions for the fate of Inez than such as grew out of his knowledge of the superstitious opinions she entertained of his own church. It is needless to dwell on the mental tortures that he endured, or all the various surmises, hopes and disappointments, that he was fated to experience in the first few weeks of his misery. A jealous distrust of the motives of Inez, and a secret, lingering hope that he should yet find her, had tempered his inquiries, without however causing him to abandon them entirely. But time was beginning to deprive him, even of the mortifying reflection that he was intentionally, though perhaps temporarily, deserted, and he was gradually yielding to the more painful conviction that she was dead,when his hopes were suddenly revived in a new and singular manner.

The young commander was slowly and sorrowfully returning from an evening parade of his troops, to his own quarters, which stood at some little distance from the place of the encampment, and on the same high bluff of land, when his vacant eyes fell on the figure of a man, who by the regulations of the place, was not entitled to be there at that forbidden hour. The stranger was meanly dressed, with every appearance about his person and countenance of squalid poverty and of the most dissolute habits. Sorrow had softened the military pride of Middleton, and, as he passed the crouching form of the intruder, he said, in tones of great mildness, or rather of kindness——

"You will be given a night in the guard–house, friend, should the patrole find you here——there is a dollar——go, and get a better place to sleep in, and something to eat!"

"I swallow all my food, captain, without chewing;" returned the vagabond, with the low exultation of an accomplished villain, as he eagerly seized the silver. "Make this Mexican twenty, and I will sell you a secret."

"Go, go," said the other with a little of a soldier's severity, returning to his manner. "Go, before I order the guard to seize you."

"Well, go it is then——but if I do go, captain, I shall take my knowledge with me; and then you may live a widower bewitched till the tattoo of life is beat off."

"What mean you, fellow?" exclaimed Middleton, turning quickly towards the wretch, who was already dragging his diseased limbs from the place.

"I mean to have the value of this dollar in Spanish brandy, and then come back and sell you my secret for enough to buy a barrel."

"If you have any thing to say, speak now;" continued Middleton, restraining with difficulty the impatience that urged him to betray his feelings.

"I am a–dry, and I can never talk with elegance when my throat is husky, captain. How much will you give to know what I can tell you; let it be something handsome; such as one gentleman can offer to another."

"I believe it would be better justice to order the drummer to pay you a visit, fellow. To what does your boasted secret relate?"

"Matrimony; a wife and no wife; a pretty face and a rich bride; do I speak plain now, captain?"

"If you know any thing relating to my wife, say it at once; you need not fear for your reward."

"Ay, captain, I have drove many a bargain in my time, and sometimes I have been paid in money, and sometimes I have been paid in promises: now the last are what I call pinching food."

"Name your price."

"Twenty——No, damn it, it's worth thirty dollars, if it's worth a cent."

"Here, then, is your money; but remember, if you tell me nothing worth knowing, I have a force that can easily deprive you of it again, and punish your insolence in the bargain."

The fellow examined the bank–bills he received with a jealous eye, and then pocketed them, apparently well satisfied of their being genuine.

"I like a northern note," he said very coolly; "they have a character to lose like myself. No fear of me, captain; I am a man of honour, and I shall not tell you a word more, nor a word less than I know of my own knowledge to be true."

"Proceed then without further delay, or I may repent and order you to be deprived of all your gains; the silver as well as the notes."

"Honour, if you die for it!" returned the miscreant, holding up a hand in affected horror at so treacherous a threat. "Well, captain, you must know that gentlemen don't all live by the same calling; some keep what they've got, and some get what they can."

"You have been a thief."

"I scorn the word. I have been a humanity hunter. Do you know what that means? Ay, it has many interpretations. Some people think the woolly-heads are miserable, working on hot plantations under a broiling sun——and all such sorts of inconveniences. Well, captain, I have been, in my time, a man who has been willing to give them the pleasures of variety, at least, by changing the scene for them. You understand me?"

"You are, in plain language, a kidnapper."

"Have been, my worthy captain——have been; but just now a little reduced, like a merchant who leaves off selling tobacco by the hogshead, to deal in it by the yard. I have been a soldier, too, in my day. What is said to be the great secret of our trade, now can you tell me that?"

"I know not," said Middleton, beginning to tire of the fellow's trifling; "courage?"

"No, legs——legs to fight with, and legs to run away with——and therein you see my two callings agreed. My legs are none of the best just now, and without legs a kidnapper would carry on a losing trade; but then there are men enough left, better provided than I am."

"Stolen!" groaned the horror-struck husband.

"On her travels, as sure as you are standing still!"

"Villain, what reason have you for believing a thing so shocking?"

"Hands off——hands off——do you think my tongue can do its work the better for a little squeezing ofthe throat! Have patience, and you shall know it all; but if you treat me so ungenteelly again, I shall be obliged to call in the assistance of the lawyers."

"Say on; but if you utter a single word more or less than the truth, expect my instant vengeance!"

"Are you fool enough to believe what such a scoundrel as I am tells you, captain, unless it has probability to back it? No, I know you are not: Therefore I will give my facts and my opinions, and then leave you to chew on them, while I go and drink of your generosity. I know a man who is called Abiram White.——I believe the knave took that name to shew his enmity to the race of blacks! But this gentleman is now, and has been for years, to my certain knowledge, a regular translator of the human body from one State to another.——I have dealt with him in my time, and a cheating dog he is! No more honour in him than meat in my stomach.——I saw him here in this very town, the day of your wedding. He was in company with his wife's brother, and pretended to be a settler on the hunt for new land. A noble set they were, to carry on business——seven sons, each of them as tall as your sergeant with his cap on. Well, the moment I heard that your wife was lost, I saw at once that Abiram had laid his hands on her."

"Do you know this——can this be true? What reason have you to fancy a thing so wild?"

"Reason enough; I know Abiram White. Now, will you add a trifle just to keep my throat from parching?"

"Go, go; you are stupified with drink already, miserable man, and know not what you say. Go; go, and beware the drummer."

"Experience is a good guide"——The fellow called after the retiring Middleton, and then turning with a chuckling laugh, like one well satisfied with himself, he made the best of his way towards the shop of the suttler.

A hundred times in the course of that night did Middleton fancy that the communication of the miscreant was entitled to some attention, and as often did he reject the idea as too wild and visionary for another thought. He was awakened early on the following morning, after passing a restless and nearly sleepless night, by his orderly, who came to report that a man was found dead on the parade, at no great distance from his quarters. Throwing on his clothes he proceeded to the spot, and beheld the individual, with whom he had held the preceding conference, in the precise situation in which he had first been found.

The miserable wretch had fallen a victim to his intemperance. This revolting fact was sufficiently proclaimed by his obtruding eye-balls, his bloated countenance, and the nearly insufferable odours that were even then exhaling from his carcass. Disgusted with the odious spectacle, the youth was turning from the sight, after ordering the corpse to be removed, when the position of one of the dead man's hands struck him. On examination, he found the fore-finger extended, as if in the act of writing in the sand, with the following incomplete sentence, nearly illegible, but yet in a state to be deciphered: "Captain, it is true, as I am a gentle——" He had either died, or fallen into a sleep which was the forerunner of his death, before the latter word was finished.

Concealing this fact from the others, Middleton repeated his orders and departed. The pertinacity of the deceased, and all the circumstances united, induced him to set on foot some secret inquiries. He found that a family, answering the description which had been given him, had in fact passed the place the very day of his nuptials: They were traced along the margin of the Mississippi for some distance, until they took boat and ascended the river to its confluence with the Missouri. Here they had disappeared, like hundreds of others, in pursuit of the hidden wealth of the interior.

Furnished with these facts, Middleton detailed a small guard of his most trusty men, took leave of Don Augustin, without declaring his hopes or his fears, and having arrived at the indicated point, he pushed into the wilderness in pursuit. It was not difficult to trace a train like that of Ishmael until he was well assured its object lay far beyond the usual limits of the settlements. This circumstance in itself quickened his suspicions, and gave additional force to his hopes of final success.

After getting beyond the assistance of verbal directions, the anxious husband had recourse to the usual signs of a trail, in order to follow the fugitives. This he also found a task of no difficulty until he reached the hard and unyielding soil of the rolling prairies. Here, indeed, he was completely at fault. He found himself, at length, compelled to separate his followers, appointing a place of rendezvous at a distant day, and to endeavour to find the lost trail by multiplying, as much as possible, the number of his eyes. He had been alone a week, when accident brought him in contact with the trapper and the bee-hunter. Part of their interview has been related, and the reader can readily imagine the explanations that succeeded the tale he recounted, and which led, as has already been seen, to the recovery of his bride.

CHAPTER XVI.

"These likelihoods confirm her flight from hence,

Therefore, I pray you, stay not to discourse,

But mount you presently;——"

—— Shakspeare

An hour had slid by, in hasty and nearly incoherent questions and answers, before Middleton, hanging over his recovered treasure with that sort of jealous watchfulness with which a miser would regard his hoards, closed the disjointed narrative of his own proceedings by demanding——

"And you, my Inez; in what manner were you treated?"

"In every thing, but the great injustice they did in separating me so forcibly from my friends, as well perhaps as the circumstances of my captors would allow. I think the man, who is certainly the master here, is but a new beginner in wickedness. He quarrelled frightfully in my presence, with the wretch who seized me, and then they made an impious bargain, to which I was compelled to acquiesce, and to which they bound me as well as themselves by oaths. Ah! Middleton, I fear the heretics are not so heedful of their vows as we who are nurtured in the bosom of the true church!"

"Believe it not; these villains are of no religion; did they forswear themselves?"

"No, not perjured: but was it not awful to call upon the good God to witness so sinful a compact?"

"And so we think, Inez, as truly as the most virtuous cardinal of Rome. But how did they observe their oath, and what was its purport?"

"They conditioned to leave me unmolested, and free from their odious presence, provided I would give a pledge to make no effort to escape; and that I would not even shew myself,

170

until a time that my masters saw fit to name."

"And that time?" demanded the impatient Middleton, who so well knew the religious scruples of his wife——"That time?"

"It is already passed. I was sworn by my patron saint, and faithfully did I keep the vow, until the man they call Ishmael forgot the terms by offering violence. I then made my appearance on the rock, for the time too was passed; though I even think father Ignatius would have absolved me from the vow, on account of the treachery of my keepers."

"If he had not," muttered the youth between his compressed teeth, "I would have absolved him forever from his spiritual care of your conscience!"

"You, Middleton!" returned his wife looking up into his flushed face, while a bright blush suffused her own sweet countenance; "you may receive my vows, but surely you can have no power to absolve me from their observance!"

"No, no, no. Inez, you are right. I know but little of these conscientious subtilties, and I am any thing but a priest: yet tell me, what has induced these monsters to play this desperate game——to trifle thus with my happiness?"

"You know my ignorance of the world, and how ill I am qualified to furnish reasons for the conduct of beings so different from any I have ever seen before. But does not love of money drive men to acts even worse than this? I believe they thought that an aged and wealthy father could be tempted to pay them a rich ransom for his child; and, perhaps," she added, stealing an inquiring glance, through her tears, at the attentive Middleton, "they counted something on the fresh affections of a bridegroom."

"They might have extracted the blood from my heart, drop by drop!"

"Yes," resumed his young and timid wife, instantlywithdrawing the stolen look she had hazarded, and hurriedly pursuing the train of the discourse, as if glad to make him forget the liberty she had just taken, "I have been told, there are men so base as to perjure themselves at the altar, in order to command the gold of ignorant and confiding girls; and if love of money will lead to such baseness, we may surely expect it will hurry those, who devote themselves to gain, into acts of lesser fraud."

"It must be so; and now Inez, though I am here to guard you with my life, and we are in possession of this rock, our difficulties, perhaps our dangers are not ended. You will summon all your courage to meet the trial and prove yourself a soldier's wife, my Inez?"

"I am ready to depart this instant. The letter, you sent by the physician, had prepared me to hope for the best, and I have every thing arranged for flight, at the shortest warning."

"Let us then leave this place and join our friends."

"Friends!" interrupted Inez, glancing her eyes around the little tent in quest of the form of Ellen. "I, too, have a friend who must not be forgotten, but who is pledged to pass the remainder of her life with us. She is gone!"

Middleton gently led her from the spot, as he smilingly answered——

"She may have had, like myself, her own private communications for some favoured ear."

The young man had not however done justice to the motives of Ellen Wade. The sensitive and intelligent girl had readily perceived how little her presence was necessary in the interview that has just been related, and had retired with that intuitive delicacy of feeling which seems to belong more properly to her sex. She was now to be seen seated on a point of the rock, with her person so entirely enveloped in her dress as entirely to conceal her features. Here she had remained for near an hour, no one approaching to address her, and as it appeared to her own quick and jealous eyes, totally unobserved. In the latter particular, however, even the vigilance of the quick–sighted Ellen was deceived.

The first act of Paul Hover, on finding himself the master of Ishmael's citadel, had been to sound the note of victory, after the quaint and ludicrous manner that is so often practised among the borderers of the West. Flapping his sides with his hands, as the conquering game–cock is wont to do with his wings, he raised a loud and laughable imitation of the exultation of this bird; a cry which might have proved a dangerous challenge had any one of the athletic sons of the squatter been within hearing.

"This has been a regular knock–down and dragout," he cried, "and no bones broke! How now, old trapper, you have been one of your training, platoon, rank and file soldiers in your day, and have seen forts taken and batteries stormed before this—— am I right?"

"Ay, ay, that have I," answered the old man, who still maintained his post at the foot of the rock, so little disturbed by what he had just witnessed, as to return the grin of Paul, with a hearty indulgence in his own silent and peculiar laughter; "you have gone through the exploit like men!"

"Now tell me, is it not in rule, to call over the names of the living, and to bury the dead, after every bloody battle?"

"Some did and other some didn't. When Sir William push'd the German, Dieskau, thro' the defiles at the foot of the Hori——"

"Your Sir William was a drone to Sir Paul, and knew nothing of regularity. So here begins the roll-call——by-the-bye old man, what between bee-hunting and buffaloe humps and certain other matters, I have been too busy to ask your name, for I intend to beginwith my rear guard, well knowing that my man in front is too busy to answer."

"Lord, lad, I've been called in my time by as many names as there are people among whom I've dwelt. Now, the Delawares nam'd me for my eyes, and I was called after the far-sighted hawk. Then, ag'in, the settlers in the Otsego hills christened me anew, from the fashion of my leggings; and various have been the names by which I have gone through life; but little will it matter when the time shall come, that all are to be muster'd, face to face, by what titles a mortal has played his part! I humbly trust I shall be able to answer to any of mine in a loud and manly voice."

Paul paid little or no attention to this reply, more than half of which was lost in the distance, but pursuing the humour of the moment, he called out in a stentorian voice to the naturalist to answer to his name. Dr. Battius had not thought it necessary to push his success beyond the comfortable niche, which accident had so opportunely formed for his protection, and in which he now reposed from his labours with a pleasing consciousness of security, added to great exultation at the possession of the botanical treasure, already mentioned.

"Mount, mount, my worthy mole-catcher! come and behold the prospect of skirting Ishmael; come and look nature boldly in the face, and not go sneaking any longer, among the prairie grass and mullein tops, like a gobbler nibbling for grasshoppers."

The mouth of the light–hearted and reckless bee–hunter was instantly closed, and he was rendered as mute, as he had just been boisterous and talkative, by the appearance of Ellen Wade. When the melancholy maiden took her seat on the point of the rock as mentioned, Paul affected to employ himself in conducting a close inspection of the household effects of the squatter. He rummaged the drawersof Esther with no delicate hands, scattered the rustic finery of her girls on the ground, without the least deference to its quality or elegance, and tossed her pots and kettles here and there, as though they had been vessels of wood instead of iron. All this industry was however manifestly without an object. He reserved nothing for himself, not even appearing to be conscious of the nature of the articles which suffered by his familiarity. When he had examined the inside of every cabin, taken a fresh survey of the spot where he had confined the children, and where he had thoroughly secured them with cords, and kicked one of the pails of the woman, like a football, fifty feet into the air, in sheer wantonness, he returned to the edge of the rock, and thrusting both his hands through his wampum belt, he began to whistle the 'Kentucky Hunters' as diligently as if he had been hired to supply his auditors with music by the hour. In this manner passed the remainder of the time, until Middleton, as has been related, led Inez forth from the tent, and gave a new direction to the thoughts of the whole party. He summoned Paul from his flourish of music, tore the Doctor from the study of his plant, and, as acknowledged leader, gave the necessary orders for their immediate departure.

In the bustle and confusion that were likely to succeed such a mandate, there was little opportunity to indulge in complaints or reflections. As the adventurers had not come unprepared for victory, each individual employed himself in such offices as was best adapted to his strength and situation. The trapper had already made himself master of the patient Asinus, who was quietly feeding at no great distance from the rock, and he was now busy in fitting his back with the complicated machinery that Dr. Battius saw fit to term a saddle of his own inventionThe naturalist himself seized upon his port–folios, herbals, and collection of insects, which he quickly transferred from the encampment of the squatter to certain pockets in the aforesaid ingenious invention, and which the trapper as uniformly cast away the moment his back was turned. Paul shewed his dexterity in removing such light articles as Inez and Ellen had prepared for their flight to the foot of the citadel, while Middleton, after mingling threats and promises, in order to induce the children to remain quietly in their bondage, assisted the females to descend. As time began to press upon them, and there was great danger of Ishmael's returning, these several movements were made with singular industry and despatch.

The trapper bestowed such articles as he conceived were necessary to the comfort of the weaker and more delicate members of the party in those pockets, from which he had so unceremoniously expelled the treasures of the unconscious naturalist, and then gave way for Middleton to place Inez in one of those seats, which he had prepared on the back of the animal for her and her companion.

"Go, child," the old man said, motioning to Ellen to follow the example of the lady, and turning his head a little anxiously to examine the waste behind him. "It cannot be long afore the owner of this place will be coming to look after his household; and he is not a man to give up his property, however obtained, without complaint!"

"It is true," cried Middleton; "we have wasted moments that are precious, and have the utmost need of all our industry."

"Ay, ay, I thought it; and would have said it, captain; but I remembered how your grand'ther used to love to look upon the face of her he led away for a wife, in the days of his youth and hishappiness. 'Tis natur', 'tis natur', and 'tis wiser to give way a little before its feelings, than to try to stop a current that will have its course."

Ellen advanced to the side of the beast, and seizing Inez by the hand, she said, with heart–felt warmth, after struggling to suppress an emotion that nearly choked her——

"God bless you, sweet lady! I hope you will forget and forgive the wrongs you have received from my uncle——"

The humbled and sorrowful girl could say no more, her voice becoming entirely inaudible in an ungovernable burst of grief.

"How is this?" cried Middleton; "did you not say, Inez, that this excellent young woman was to accompany us, and to live with us for the remainder of her life; or, at least, until she found some more agreeable residence for herself?"

"I did; and I still hope it. She has always given me reason to believe, that after having shown so much commiseration and friendship in my misery, she would not desert me, should happier times return."

"I cannot——I ought not," continued Ellen, getting the better of her momentary weakness. "It has pleased God to cast my lot among these people, and I ought not to quit them. It would be adding the appearance of treachery to what will already seem bad enough, with one of his opinions. He has been kind to me, an orphan, after his rough customs, and I cannot steal from him at such a moment."

"She is just as much a relation of skirting Ishmael, as I am a bishop!" said Paul, with a loud hem, as if his throat wanted clearing. "If the old fellow has done the honest thing by her in giving her a morsel of venison, now and then, or a spoon around his homminy dish, hasn't she pay'd him in teaching the young devils to read their bible, or in helping oldEsther to put her finery in some shape and fashion. Tell me that a drone has a sting, and I'll believe you as easily as I will that this young woman is a debtor to any of the tribe of Bush!"

"It is but little matter who owes me, or where I am in debt. There are none to care for a girl who is fatherless and motherless, and whose nearest kin are the offcasts of all honest people. No, no; go, lady, and Heaven for ever bless you! I am better here, in this desert, where there are none to know my shame."

"Now, old trapper," retorted Paul, "this is what I call knowing which way the wind blows! You ar' a man that has seen life, and you know something of fashions; I put it to your judgment, plainly, isn't it in the nature of things for the hive to swarm when the young get their growth, and if children will quit their parents, ought one who is of no kith nor kin——"

"Hist!" interrupted the man he addressed, "Hector is discontented. Say it out, plainly, pup; what is it dog——what is it?"

The venerable hound had risen, and was scenting the fresh breeze which continued to sweep heavily over the prairie. At the words of his master he growled and contracted the muscles of his lips, as if half disposed to threaten with the remnants of his teeth. The younger dog, who was resting after the chace of the morning, also made some signs that his nose detected a taint in the air, and then the two resumed their slumbers, as though they had done enough.

The trapper seized the bridle of the ass and cried, as he urged the beast onward——

"There is no time for words. The squatter an his brood are within a mile or two of this blessed spot."

Middleton lost all recollection of Ellen, in the danger which now so imminently beset his recoveredbride again, nor is it necessary to add that Dr. Battius did not wait for a second admonition to commence his retreat.

Following the route indicated by the old man, they turned the rock in a body, and pursued their way as fast as possible across the prairie, under the favour of the cover the light afforded.

Paul Hover, however, remained in his tracks, sullenly leaning on his rifle. Near a minute had elapsed before he was observed by Ellen, who had buried her face in her hands, as if to conceal her fancied desolation from herself.

"Why do you not fly?" the weeping girl exclaimed, the instant she perceived that she was not alone.

"I'm not used to it."

"My uncle will soon be here! you have nothing to hope from his pity."

"Nor from that of his niece, I reckon. Let him come; he can only knock me on the head."

"Paul, Paul, if you love me, fly."

"Alone!——if I do may I be——."

"If you value your life, fly!"

"I value it not, compared to you."

"Paul!"

"Ellen!"

She extended both her hands and burst into another and a still more violent flood of tears. The bee-hunter put one of his sturdy arms around her thin waist, and in another moment he was urging her over the plain, in rapid pursuit of their flying friends.

CHAPTER XVII.

"Approach the chamber, and destroy your sight

With a new Gorgon:——Do not bid me speak;

See, and then speak yourselves."

—— Shakspeare

The little run, which supplied, the family of the squatter with water, and had nourished the trees and bushes that had grown near the base of the rocky eminence, took its rise at no great distance from the latter, in a small thicket of cotton-wood and vines. Hither, then, the trapper directed the flight, as to the place affording the only available cover in so pressing an emergency. It will be remembered, that the sagacity of the old man, which, from long practice in similar scenes, amounted nearly to an instinct in all cases of sudden danger, had first induced him to take this course, as it placed the hill between them and the approaching party of their enemies. Favoured by this circumstance he succeeded in reaching the bushes in sufficient time, and Paul Hover had just hurried the breathless Ellen into the tangled brush, as Ishmael gained the summit of the rock, in the manner already described, where he stood like a man momentarily bereft of his senses, gazing at the confusion which had been created among his chattles, or at his gagged and bound children, who had been safely bestowed by the forethought of the bee-hunter under the cover of a bark roof, in a sort of irregular pile. A long rifle would have thrown a bullet from the height, on which the squatter now stood, into the very cover where the fugitives, who had wrought all this mischief, were clustered.

The trapper was the first to speak, as the man on whose intelligence and experience they all depended for counsel, after running his eye, over the different individuals who gathered about him, in order to see that none were missing.

"Ah! natur' is natur', and has done its work!" he said, nodding to the exulting Paul, with a smile of approbation. "I thought it would be hard for those, who had so often met in fair and foul, by starlight and under the clouded moon, to part at last in anger. Now is there little time to lose in talk, and every thing to gain by industry! It cannot be long afore some of yonder brood will be nosing along the 'arth for our trail, and should they find it, as find it they surely will, and should they push us to stand on our courage, the dispute must be settled with the rifle; which may He in heaven forbid! Captain, can you lead us to the place where any of your warriors lie?——For the stout sons of the squatter will make a manly brush of it, or I am but little of a judge in warlike dispositions!"

"The place of rendezvous is many leagues from this on the banks of La Platte."

"It is bad——it is bad. If fighting is to be done, it is always wise to enter on it on equal terms. But what has one so near his time to do with ill–blood and hot–blood at his heart! Listen to what a gray head and some experience have to offer, and then if any among you can point out a wiser fashion for a retreat, we can just follow his design, and forget that I have spoken. This thicket stretches for near a mile, as it may be slanting, from the rock, and leads towards the sunset instead of the settlements."

"Enough, enough," cried Middleton, too impatient to wait until the deliberative and perhaps loquacious old man could end his minute explanation. "Time is too precious for words. Let us fly."

The trapper made a gesture of compliance, and turning in his tracks, he led Asinus across the trembling earth of the swale and quickly emerged on thehard ground, on the side opposite to the encampment of the squatter.

"If old Ishmael gets a squint at that highway through the brush," cried Paul, casting, as he left the place, a hasty glance at the broad trail the party had made through the thicket, "he'll need no finger–board to tell him which way his road lies. But let him follow! I know the vagabond would gladly cross his breed with a little honest blood, but if any son of his ever gets to be the husband of——"

"Hush, Paul, hush," said the blushing and terrified young woman, who leaned on his arm for support, "your voice might be heard."

The bee—hunter was silent, though he did not cease to cast certain ominous looks behind him, as they flew along the edge of the run, which sufficiently betrayed the belligerent condition of his mind. As each one was busy for himself, but a few minutes elapsed before the party rose a swell of the prairie and descending without a moment's delay on the opposite side, they were at once removed from every danger of being seen by the sons of Ishmael, unless the pursuers should happen to fall upon their trail. The old man now profited by the formation of the land to take another direction, with a view to elude pursuit, as a vessel changes her course in fogs and darkness, to escape from the vigilance of her enemies.

Two hours, passed in the utmost diligence, had enabled them to make a half circuit around the rock, and to reach a point that was exactly opposite to the original direction of their flight. To most of the fugitives their situation was as entirely unknown as is that of a ship in the middle of the ocean to the uninstructed voyager: but the old man proceeded at every turn, and through every bottom, with a decision that inspired his followers with confidence, as it spoke favourably of his own knowledge of the localities. His hound, stopping now and then, to catch the expression of his eye, had preceded the trapper throughout the whole distance, with as much certainty as though a previous and intelligible communion between them had established the route by which they were to proceed. But at the expiration of the time just named, the dog suddenly came to a stand, and then seating himself on the prairie, he snuffed the air a moment, and began a low and piteous whining.

"Ay——pup——ay. I know the spot——I know the spot, and reason there is to remember it well!" said the old man, stopping by the side of his uneasy associate, until those who followed had time to come up. "Now, yonder, is a thicket before us," he continued, pointing forward, "where we may lie till tall trees grow on these naked fields, afore any of the squatter's kin will venture to molest us."

"This is the spot, where the body of the dead man lay!" cried Middleton, examining the place with an eye that revolted at the recollection.

"The very same. But whether his friends have put him in the bosom of the ground or not, remains to be seen. The hound knows the scent, but seems to be a little at a loss, too. It is therefore necessary that you advance, friend bee–hunter, to examine, while I tarry to keep the dogs from complaining in too loud a voice."

"I!" exclaimed Paul, thrusting his hand into his shaggy locks, like one who thought it prudent to hesitate before he undertook so formidable an adventure; "Now heark'ee, old trapper; I've stood in my thinnest cottons in the midst of many a swarm that has lost its queen–bee, without winking, and let me tell you, the man who can do that, is not likely to fear any living son of skirting Ishmael; but as to meddling with dead men's bones, why it is neither my calling nor my inclination; so, after thankingyou for the favour of your choice, as they say, when they make a man a corporal in the Kentucky militia, I decline serving."

The old man turned a disappointed look towards Middleton, who was too much occupied in solacing Inez to observe his embarrassment, which was, however, suddenly relieved from a quarter, whence, from previous circumstances, there was little reason to expect such a demonstration of fortitude.

Doctor Battius had rendered himself a little remarkable, throughout the whole of the preceding retreat, for the exceeding diligence with which he had laboured to effect that desirable object. So very conspicuous was his zeal indeed, as to have entirely gotten the better of all his ordinary predilections. The worthy naturalist belonged to that species of discoverers, who make the worst possible travelling–companions to a man who has reason to be in a hurry. No stone, no bush, no plant is ever suffered to escape the examination of their vigilant eyes, and thunder may mutter, and rain fall, without disturbing the pleasing abstraction of their reveries. Not so, however, with the disciple of Linnæus, during the momentous period that it remained a mooted point at the tribunal of his better judgment, whether the stout descendants of the squatter were not likely to dispute his right to traverse the prairie in freedom. The highest blooded and best trained hound, with his game in view, could not have run with an eye more riveted than that with which the Doctor had pursued his curvilinear course. It was perhaps lucky for his fortitude that he was ignorant of the artifice of the trapper in leading them around the citadel of Ishmael, and that he had imbibed the soothing impression that every inch of prairie he traversed was just so much added to the distance between his own person and the detested rock. Notwithstanding the momentary shock he certainly experienced, when he discovered this error, he was the man who now so boldly volunteered to enter the thicket in which there was some reason to believe the body of the murdered Asa still lay. Perhaps the naturalist was urged to show his spirit, on this occasion, by some secret consciousness that his excessive industry in the retreat might be liable to misconstruction; and it is certain that, whatever might be his peculiar notions of danger from the quick, his habits and his knowledge had placed him far above the apprehension of suffering harm from any communication with the dead.

"If there is any service to be performed, which requires the perfect command of the nervous system," said the man of science, with a look that was slightly blustering, "you have only to give a direction to his intellectual faculties, and here stands one on whose physical powers you may depend."

"The man is given to speak in parables," muttered the single–minded trapper, "but I conclude there is always some meaning hidden in his words, though it is as hard to find sense in his speeches, as to discover three eagles on the same tree. It will be wise, friend, to make a cover, lest the sons of the squatter should be out skirting on our trail, and, as you well know, there is some reason to fear yonder thicket contains a sight that may horrify a woman's mind. Are you man enough to look death in the face; or shall I run the risk of the hounds raising an outcry, and go in myself? You see the pup is willing to run with an open mouth, already."

"Am I man enough? Venerable trapper, our communications have a recent origin, or thy interrogatory might have a tendency to embroil us in an angry disputation. Am I man enough? I claim to be of the class, mammalia; order, primates; genus, homo! such are my physical attributes; of my moralproperties, let posterity speak; it becomes me to be mute."

"Physic may do for such as relish it; to my taste and judgment it is neither palatable nor healthy; but morals never did harm to any living mortal, be it that he was a sojourner in the forest or a dweller in the midst of glazed windows and smoking chimneys. It is only a few hard words that divide us, friend, for I am of an opinion that, with use and freedom, we should come to understand one another, and mainly settle down into the same judgments of mankind, and of the ways of the world. Quiet, Hector, quiet; what ruffles your temper, pup; is it not used to the scent of human blood?"

The Doctor bestowed a gracious but commiserating smile on the philosopher of nature, as he retrograded a step or two from the place whither he had been impelled by his excess of spirit, in order to reply with less expenditure of breath and with a greater freedom of air and attitude.

"A homo is certainly a homo," he said, stretching forth an arm in an imposing and argumentative manner; "so far as the animal functions extend, there are the connecting links of harmony, order, conformity and design between the whole genus; but there the resemblance ends. Man may be degraded to the very margin of the line which separates him from the brute, by ignorance; or he may be elevated to a communion with the great master–spirit of all, by knowledge; nay I know not, if time and opportunity were given him, but he might become the master of all learning, and consequently equal to the great moving principle."

The old man, who stood leaning on his rifle in a thoughtful attitude, shook his head, as he answered with a native steadiness, that entirely eclipsed the imposing air which his antagonist had seen fit to assume——

'This is neither more than less than mortal wickedness! Here have I been a dweller on the earth for fourscore and six changes of the seasons, and all that time have I look'd at the growing and the dying trees, and yet do I not know the reasons why the bud starts under the summer sun, or the leaf falls when it is pinch'd by the frosts. Your l'arning, though it is man's boast, is folly in the eyes of Him, who sits in the clouds, and looks down, in sorrow, at the pride and vanity of his creatur's. Many is the hour that I've passed, lying in the shades of the woods, or stretch'd upon the hills of these open fields, looking up into the blue skies, where I could fancy the Great One had taken his stand, and was solemnizing on the waywardness of man and brute, below, as I myself had often look'd at the ants tumbling over each other in their eagerness, though in a way and a fashion more suited to His mightiness and power. Knowledge! It is his plaything. Say, you who think it so easy to climb into the judgment–seat above, can you tell me any thing of the beginning and the end? Nay, you're a dealer in ailings and cures: what is life, and what is death? Why does the eagle live so long, and why is the time of the butterfly so short? Tell me a simpler thing: why is this hound so uneasy, while you, who have passed your days in looking into books, can see no reason to be disturbed?"

The Doctor, who had been a little astounded by the dignity and energy of the old man, drew a long breath, like a sullen wrestler who is just released from the throttling grasp of his antagonist, and seized on the opportunity of the pause to reply——

"It is his instinct."

"And what is the gift of instinct?"

"An inferior gradation of reason. A sort of mysterious combination of thought and matter."

"And what is that which you call thought?"

"Venerable venator, this is a method of reasoning which sets at nought the uses of definitions, and such as I do assure you is not at all tolerated in the schools."

"Then is there more cunning in your schools than I had thought, for it is a certain method of showing them their vanity;" returned the trapper, suddenly abandoning a discussion, from which the naturalist was just beginning to anticipate great delight, by turning to his dog, whose restlessness he attempted to appease by playing with his ears. "This is foolish, Hector; more like an untrained pup than a sensible hound; one who has got his education by hard experience, and not by nosing over the trails of other dogs, as a boy in the settlements follows on the track of his masters, be it right or be it wrong. Well, friend; you who can do so much, are you equal to looking into the thicket? or must I go in myself?"

The Doctor again assumed his air of resolution, and, without further parlance, proceeded to do as desired. The dogs were so far restrained, by the remonstrances of the old man, as to confine their noise to low but often-repeated whinings. When they saw the naturalist advance, the pup, however, broke through all restraint, and made a swift circuit around his person, scenting the earth as he proceeded, and then, returning to his companion, he howled aloud.

"The squatter and his brood have left a strong scent on the earth," said the old man, watching as he spoke for some signal from his learned pioneer to follow; "I hope yonder-school bred man knows enough to remember the errand on which I have sent him."

Doctor Battius had already disappeared in the bushes, and the trapper was beginning to betray additional evidences of impatience, when the person of the former was seen retiring from the thicket backwards, with his face fastened on the place he had just left as though his look was bound in the thraldom of some charm.

"Here is something skeary, by the wildness of the creatur's countenance!" exclaimed the old man relinquishing his hold of Hector, and moving stoutly to the side of the totally unconscious naturalist. "How is it, friend; have you found a new leaf in your book of wisdom?"

"It is a basilisk!" muttered the Doctor, whose altered visage betrayed the utter confusion which had beset his faculties. "An animal of the order serpens. I had thought its attributes were fabulous, but mighty nature is equal to all that man can imagine!"

"What is't? What is't? The snakes of the prairies are harmless, unless it be now and then an angered rattler, and he always gives you notice with his tail, afore he works his mischief with his fangs. Lord, Lord, what a humbling thing is fear! Here is one who in common delivers words too big for a humble mouth to hold, so much beside himself, that his voice is as shrill as the whistle of the whip–poor–will! Courage! what is it, man? what is it?"

"A prodigy! a lusus naturæ! a monster, that nature has delighted to form in order to exhibit her power! Never before have I witnessed such an utter confusion in her laws, or a specimen that so completely bids defiance to the distinctions of class and genera. Let me record its appearance," fumbling for his tablets with hands that trembled too much to perform their office, "while time and opportunity are allowed——eyes, enthrallling; colour, various complex, and profound

"One would think the man was craz'd, with his enthralling looks and pieball'd colours!" interrupted the discontented trapper, who began to grow a little uneasy that his party was all this time neglectingto seek the protection of some cover. "If there is a reptile in the brush, show me the creatur', and should it refuse to depart peaceably, why there must be a quarrel for the possession of the place."

"There!" said the Doctor, pointing into a dense mass of the thicket, to a spot within fifty feet of where they both stood. The trapper turned his look, with perfect composure, in the required direction, but the instant his keen and practised glance met the object which had so utterly upset the philosophy of the naturalist, he gave a start himself, and threw his rifle rapidly forward, and as instantly recovered it, as though a second flash of thought convinced him he was wrong. Neither the instinctive movement nor the sudden recollection was without a sufficient object. At the very margin of the thicket, and in absolute contact with the earth, lay an animate ball, that might easily, by the singularity and fierceness of its aspect, have justified the disturbed condition of the naturalist's mind. It were difficult to describe the shape or colours of this extraordinary substance, except to say, in general terms, that it was nearly spherical, and exhibited all the hues of the rainbow, intermingled without reference to harmony, and without any very ostensible design. The predominant hues were a black and a bright vermilion. With these, however, the several tints of white, yellow, and crimson, were strangely and wildly blended. Had this been all, it would have been difficult to have pronounced that the object was possessed of life, for it lay as motionless as any stone; but a pair of dark, glaring, and moving eyeballs which watched with jealousy the smallest movements of the trapper and his companion, sufficiently established the important fact of its possessing vitality.

"Your reptile is a scouter, or I'm no judge of Indian paints and Indian deviltries!" muttered the old man, dropping the butt of his weapon to the ground, and gazing with a steady eye at the frightful object, as he leaned on its barrel, in an attitude of great composure. "He wants to face us out of sight and reason, and make us think the head of a red-skin is a stone covered with the autumn leaf; or he has some other devilish artifice in his mind!"

"Is the animal human?" demanded the Doctor, "of the genus, homo? I had fancied it a non-descript."

"It's as human, and as mortal too, as a warrior of these prairies is ever known to be. I have seen the time when a red-skin would have shewn a foolish daring to peep out of his ambushment in that fashion on a hunter I could name, but who is too old now, and too near his time, to be any thing better than a miserable trapper. It will be well to speak to the imp, and to let him know he deals with men whose beards are grown. Come forth from your cover, friend," he continued in the language of the extensive tribes of the Dahcotahs; "there is room on the prairie for another warrior."

The eyes appeared to glare more fiercely than before, but the mass which, according to the trapper's opinion, was neither more nor less than a human head, shorn, as usual among the warriors of the west, of its hair, still continued without motion or any other sign of life.

"It is a mistake!" exclaimed the Doctor. "The animal is not even of the class, Mammalia, much less a man."

"So much for your knowledge!" returned the trapper, laughing with great inward exultation. "So much for the l'arning of one who has look'd into so many books, that his eyes are not able to tell a moose from a wild–cat. Now my Hector, here, is a dog of education after his fashion, and, though the meanest primer in the settlements would puzzle his information, you could not cheat the hound in a matterlike this. As you think the object an't a man, you shall see his whole formation, and then let an ignorant old trapper, who never willingly pass'd a day within reach of a spelling–book in his life, know by what name to call it. Mind, I mean no violence; but just to start the devil from his ambushment."

The trapper now very deliberately examined the priming of his rifle, taking care to make as great a parade as possible of his hostile intentions, in going through the necessary evolutions with the weapon. When he thought the stranger began to apprehend some danger, he very deliberately presented the piece, and called aloud——

"Now, friend, I am all for peace, or all for war, as you may say. No! well it is no man, as the wiser one, here, says, and there can be no harm in just firing into a bunch of leaves."

The muzzle of the rifle fell as he concluded, and the weapon was gradually settling into a steady, and what would easily have proved a fatal aim, when a tall Indian sprang from beneath that bed of leaves and brush, which he had probably collected about his person at the approach of the party, and stood upright, uttering the sententious exclamation,

"Wagh!"

END OF VOLUME I.

J. M. HODGES LEARNING CENTER
WHARTON COUNTY JUNIOR COLLEGE
WHARTON, TEXAS 77488

Printed in the United States
51247LVS00004B/27

9 781419 178467